BROKEN LINES

BROKEN LINES

Jo Bannister

St. Martin's Press

New York

Library of Congress Cataloging-in-Publication Data

Bannister, Jo.
    Broken lines / Jo Bannister.
        p. cm.
        ISBN 0-312-19842-6
        I. Title.
    PR6052.A497B76   1999
    823'.914
                                                    98-50899
                                                        CIP

First published in Great Britain by Macmillan Publishers Ltd.

First U.S. Edition: March 1999

10 9 8 7 6 5 4 3 2 1

BROKEN LINES

I

Chapter One

Donovan was thinking about women. He often found himself thinking about women when he was riding his motorbike. It might have been the perfect balance of the machine between his thighs, it might have been the way it responded instantly to his every desire; it might even have been the way that keeping it tanked up ate holes in his salary. The fuel gauge was getting low now. Donovan's idea of a perfect Sunday was getting on the bike and travelling: not going anywhere, just riding. He avoided beauty spots, preferred having somewhere less pretty to himself.

He'd been to the north shore of Norfolk, to bathe his soul in an icy gale that had crossed no other land on its journey from the Arctic. Even in summer it's a quiet bit of coast: in January it's desolate. Donovan liked desolate. He'd cruised empty roads and gritty lanes with the frost still crisp in the verges, and ended up on a shingle beach miles long where the only other living souls were a man and his dog. Brian Boru would have liked it too, but Donovan still hadn't figured out how to carry a pit bull terrier on a motorcycle.

And what he was thinking about women was, how few there were who thought it was worth being cold and wet, bent double on a motorbike for hours at a time, in order to stroll on a pebble beach in the dead of winter. Off hand he could only think of one who might have enjoyed it, and not only was she married to someone else but she was his boss. Otherwise he'd have asked her along. Cal Donovan was a loner by nature and custom but he liked women, in principle. It was the practice he had difficulties with; mainly, getting enough. He wasn't good at personal relationships. He knew what the problem was: being too intense when a degree of flexibility was called for, and letting his mind wander when it wasn't. Like thinking about women when he was riding his bike. He also did it the other way round.

A mile from home, coming into Castlemere down the Cambridge Road, he checked the fuel again and thought he'd fill up before the garage closed. He probably wouldn't need the bike until tomorrow but in his line of work you couldn't count on it.

An early dusk had set in before he left Norfolk, by now it was entirely dark. The lights of the filling station rose on the tarmac horizon like a liner at sea. Donovan swung off the road and gunned to a halt by a pump. He had all four to choose from. The place was empty, there was just him, the attendant in his brilliant emporium and a small red van left slantwise across the forecourt, the engine still running, presumably by someone who only wanted a packet of cigarettes.

Donovan had noticed how people buying fish, paint or a bottle of wine would park a car but those who wanted only a packet of cigarettes would abandon it where it stopped. Donovan could get quite ratty about inconsiderate parking. People who knew him slightly, enough to know he lived on a narrow-boat and rode a motorbike and visited the barber about as often as other people visit the dentist, had him down as a Hell's Angel. In fact he was a bit of a puritan.

When the bike was fed he padded across the fore-court, his helmet over his arm, unzipping the pockets of his leathers until he found one with some money in. On an impulse, as he passed the red van he reached inside and turned off the engine, taking the key with him.

There were only two people in the shop, the assistant behind the till and the customer he was serving, muffled against the weather in a long coat and balaclava. Donovan dropped the keys over his shoulder. 'Don't leave it running,' he growled, 'somebody might steal it.'

The only warning he got that he'd misread the situation was the look on the assistant's face. He knew Ash Kumani well enough to expect a nod of recognition or maybe a grin in reply. Instead the man's eyes flicked briefly at him, rimed with fear.

Donovan frowned, and his lips pursed to say 'What—?' But before he got the word out the man in front of him, the small man muffled up against the icy New Year, spun on his heel like a dancer and hit him in the face hard enough to floor him.

Donovan had been a policeman for more than ten years, he'd been hit more times than he could remember. He'd taken systematic beatings from men who knew just how to do it, and collected black eyes simply for being in the wrong place at the wrong time. But he didn't remember being taken so totally by surprise before. Pain exploded up the side of his face, and even as he reeled against the videos he was dimly aware that no fist had done that. Then he hit the tiles; the coloured lights bled together and faded to black.

It was more a lapse than a loss of consciousness, though, because when the world started to come back he knew he'd only been away a few seconds. He saw Ash Kumani coming round the counter and bending over him anxiously, and heard the roar of an engine mount and diminish as the van shot off with a Grand-Prix flourish. His hand, wandering vaguely to his face, met the cool slickness of blood.

'What did he hit me with?' Somehow that was important to him, that he hadn't been felled by a man smaller than himself equipped with nothing more than his bare fists.

'A gun. A pistol.' Kumani gestured at Donovan's face, the skin split over the outer edge of the high cheekbone. 'You'll need a stitch in that. Sit still, I'll call 999 and then I'll fix you a dressing.' Kumani kept an eclectic garage shop, lint and sticking plaster were no strain on his resources, and by keeping busy he could fend off the reaction he felt as an incipient tremble in his knees. He'd be all right until he had time to acknowledge the fact that he'd just lost his weekend takings to an armed robber in a ski mask.

But Donovan was on his feet and heading for the door before the diminishing roar of the engine had entirely died. Cambridge Road offered only two possi-bilities: into Castlemere or out to The Levels. The

6

police would come up the road from town so the van had headed east.

He paused just long enough to find his helmet and jam it on. 'Pay you later.' He headed for his bike at a slightly unsteady jog.

Kumani's horrified exclamation – 'You can't ride like that!' – was lost on him, and he had the bike under way before anyone arrived from Queen's Street to stop him.

He'd been riding motorbikes since he was twelve, always said he could do it in his sleep; now he was going to find out. If he'd been any less stunned he'd have recognized that it wasn't only his own neck he was risking. But that was sophisticated thinking for a man who'd just been pistol-whipped, and he was heading for The Levels at sixty miles an hour before he'd wondered if he should or even could.

After the slightly shabby Victorian suburbs around the garage Cambridge Road gave way first to a classy semi-rural area of big expensive houses in extensive grounds and then to farmland. At this time of year the fields were either in stubble or in plough and there was nothing to hide the distant lights of a speeding van; a fact which was probably not appreciated by the driver. When he turned off towards the dozen houses and a church that constituted Chevening village his only purpose could be to evade pursuit. There was nothing that way that could be of any use to him, but there weren't so many roads out here that he could afford to pass one if he wanted to break his trail.

All the same, he'd have been better passing that one. Donovan gave a little grunt of satisfaction:

'Gotcha!' Narrow and cornering sharply round fields that predated the internal combustion engine, Chevening Moss Road was impossible for a four-wheeled vehicle to take at speed. If he met another vehicle coming the other way the raider would have to slow to a crawl should every squad car Queen's Street could muster be behind him. As long as Donovan kept the rhythm of his cornering fluent, which wouldn't normally be a problem but just might be this time, he could cut that half-mile lead back to nothing about the time the van reached the village.

In daylight the spire of Chevening Parish Church was visible from far out across The Levels. When the fens were trackless wetland church spires served the same purpose as lighthouses to ships at sea. But in the dark the first you knew was the road doing a sudden switchback round the graveyard wall. Donovan saw the van's brake lights flare, and the beam of the headlamps raked wildly as the rear end broke away. He braked too, ready to stop, but somehow the van recovered, vanishing out of the dog-leg turn as Donovan came into it.

Though he was unsighted for a few seconds then, Donovan got a moment's warning of what was going to happen. Headlights gleamed off the reflectors on the corner: another car was on the roundabout immediately beyond the church. Donovan just had time to think, 'Please God, let it be coming this way.' Then the reflectors went dark as the lights veered off, the vehicle crossing the path of the speeding van.

The raider must have seen the other vehicle, must have known it had right of way. He might have thought he could beat it across the roundabout, that it would brake when he failed to; or he may have been checking his mirror at the critical moment, aware of the single light gaining on him from behind and wondering if it was pursuit or coincidence. For whatever reason he kept going and, instead of meshing like the cogs on a wheel, momentarily the two vehicles tried to occupy the same space.

Through his helmet Donovan heard the squeal of brakes swallowed almost instantly in an impact like an explosion. Lights cartwheeled across the sky. Afraid he'd swing round the last corner and pile into them he braked again, harder, and fought the resentful machine under him to a more-or-less controlled halt. The crash scene opened up before him, lit by the three Victorian lamp-posts that constituted Chevening's public lighting scheme.

The red van had hit a white saloon and bowled it across the roundabout like rolling a bottle. Between rolling and sliding it must have covered forty metres, the tortured metal shrieking in agony, before coming to rest on its side against an oak tree overhanging the road.

The van itself had veered left into Fletton Road. Somehow it had stayed upright as it ricocheted like a pin-ball off the churchyard wall, but the whole nearside had been stripped to the metal before it ended its career under the backside of a parked digger. Now it looked as if the digger had sat on its bonnet. The van's engine had gone as far under as it could and then come back into the cab.

'God almighty!' whispered Donovan. All at once a cut face seemed small beer. He couldn't see how the occupants of either vehicle could have escaped with their lives.

But he had to be sure. Carefully now – he was probably the only one left for whom things could get any worse – he rode on to the roundabout and left the bike with its light shining back at the blind corner to warn anyone coming in his wake. He threw off his helmet and, fighting the weakness that adrenalin had thus far kept at bay, crossed the road to the white saloon.

It had been a good car once but it was done now. There might be a few parts deep in the engine block that could be salvaged, but in every way that counted it was a write-off. If it had had furry dice, the furry dice would have been a write-off.

Or just possibly not. Because modern cars are constructed in such a way that everything collapses and crumples and falls apart in order to safeguard the passengers inside. When Donovan steeled himself to look he met not a shatter of blood and bones and grey flesh forced into impossible contortions but shock-dilated eyes in the white face of a woman who, so far as he could see, hadn't a mark on her.

Her mouth opened and closed a couple of times before anything came out. Then she said – whispered, rather, but with the exquisite politeness that a totally unfamiliar situation engenders – 'Please, could you help me?'

Relief almost made Donovan laugh. It certainly made him forget his manners. 'Jesus, lady, I thought you were mincemeat!' The offside doors were under the car. He found the nearside handle sandwiched into a concertina fold of the door and pulled but nothing happened, and judging from the seized-solid feel of it nothing was going to. Without much hope Donovan tried the rear door but the whole frame was distorted, it would take cutting equipment to shift it.

He thought for a moment, sniffing the air like a dog. He couldn't smell petrol. The engine was dead. 'Can you turn the ignition off?' She didn't answer. He tried again. 'The ignition. The key. Can you reach it to turn it off?'

'Oh – yes.' Donovan saw her right hand move, awkwardly because her body was tipped on her right side, held there by the seat-belt. He heard the key turn.

'OK, good. Now, are you hurt?'

She needed a moment's notice of that too. 'I don't know. I don't think so.'

'Can you move your legs?'

'Y-yes. But not much, there's something in the way.'

From the state of the car it could have been anything including the tow bar. Donovan wiped his forearm across his eyes. 'Listen, you'd best stay where you are till help gets here. It won't be long, and they'll be able to force the door and get you out easy. The only way out right now is through the windscreen, and if you are hurt I could do some damage pulling you about. Keep still and be patient. You're in no danger, there's no need to be frightened. I have to go check the other vehicle.'

That seemed to bring home to her what had happened. Until then she was the victim of some incomprehensible disaster as impersonal as a lightning strike or an avalanche, and all she knew was to be grateful there was someone on hand to help her. But that brought it back. Another vehicle? – she was hit by another vehicle! She was driving round the roundabout when a red van that should have stopped at the broken line came straight on and hit her at full tilt. It wasn't an accident, not in any real sense – someone did this to her! Outrage flooded through her. 'He hit me! I was on the roundabout, and he crossed the line and hit me!'

Donovan nodded. 'He's pretty maced up too, by the look of it. Worse than you. If there's nothing I can do there I'll come straight back.'

'Don't leave me!' From a whisper her voice rose to a wail.

Donovan flinched. 'I have to. Look, there are people coming now – I'll get someone to wait with you. I'll be back as soon as I can.'

Her free left hand came towards him through the broken windscreen, imploring, seeking contact. He stepped back quickly, then, feeling like a worm, turned his back on her.

People were coming from the little knot of houses round the church. He sent the first to phone for the police, Fire Brigade and Ambulance – the cars from Queen's Street wouldn't be able to do much more in this situation than he could – and the second to keep the woman company. 'I don't think there's any chance of a fire now, but if I'm wrong yell for me and get out of the way.'

'What about her?'

But he had no answer. He took off at an uncertain run towards Fletton Road.

Even more than the car the van looked as if it had

been through one of those compactors that reduce a ton of engineering to an Art Deco coffee-table. There was hardly enough paint left to show what colour it had been. The bonnet was crushed downwards and the pillars of the windscreen inwards. The height of the front portion of the cab had been halved.

Again Donovan gritted his teeth to look. This was a man who'd hit him in the face with a gun, but that didn't make it any easier to see him reduced to the filling in a steel sandwich.

And again he didn't see what he expected to. Firstly, though the driver had certainly come off worse than the woman in the car – there was blood on his forehead and bubbling through a rent in the leg of his jeans – he was surprisingly active, struggling to haul his legs out of the compacted well of the van on to the front seats. He was also too noisy for someone at death's door, sobbing in shock and terror and pain.

The second thing Donovan noticed was that he knew this man. Mikey Dickens was a junior member of The Jubilee's leading crime family, and if there'd been any time in the last ten minutes for the policeman to ask himself who was most likely to have robbed Ash Kumani at gunpoint, Mikey Dickens was the answer he'd have come up with. The small stature and ready violence should have been enough to tell him.

And the third thing he noticed was that, unlike the white saloon, all around the van stank of petrol.

Chapter Two

There was a long moment in which Donovan was close to walking away. Mikey Dickens was in a situation entirely of his own making. It was a miracle he hadn't killed the woman in the car; and if he'd hit Donovan any harder he wouldn't have been in this quandary, he'd still have been crawling round Ash Kumani's floor wondering which end of the sky fell on him. He couldn't think of a single good reason to risk his life for the likes of Mikey Dickens.

Because that was what he'd have to do to get him out. Both wings of the van had been forced back by the impact, reducing the doors to mere jagged slashes in the wreckage. Not even a weasel like Mikey was coming out that way. The windscreen had been crushed by the digger to a letter-box slit. The only other exit, unless the Fire Brigade got here with cutting equipment before the thing went up like a bomb, was the back doors. And to get out that way, Mikey was going to need help.

There were limits to what flesh and blood could do. If Donovan waited for the emergency services, and put in his report that he was unable to render assistance due to the damage sustained by the vehicle, no one would challenge it. Certain risks, even serious

14

risks, came with the territory but this wasn't one: crawling over a ruptured petrol tank that could explode at any second. There were police officers who went that far beyond the call of duty – Donovan had before now – but nobody had a right to expect it. It would be noted that he was concussed, and also how he came by that concussion. Senior ranks would support his decision, and even in the canteen no one would dare suggest they'd have handled it better for fear that some time they'd get the chance to prove it.

So it was neither peer pressure nor official expectation that made his mind up. Mostly it was lacking the time and the strength of will to hammer out a rational decision. It was easier and quicker to go by gut instinct, and instinct said he couldn't leave a man to burn, not even Mikey Dickens, not even in a conflagration of his own making.

Where the door had been was a gap sufficient to take Donovan's hand but not enough of his arm for him to reach the ignition. 'Give me your keys. Mikey! – the keys. I have to get the back door open.' Mikey's pinched little face, the ski mask discarded now, was white with terror. But intelligence glimmered in the hunted-animal eyes, and he crawled on his elbows towards the sound of Donovan's voice. 'Mr Donovan, is that you? Oh thank Christ. Get me out of here, for pity's sake!'

'I will,' promised Donovan. 'But you have to reach me the keys. Then get yourself into the gap between the seats, and I'll come in and pull you out.'

Put like that it sounded nothing at all. He could have Mikey out of there in just a few seconds. Only the stench of petrol turned it from an exercise in logic into a trial of nerves, and even then there was only a problem if the petrol met a spark. The stink alone would do neither of them any harm. Donovan tried hard to hold that thought.

Mikey was bloodier but less shocked than the woman in the car. He understood immediately what Donovan intended and what he needed. He squirmed round as best he could in the space remaining over the front seats and groped for the ignition with one gloved hand. When he had the key he put it into Donovan's fingers as carefully as if his life depended on it.

And Donovan dropped it. It wasn't just nerves making him clumsy. He'd taken his own gloves off in order to reach through the crack, and the metal key seared his palm as if it had been among hot coals.

Fortunately he was already withdrawing his hand when the heat got through to him and it fell at his feet. If it had fallen among the twisted debris inside the car it would never have been found in time.

Mikey had his gloves on, he didn't know that the key was hot and what that meant. Donovan did: it meant there was a fire in the engine compartment. It meant that there was no longer a margin of safety, however slim. But Mikey didn't need to know. The man couldn't have wanted to get out of that van any more if there'd been a kilo of Semtex under his seat and a Des O'Connor song on the radio: scaring him even more would be counter-productive. Donovan bent quickly and picked up the key with his finger-tips. Mikey was in no position to notice. 'OK, I'll have it open in a second. Get you over them seats as best you can.'

It wasn't the Queen's English but Mikey knew
what he meant. Both front seats had head restraints
which had halted the collapse of the roof: the space
between them was the only way out. A bigger man
would never have done it. An injured man in less
immediate peril would not have thought he could do
it. But Mikey was coming through that gap if he had
to strip naked to do it: somehow, in the narrow place,
he wriggled out of his heavy coat and wormed his
way into the tight channel that was his only exit from
hell.

He got just far enough to think he had it licked,
then he stuck fast. Even with his mind racing it took
him a second to figure out how. His shoulders were
already through the gap and they were the widest part
of him: the rest should have followed. But whatever it
was that stabbed into his thigh had torn a rent in his
jeans that had now become snagged on the gearstick.

He fought so fiercely to free himself that anything
other than denim would have given way. But Mikey
robbed petrol stations to keep himself in a manner
which included top quality jeans and the fabric
resisted all his efforts to rip it. When Donovan got the
key turned in the back door he met the frantic waving
hands and terrified face of a man trapped in his worst
nightmare.

And the reason he could see the terror on Mikey's
face was that there was now some light inside the
wrecked van. A flickering rosy glow was emanating
from under the remains of the dashboard.

There was no time left: either he went in or
he got out. It wasn't a conscious heroism that made
him kneel on the platform immediately above the

punctured tank and grab one of Mikey's hands in his own, but it was heroism just the same. He knew what could happen – what *would* happen, the only question was when. But the longer he waited the more danger he was in, so he flung the door out of his way, got just as far into the van as he had to to reach the trapped man, gripped the gloved hand tight and yanked with all his strength.

With the leverage he had Mikey's jeans stood no chance. There was a ripping sound, a sudden loss of resistance, and Mikey came at him as if he'd been shot from a cannon. Donovan had no time to avoid him: their heads clashed – sending new stars spinning through Donovan's vision – their limbs tangled and they fell out of the back of the van like a pair of over-excited wrestlers falling out of a ring. Donovan landed on his back with Mikey on top of him and all the breath gushed out of him. Mikey, his injuries notwith-standing, hit the ground running.

He travelled three, maybe four paces, and then he slid to a halt and looked back. Donovan was still on the ground, plainly stunned, sitting up now but either unaware of the giant petrol bomb he was sitting beside or unable to get away from it. The leaked fuel was all around him.

Mikey screamed his name and Donovan looked round, a little vaguely, as if he didn't quite know where he was.

Then Mikey Dickens did something no one would have anticipated – not his father, not his best friend, least of all himself. He went back. He wasted no time. He grabbed Donovan without ceremony and dragged him away, stumbling on his hands and knees and then at least approximately on his feet.

And the van blew up.

Flame fountained into the dark sky. Bits of the van lanced through the air like fighter planes. When the force-front of the explosion caught the stumbling men it hurled them forward then slammed them down face-first on the tarmac and poured over them in a maelstrom of sound and smoke and shrapnel and flames.

The first Donovan knew that he was on fire was Mikey battling to get his jacket off. It was leather, it protected him from injury, but there were a lot of fastenings to unclip and unbuckle, and by the time he was out of it the jacket was past saving. Mikey flung it away from them, back into the inferno, along with his own gloves that had caught light while they struggled. Then, keeping low, they helped one another out of range.

By then the first of the cars from Queen's Street had arrived. WPC Flynn took in the mayhem open-mouthed, then busied herself at the white saloon whose occupant was still lying trapped on her side. Helpless to escape or protect herself, the explosion had terrified her; now she was crying hysterically.

While Cathy Flynn did what she could to calm her, PC Stark hurried towards the burning van, meeting the men staggering away from it half-way. 'Was there anyone else? Donovan! – was there anyone else inside?'

It would have been too late to matter if there had been. Donovan shook his head wearily, then wished he hadn't. 'Just your man.' In moments of stress he reverted to an almost impenetrable Ulster vernacular.

'There's an ambulance on its way,' said Stark. 'You'd better sit down till it gets here.' He'd spotted the blood still pulsing from Mikey's leg. 'I'll stick a bandage on that while we wait. What about you, Serg – are you hurt?' The gaping wound on Donovan's cheek that had so alarmed Ash Kumani had disappeared under the smoke and dirt.

Donovan considered for a moment. 'Nothing a cup of tea won't cure.' But he lurched against Jim Stark as if he had no idea whether his feet were touching the ground.

'Right, sure,' agreed Stark, steering him to the bench against the wall where Chevening's three senior citizens waited for the bus on pension day. 'They make a decent brew down Castle General, so I've heard.'

Donovan cranked up an eyelid in order to scowl at him. He knew he wasn't going to win this argument, but nor was he going to let a downright lie pass unchallenged. 'I've had better tea out of a gypsy's welly.'

Stark applied himself to Mikey's leg. 'Is somebody going to tell me what happened here?'

Mikey Dickens, discovering a sudden interest in church architecture, couldn't take his eyes off the lych-gate. Donovan sighed. 'Mikey made a slight error of judgement: he mistook Chevening roundabout for the straight at Silverstone. I yanked him out of the van, he yanked me out of the explosion. Jesus, he threw my jacket in the fire! That's why I'm so cold. I thought it was shock.'

Cathy Flynn came over with a blanket which Donovan shrugged around himself. He sat on the bench looking like a vulture whose last antelope disagreed with him.

Soon after that the ambulance arrived, and on its tail the fire engine. When the fire was out no more remained of the red van than a few tangled spars of blackened metal sitting in a hole in the road.

The paramedics helped Mikey into the back of the ambulance. By then firemen with cutting equipment had freed the woman from the white saloon and they went to check that she too was fit to be moved. She was: she had escaped virtually without injury. With a little support she was able to walk to the ambulance.

One of the paramedics peered at the angular figure on the bench with its smoke-blackened face and blanket. 'It's Detective Sergeant Donovan, isn't it? Are you coming with us?'

Donovan nodded and climbed creakily to his feet. 'Better had. There's something I have to say to Mikey.'

His head was clearing all the time. In the ambulance he found a seat opposite where Mikey Dickens was stretched out. His battered face ventured a fractional smile. 'Mikey—'

Now he was out of danger Mikey was high on adrenalin. For possibly the first time in his life he'd behaved better and achieved more than anyone could have expected. For possibly the first time in his life he was not merely pleased with himself but proud of himself.

He propped himself up on one elbow and his

pinched little face glowed. 'That's all right, Mr Donovan, you don't need to say it.'

But Donovan did. 'Michael Dickens, I am arresting you for the armed robbery of Ashog Kumani's Garage, Cambridge Road, on January the fifth. You are not obliged to say anything. But it may harm your defence if you do not mention now . . . er . . . something which you later wish to rely on . . . um . . . Will be taken down.' Even when he wasn't concussed he had trouble with the new caution. He thought for a moment longer, then gave up. 'Hell, Mikey, you've heard it before, you know what it means. It means you're nicked.'

Chapter Three

'You do not have to say anything,' said Detective Superintendent Frank Shapiro sternly. 'But I must caution you that if you do not mention when questioned something which you later rely on in court it may harm your defence. If you do say anything it may be given in evidence.'

'Uhhuh,' said Donovan.

Shapiro bristled. 'Never mind Uhhuh: this matters. The first time I have a case thrown out of court because you couldn't be bothered to caution the suspect correctly I'll have you directing traffic. *Why* is it a problem, anyway? Twenty-year-old kids in their first week of basic training have it off word-perfect. So, for that matter, have old codgers like me and Sergeant Bolsover who learned the old one when Adam was under the age of criminal responsibility. In God's name, Sergeant, what is your problem?'

Donovan mumbled something, avoiding his eyes. '*What?*'

'I was concussed,' Donovan said defensively. The cut over his cheekbone was held together by butterfly plasters and the whole orbit of his eye was black. 'First the sod hit me in the face, then we clashed heads. I'm sorry I wasn't up to giving the Gettysburg

Address under these circumstances but I have to say, I doubt Lincoln would have been either.'

Shapiro sighed. Tearing strips off Detective Sergeant Donovan was a thankless task. For one thing, it was like painting the Forth Bridge: you'd barely finished when it was time to start again. For another, although you could always find something to criticize about the way Donovan did his job he did it well. He put himself out, he got results, in all the important ways he was a good policeman. Whenever Shapiro was dragging him over the coals, which he did at regular intervals, half-way through he started feeling foolish because what he was complaining about didn't matter as much as the things Donovan got right.

'How's the head now?' he asked.

'Fine,' said Donovan. 'I'll be in to work tomorrow.'

It was Monday evening, they were talking in the saloon of Donovan's boat on the Castlemere Canal. In January only a handful of boats remained on the water and only one other was occupied so Broad Wharf seemed like a ghost town. Shapiro had left his car on Brick Lane and cut through on the footpath. It always made him nervous, leaving his car so close to The Jubilee. The half-dozen streets of black Victorian brick made a sort of walled city which much of Castlemere's criminal fraternity, the Dickens clan among them, called home. In fact, the car was quite safe. The nice thing about old-fashioned criminals, as distinct from the yuppie kind who used mobile phones and joined golf clubs, was that they had a sort of respect for the enemy. They called him Mr Shapiro. They even called Donovan *Mr* Donovan.

'There's no rush,' said Shapiro. 'Apart from Mikey the ungodly are still on their holidays.'

'Just the same.' Donovan only took today off because the doctor insisted. He hated being sidelined. He seemed to think crime would grind to a halt if he wasn't there.

Shapiro nodded and struggled to his feet. Donovan favoured low furniture because of *Tara's* low ceilings, but Shapiro had reached an age and a shape which called for a nice upright chair with stout arms. 'Good enough. I just thought I'd stick my head in, see how you were.'

Donovan uncoiled from the low sofa like a snake rising; behind him, shadow-silent, rose the dark shape of the dog.

Shapiro said, 'Lost any fingers yet?'

Donovan gave his saturnine grin. 'Him? He's a pussycat.'

'Sure he is,' agreed Shapiro. 'Till one morning you're late with his breakfast.' He smiled into his chest. 'Never mind, those big white gloves cover a multitude of sins.'

Donovan didn't understand. 'Big white gloves?'

'The ones for directing the traffic.'

Detective Inspector Liz Graham was in charge of the investigation, and a baffling case it was too. One minute the room had been full of valuables, a flick of the curtain later they were all gone. The open boxes full of diamonds and rubies, the stacks of gold ingots, the strings of pearls: all vanished as if by magic.

At least she had a suspect: a thirteen-year-old

wearing a cut-down Lurex evening dress and a pink velvet turban. She herself was wearing a plastic helmet held under her chin by a length of elastic. 'Ali Baba,' she intoned solemnly, 'I'm arresting you for the theft of the Wazir's treasure. You do not have to say anything, but I must caution you that if you do not mention when questioned something which you later rely on in court . . .' One thing about Castle High School pantomimes: they were good on detail.

Another thing about them was that, by and large, the adults involved enjoyed them more than the children. More into pop groups than Middle Eastern myths, they went along with the nonsense amiably enough because it amused their parents and teachers and was a high point of the Christmas holidays for younger siblings. For themselves, they'd just as soon have been in Philadelphia.

After the children had been packed off home, those unencumbered by sprogs with bedtimes gathered round some bottles of wine and some cheese straws in the staffroom. They were still in costume. Brian Graham, who was the Wazir, was wearing burnt-cork whiskers, a long brocade waistcoat and something that might have been a Victorian smoking cap. Liz thought he looked more like Mr Mole than the Wazir of Baghdad. But then, she didn't look much like a chief of detectives either.

The part does not figure prominently in the original story. It was created specially for her when she saw a rehearsal a couple of weeks ago and laughed herself silly. It was the funniest thing she'd seen since Donovan took her to a pub where folk music was perpetrated. She only came to admire the scenery

– as head of the art department Brian had a dual contribution to make to the festivities. But by the time she'd hooted her way through a couple of scenes – comedy, love interest, the death of Ali Baba's mother, the lot – it was generally agreed that she'd better be given a part to play since the alternative was probably having her in the audience.

Now it was over, and unless a theatrical agent was waiting with a contract at the stage door it was back to Castlemere's generally less picturesque crime scene tomorrow morning. For Ali Baba's mother read Mikey Dickens's grandma Thelma; for the Wazir's treasure read a nice little earner in second-hand car stereos with the serial numbers unaccountably missing.

She liked Brian's colleagues. She'd met most of them at one time or another, but dressing up in false beards and discarded curtains showed them in a whole new light. Who'd have thought that the best education in Castlemere was being purveyed by people whose idea of entertainment was I-say-I-say-I-say jokes and sand dancing?

Brian spotted someone he wanted to talk to and left her to the tender mercies of Slasher Siddons, head of Religious Studies. The Reverend Simon Siddons was a fencer in his youth: thirty years later the nickname still gave him so much pleasure he made sure no one forgot it. He'd played the part of Mrs Baba, in drag.

He looked over the heads of the assembly – he was the tallest person present as well as, at least temporarily, the best endowed bosom-wise – and saw Brian talking to a mousy woman in the last dirndl skirt in England. 'Marion Cully,' he said, for Liz's benefit. 'She's Mrs Taylor's deputy in the English department, she went round with some flowers this afternoon to see how she was. After the accident.'

'Accident?' Liz hadn't been at Queen's Street today or she'd have known.

'She was run off the road by some young tearaway last night. She wasn't hurt, apparently, just very shaken. But it must have been a close thing. One of the cars caught fire.'

'The accident in Chevening? I heard something about it on the radio. They said three people were taken to hospital but that none of the injuries was serious. Do you know who the others were?'

She wondered why Mr Siddons was regarding her oddly, as if he thought she might be fibbing and couldn't work out why. 'One of them was the boy involved – one of the Dickenses, I think. The other was your sergeant. The Irish one.'

Liz had a sort of reflex action for when people mentioned Donovan: her heart sank and her chin rose, ready to defend him. In the three years he'd worked for her she'd called him every name under the sun, but never in front of third parties. In front of third parties, which included all the general public except Brian and all the police except Shapiro, she backed him to the hilt because she knew he did the same for her.

'Donovan was in one of the cars?'

'I think he came on the scene right after the crash. He pulled young Dickens clear in the nick of time.'

Liz nodded slowly. That sounded like Donovan. If the man went into a florist's he'd walk in on the world's first Great Chrysanthemum Robbery.

Later, driving home, she asked Brian how Miss Cully had found the head of the English department.

'Well, she's at home. The hospital didn't keep her, just checked her over and discharged her. Marion said she was still pretty tearful. Shock, I suppose. I mean, that's about as close as you ever want to come.'

'Did you know Donovan was involved?'

'Donovan?' Brian stared at her so long Liz thought there was going to be another accident. Then the cork whiskers spread in a wry grin. 'Typical. No, I didn't know it was him. Somebody said there was a policeman on the scene, but I thought they meant afterwards. Was he hurt?'

'I'll get the gory details tomorrow. Slasher reckons he pulled the kid responsible out of the wreckage just before it blew up.'

This time Brian nodded without taking his eye off the road. 'More guts than sense; but then, so have lemmings.'

Liz chuckled. 'True, but not kind.'

Brian glanced at her from the corner of his eye. 'It wasn't me said it. It was you.'

She wanted him to leave the whiskers on – 'I've never slept with a Wazir before' – but Brian thought of the mess they'd make of the sheets. So he washed off the whiskers but kept the smoking cap on.

He also kept the Wazir's voice, though with a salacious undertone that would have frightened the younger members of the evening's audience and made the older ones seriously uneasy. 'Now you are my odalisque, my pretty, with your white skin and your golden hair and your green, green eyes, and I shall have my wicked way with you.'

29

'Oh but sir,' protested Liz, 'whatever will my husband think?'

'Him? He's only an art teacher, and I am the Wazir of Old Baghdad!'

She thought for a moment, then nodded. 'Fair enough.'

Later, as they drifted becalmed off the shores of sleep, she wove her arm through his and said, 'Brian – do you ever wish we'd had children?'

He rolled on his side and in the darkness looked at where she was. Neither of them turned the light on. 'What's brought this on?'

Liz squirmed the curves of her body into his. 'Just, seeing you with the kids made me wonder. You're so good with them, I wondered if you were sorry you'd none of your own.'

It was an honest enquiry and he tried to answer honestly. 'Most of the time I never give it a thought. Sometimes I'm very glad that children are my work and I can leave them behind when I come home. But yes, just occasionally I think it would have been nice if it had happened. Christ!' He sat bolt upright. 'Liz – you aren't trying to tell me something?'

She shook her head. Unseen, the long fair hair stroked his skin. 'No, I rather think we've left it too late. My fault, I suppose. I wanted to get my career on track without any distractions, and by then the biology was fighting an uphill battle. I'm sorry if it matters to you, even a little bit.'

His long arm was around her bare shoulders. They couldn't have been closer if he'd been inside her. 'But it's not the little bits that count, it's the whole package. Sure I could have had children. But not with you –

not with you as you are. If you'd made different choices you'd have been a different woman, and it wasn't anyone else I wanted. Yes, sometimes I wish I had children. Sometimes I wish I had a Porsche, a yacht and a villa in the Algarve. Then I wonder what I've got that I'd be willing to give up for them, and the answer is nothing.

'I've got the top three items on my list: you, you and you. Anything more than that's icing on the cake. Sure it looks nice, it tastes sweet, but it's the cake that counts.' He gave a lugubrious sniff. 'Besides, any time I'm feeling broody I can always take 3b for extra art. It's a complete cure. An afternoon with 3b and you realize Darwin got it wrong. The apes isn't where we came from – it's where we're heading.'

Chapter Four

To reach her office the next morning Liz had to cross a battlefield centred on the station sergeant's desk. The protagonists were a middle-aged man and a woman in her twenties, though a small child was watching with a wide-eyed innocence that suggested it had played a prominent role in the dispute.

Sergeant Bolsover too had become embroiled, rising from his paperwork to interpose his bulk between the warring parties. Kevin Tufnall already had one black eye, it went against the spirit of the Police and Criminal Evidence legislation to let him get another within the confines of the police station.

Because it was Kevin who was in danger, even though the woman came barely up to his shoulder. Her face was red with fury and her fists knotted, and if the Station Sergeant had stepped aside she would undoubtedly have knocked the stuffing out of Castlemere's least gifted professional criminal.

It wasn't just the arthritis in his hands, though in recent times that had put dipping and even basic shimming-a-lock-with-22-'loid beyond his capabilities. He was also handicapped in his chosen career by fallen arches, which meant that little old ladies collecting their pensions could outrun him, and by adenoids which made his voice so distinctive blind men could pick him out of identity parades. Buck teeth made him immediately recognizable from almost any angle.

Magistrates had commented on his unfitness for a life of crime and wondered if invalidity benefit might prove a cost-effective means of keeping him out of court. But Kevin Tufnall was a proud man. He wouldn't take charity when he could still take most other things that weren't nailed down.

Liz greeted him like an old friend. She'd been arresting him at regular intervals for the last three years. 'Hello, Kevin, how's tricks?'

He gave her a hurt spaniel look. He had a touch of conjunctivitis. 'I've been misunderstood, Mrs Graham. Again.'

She bit her lip. 'What happened this time?'

Bella Willis had been through one of the worst half-minutes a mother can when she glanced up from the cheese counter in Tesco's to see a shabbily dressed man reaching into the pram where young Dean Willis was attempting to swallow one foot.

There wasn't much of Bella. Girls who were at school with her would have said she was a shy little thing who preferred to watch anything more robust than flower-arranging from a safe distance. But now her child was at risk. She let out a howl of rage that transfixed everyone between Ready Meals and Best Cambridge King Edwards, and flew at him.

Liz could have told her, had she been there, that a ten-month-old baby was the last thing Kevin Tufnall needed or wanted. But Bella thought her child was being abducted, and nothing Kevin could have done that left her standing would have protected him from her fury. Her hard little fists blackened his eye and split his lip. When he tried to turn away she tore out a handful of his hair. If people hadn't restrained her, shy little Bella Willis would have ripped him limb from limb.

Liz sighed. 'All right, Kevin, what were you after? Not the baby, I know that – too hard to fence. Did you have some earlier shopping in the pram, Mrs Willis? Had you tucked your purse under the covers?'

By now Bella had realized that this man, though he was plainly known to the police, was not known for abducting infants. She'd misread the situation. It hardly mattered. A man she didn't know had trespassed on her most precious property. Huge, primitive emotions burgeoned within her. She could have done anything – she could have killed him. Even now the rage shielded her from embarrassment. She would have scurried away apologizing from someone who jostled her on a bus; she would have been too mortified to complain if someone hijacked her drier at the laundrette. But this man had made her think her baby was in danger, and it was impossible to overreact to that. She had trouble speaking civilly even to Liz. 'Of course not.'

'There must have been something,' said Liz reasonably. 'He steals – that's what he does, nothing else. Do you want to tell us, Kevin? If you don't admit attempted theft it's going in the book as a suspected abduction.'

Kevin thought a bit longer, but a man who goes to prison every few months wants nothing on his record that smacks of child abuse. Being that misunderstood could get him killed. Finally he nodded, and mumbled something out of the corner of his mouth like a spy giving a password in a public place.

It wasn't a deliberate ploy to embarrass him further, Liz genuinely didn't hear. 'Sorry – what?'

With a martyred expression Kevin repeated it louder. 'I said, I was hungry. I haven't eaten since yesterday morning. There was a packet of rusks on top of the pram.'

It was too pathetic to be other than true. Liz rolled her eyes. 'You mean, you really *are* reduced to stealing from babies? Kevin, that's the pits. You have *got* to get your act together, before we find you dead in Cornmarket with a tin of cat-food clutched in your cold little hand and no can-opener.'

Her first instinct was to go and tell Frank Shapiro about her latest contribution to the clear-up rate. But actually it wasn't as funny as it was tragic. Kevin Tufnall might be an extreme case, but he was more typical of the criminal underworld than clever men with organizations behind them. Most of the people the police dealt with were more stupid, lazy and weak than they were evil. They lacked the commitment, the application, to make a success even of crime.

But she wanted to see Shapiro anyway. 'What's all this about Donovan and a car crash?'

Donovan was already there, lurking behind the door. 'Go on,' he growled, 'talk about me behind my back.'

Liz bestowed on him her sweetest smile. 'Now Sergeant, you know we wouldn't do that. You sit down right here in the middle of the room and we'll talk about you in front of you. So Frank, what's this about Sergeant Donovan here and a car crash?'

Shapiro chuckled into his double chin. That was one of his more successful gambles. It shouldn't have worked, they were too different: the taciturn sergeant from a gritty little mid-Ulster town and the cheerful, intelligent, capable woman for whom a spell as DI in Castlemere could only be a step on the way to something better. It should have been – in fact it was – antipathy at first sight. Donovan saw Liz as a Regional HQ bimbo riding a wave of positive discrimination, whose first bloody nose would see her back behind a desk except for inspirational TV appearances. Liz thought Donovan was a loose cannon, a simmering brew of grudges barely contained within a vessel as brittle as glass.

Making them work together could have been a bad mistake. If he'd had longer to think about it, and enough manpower to have a choice, probably Shapiro would have thought better of it. But there was no alternative, and in the pressure cooker of difficult and sometimes dangerous inquiries the partnership had blossomed and become fruitful.

Once she confounded his prejudices, Liz Graham was the best thing that could have happened to Donovan. She wasn't afraid of him. She could tolerate his moods, his impatience, his war of attrition with authority, for the sake of his strengths – his absolute commitment to the job and his willingness to do whatever was necessary to get it done. She also recognized that behind the romantic unpredictability of the wild Celt Detective Sergeant Donovan suffered from punishingly high expectations of himself. He didn't need driving. He needed steering.

With a little prompting he told the story again, starting with the robbery at the garage and ending with the van in flames outside Chevening Parish Church. Anti-climax had set in, leaving him flat and intolerant of all the fuss.

When Liz realized she was sitting there with her mouth open she shut it and tried to think of something intelligent to say. 'Er – has the gun been recovered?'

Shapiro was impressed. The first time he heard this story, an awareness of how closely Donovan had shaved disaster left him incapable of coherent thought for several minutes. 'SOCO have been over the van with a fine-tooth comb but they didn't find anything that might once have been a handgun.'

'Then he dumped it,' said Donovan, shortly, as if someone had accused him of something. 'Somewhere on the road between Kumani's and Chevening. It was dark, he could have dropped the window and slung it out anywhere – I wouldn't have seen, there were whole stretches where he was just a couple of tail-lights in the distance. Some of the time I couldn't see him at all, I was following by guess and by God.'

Shapiro nodded. 'Well, if that's what he did we should find it.'

Head down, Donovan growled something *sotto voce*. This was a tactical manoeuvre: if a senior officer asked him to repeat himself it was hard then to complain that he was speaking out of turn.

Shapiro knew the rules of this little game well enough. It was one of the small liberties he allowed to Donovan in order to save his energy for stamping on the larger ones. He vented a weary sigh. 'Sorry, Sergeant, what was that?'

Donovan looked up, his lips tight. 'I said, we better had. I don't want there to be any doubt about this. It was an armed robbery. Not a toy, not a replica – that was a real gun. He wouldn't have knocked me out with a toy; and Ash Kumani would have kicked him down Cambridge Road if there'd been any question in his mind what Mikey was pointing at him. It was an armed robbery, he decked me to get away, and he could have killed the woman in the car. I want that gun found. I don't want anyone saying, Well, maybe it was real and maybe it wasn't and anyway we can't prove it so how about we charge him with assault and driving without due care and attention?'

Shapiro understood his anger. It was one of the most offensive things that could happen to a police officer, to know – not to suspect, not to believe, but to *know* – that a crime had been committed and to be denied a successful prosecution by a break in the line of evidence.

It didn't depend on what you knew but on what you could prove. The Crown Prosecution Service hated losing cases, if they weren't confident of a conviction they wouldn't proceed. Placid middle-aged policemen with grandchildren and a liking for country walks could be reduced to impotent fury by the sight of some cocky young thug back on the street because a break in the evidence allowed another interpretation of the facts, if viewed from the right angle and with a following wind. It was desperately frustrating. You told yourself you'd get them next time, but it didn't make it any easier to see them swagger away. It was one of those occasions when the fact that police arms had to be authorized and issued, not just pulled from a holster, saved a lot of not very worthy lives and some rather more valuable careers.

'I've got a dozen people out looking,' said Shapiro. 'They know it's important, they'll find it if they can. At least we know where it has to be – if he threw it from the car it went out the driver's window and ended up south of the road. It's just over three miles from Kumani's to Chevening, so the search area is a twenty foot strip three miles long. I've known smaller needles found in bigger haystacks. As long as nobody's pocketed it already, they'll find it.'

Donovan was frowning. 'They're only looking now?'

Shapiro regarded him levelly. 'Yesterday I was still waiting for SOCO to tell me if it was in the car.'

Donovan knew he was being unreasonable. 'Yeah – sorry. I just—'

'I know.'

'I don't want him wriggling off the hook.'

'Yes, I know.'

When Donovan left Shapiro said, 'You know what that was about, don't you? He doesn't want people thinking Mikey Dickens got the better of him with anything smaller than a howitzer.'

Liz chuckled. 'Have you interviewed Mikey? What does he have to say for himself?'

'Not a lot,' Shapiro said ruefully. 'I saw him in the hospital: by the time he was fit to see me he'd already talked to his brief and she'd advised him to say nothing at that time. I wasn't too bothered, he wasn't going anywhere with cracked ribs and a hole in his leg. He was discharged this morning, he and his solicitor are coming in later today. Maybe we'll have the gun by then: that should help loosen his tongue.'

'And if he's still making no comment?'

'He can stew for a while, but sooner or later I'm having him for this. He's not getting away with it just by keeping his mouth shut, not when Donovan had him in sight pretty well all the way from Kumani's to where he crashed. He can't claim he was elsewhere when they picked bits of the van out of him on the operating table!'

'No,' agreed Liz, 'he'll have to come up with something a bit more imaginative than that.'

'He held me up at gunpoint, Mr Shapiro,' said Mikey Dickens, straight-faced. 'He rushed out of the garage, jumped in the van and pointed a gun in my face. He said Drive so I drove. What else could I do? What would you have done, Mr Shapiro?'

Shapiro shut his eyes. He took two or three measured breaths. His broad face, which long ago learned to mask rather than portray emotions, became positively wooden. But when he opened his eyes again they pinned Mikey Dickens to his seat. 'So Mr Kumani was robbed, and Detective Sergeant Donovan knocked down, by some *other* short, wiry individual with a liking for other people's money and a propensity for violence?'

Mikey met his gaze with wide-open, innocent,

baby-blue eyes. 'Gee, Mr Shapiro, I don't know. What's a propensity?'

Sitting beside him in the interview room, the Dickens family solicitor dug Mikey in the ribs. The last thing she needed was him getting smart with Detective Superintendent Shapiro. Ms Holloway was new to Carfax and Browne, Attorneys at Law, but almost the first thing she was told was not to under-estimate the town's senior detective. 'He only looks like a well-worn teddy bear,' said Mr Carfax darkly. 'He thinks like Machiavelli.'

Ms Holloway didn't altogether believe it, but she took the precaution of elbowing Mikey under the level of the table at which they were all sitting. She must have forgotten his damaged ribs – he winced and whined and looked reprovingly at her, which even a teddy bear could hardly have failed to notice.

She cleared her throat. A woman in her late twen-ties, she hadn't been in Castlemere long enough to switch her London lawyer's power suit for the more casual version appropriate in the sticks. 'Superin-tendent, you have my client's statement. I understand this is a full account of the events of Sunday evening, but if you need him to elaborate Mr Dickens will be happy to oblige. He's anxious to clear up any mis-understanding. He appreciates how things must have appeared to Sergeant Donovan, he has no complaints about his treatment, but he's keen to put on record those events which occurred outside the Sergeant's field of view and misled him as to the author of the attack on him.'

'By the way, Mr Shapiro,' interjected Mikey, 'how is Mr Donovan?'

It was, so far as Shapiro could tell, a genuine enquiry and he answered in the same vein. 'He's fine, thanks, Mikey. He's back at work, you'll probably see him later.'

'I was never so glad to see him as Sunday night.'

'In the garage?' Shapiro prompted innocently.

But Mikey didn't need his London brief to field that one. He smiled impishly. 'In the *van*, Mr Shapiro. After I crashed the van.'

Shapiro hadn't really expected to trip him that easily. Mikey Dickens might only have been nineteen but he'd done this before. 'All right, Mikey, tell it from the start.'

It was the cold weather, said Mikey; possibly also the springs on the van, which needed work, but mainly the cold weather that got to his bladder something rotten. He was only five minutes from home but he didn't think he'd make it: he stopped on the garage forecourt, left the van running and dashed round the back. When he returned—

'Much relieved?' suggested Shapiro, and Mikey grinned.

When he returned, much relieved, he noticed a motorbike at one of the pumps; and when he got in the van he found his keys were gone. He was still wondering where they'd got to when someone in a long dark coat and a ski mask ran out of the shop, snatched open the door of his van and leapt in beside him.

'You don't keep the passenger door locked?'

Mikey was scathing. 'Who'd steal a heap like that?'

'Somebody making a getaway from an armed robbery?'

42

Mikey nodded thoughtfully. 'Right enough, Mr Shapiro.'

'This long dark coat,' said Shapiro. 'Anything like the long dark coat you were wearing?'

'No,' Mikey said firmly. 'Mine was navy blue. His was a sort of charcoal grey.'

When he turned to remonstrate the first thing he saw was the gun; so Mikey thought he'd save the lecture on private property. The second thing he saw was his own keys being dangled under his nose. 'I went where he told me. He said to get off the main road so I headed for Chevening. He had me scared shitless, Mr Shapiro, honest. I'm not used to guns.'

'Not that end, anyway,' murmured Shapiro.

He saw the single headlight behind him, had no idea if it was pursuit or just a fellow traveller. But the man beside him told him to go faster. He saw the white car enter the roundabout, but his passenger jerked the gun at him and told him to beat it. 'I think he thought we'd make it but Mr Donovan would have to stop.'

'You knew it was Donovan, then. When did he mention that? – this passenger of yours who was wearing a coat very like yours but in charcoal grey.'

Mikey shook his head patiently. 'I didn't know *then* it was Mr Donovan. *Now* I know that's who it was.'

Everything after that happened very quickly but seemed to happen in slow motion. He couldn't beat the white saloon across the roundabout, but he felt to be waiting forever for the crash. As the van rebounded into Fletton Road he saw the digger but there seemed to be plenty of time for the van to stop.

Even the collapse of the front half of his cab seemed to happen slowly enough for him to get his legs clear. But when the van stopped the front doors were compacted to a couple of letter-boxes.

'Thin chap, was he?' asked Shapiro. 'This passenger of yours with the gun and the charcoal coat?'

Mikey frowned, puzzled. 'Didn't really notice, Mr Shapiro.'

'Only he seems to have got out through some aperture that wasn't big enough for you to follow; and without wishing to be personal, Mikey, you're not exactly Arnold Swartzer-whatsit yourself.'

Mikey's brow cleared. 'Oh, that. He got out before we hit the digger. I'm not sure if he jumped or fell, but the door opened and he was gone. I never saw him again.'

'Oddly enough,' said Shapiro, deadpan, 'neither did anyone else.'

Mikey shrugged. 'There was a lot going on, Mr Shapiro, and it was dark. And Mr Donovan was too busy trying to haul me out of there to be looking round. I don't blame him for that,' he added generously. 'He saved my life, I won't hear a word against him.'

'Oh Mikey,' said Shapiro with heavy irony, 'he *will* be touched.'

'I don't know if he had help with the story or if he's brighter than he looks.' Shapiro was stirring his coffee lugubriously, staring into the muddy vortex as if seeking wisdom. 'But actually it's quite clever. He's not saying Donovan's wrong, just that he didn't see everything. That's plausible – first he was on the floor of the shop, then he was chasing the van up the road, then he lost sight of it going into Chevening. He didn't see the crash, he could certainly have missed seeing this putative second party legging it immediately afterwards. You wouldn't have to disbelieve Donovan's account to accept Mikey's.

'Then, this putative second party looked sufficiently like Mikey that even a reliable witness could be mistaken. If I ask Kumani whether the robber was wearing a navy-blue coat or a charcoal-grey one he'll look at me askance and say that wasn't the bit he was concentrating on. And Mikey's coat and gloves were burned in the van, so we'll never know if Donovan's blood was on them. Any more than we'll know if that's why Mikey got rid of them, though we may suspect as much.'

Liz regarded him over the tray. As a Detective Superintendent Shapiro had his coffee served in cups on a tray instead of in a plastic mug with no saucer. That, and the salary, was the only difference promotion had made. 'Are you telling me you think Mikey Dickens *didn't* rob Ash Kumani at gunpoint and floor Donovan in the process?'

Shapiro's glance was dismissive. 'Of course not. Of course the little sod did it – there was no second party, he was alone in the van. But he's come up with a story that's going to take some disproving. I'd be interested to know if that was his idea or if Ms Holloway fresh from London offered suggestions.'

Liz shrugged. 'Hardly matters, does it? Whoever the Dickenses went to would need to earn their oats. We'll just have to earn ours as well. We need a witness, someone who can say if there was one man or two in the van after it left Kumani's. Someone else may have seen it earlier, but I can only think of one person who certainly saw it, and closer than anyone else. Do we have a statement from Mrs Taylor?'

'A rather cursory one. She was still pretty upset when Mary Wilson saw her, she got down the basics and left it at that. Maybe by now she's a bit calmer. Anyway, it's a simple enough question, either she saw how many people were in the van or she didn't. Do you know her, Liz? – she teaches at Brian's school.'

Liz nodded. 'We've met. A pleasant enough woman; maybe a little intense. I'll go and see her, see if she can help. If she can say there was definitely only one man in the van, we've got him.'

'And I'll tell Donovan.' Shapiro's nose wrinkled as if he'd bitten into a lemon.

'It's a tough job, but somebody has to do it,' said Liz stoutly.

Donovan took the news with a kind of savage amusement, as if life had taught him to expect no better. 'So that's it, is it? He robbed Kumani at gunpoint, he knocked me down, he damn near killed Mrs Taylor – but he says it wasn't him so we let him go. I mean, what possible reason could he have to lie?'

Shapiro had been a police officer for longer than Donovan had been alive. He'd learned much about crime and criminals, and also about policemen. He remembered when a sergeant using that tone to a superintendent would have been told to clear his locker. Even today there weren't many senior officers who'd put up with it, and those who knew Shapiro well enough to know that behind the slightly rumpled exterior dwelt a mind as sharp and clear as a cut-glass bell didn't understand why he did.

If they'd asked he'd have explained. Most detective sergeants were either on their way up the ladder or were good DCs for so long they'd earned the promotion even if they weren't up to the job. Donovan was. On his record he should have made DI; but for various reasons, some of them his fault, others not, he wasn't considered DI material. The police force hadn't changed so much in thirty years that it encouraged people who challenged its basic precepts. Which meant that Donovan would stay a detective sergeant and stay in Castlemere; and long after Liz Graham had moved on and Shapiro himself was only a memory his experience in this town would be an asset to Queen's Street CID. He was worth keeping on board for that, even if the line hadn't been drawn that he was prepared to toe.

On top of which there was the personal reason. Donovan had risked his life for this job, and he'd risked his job for Shapiro. A man didn't forget that in a hurry.

But though Shapiro allowed him some latitude, for the sake of the future and the past, his patience wasn't limitless. 'Of course that isn't it,' he snapped. 'I haven't put him on a plane to Rio: I'll have him back in here as soon as I have enough to charge him. Finding the gun will do – no jury'll believe he went on doing what he was told by a hijacker who'd thrown his gun away. No, if we find the gun we have him. He was the only one with reason to ditch it. This putative second person would have hung on to it as long as he could, so if he didn't lose it at the scene of the accident he's still got it.'

'He *hasn't* still got it,' insisted Donovan, 'because he doesn't exist! There was only ever Mikey. I know, I never saw his face. But if you smell pig, and something pig-shaped runs you down and leaves trotter-prints up your cardigan, you don't need to see the face to know it was a pig.

'It was Mikey's size and Mikey's shape, it was wearing Mikey's coat and doing what Mikey does in the characteristically vicious way that Mikey does it. Then it burnt rubber in Mikey's van, and when it crashed – away to buggery! – there was Mikey behind the wheel. It was *all* Mikey, there *was* no one else. He dumped the gun because he didn't want to be caught with it on him. The rest of it, this other man, he made it up. If there'd been a gun in his ribs that's the first thing he'd have said when I pulled him out the van. You would, wouldn't you? – It wasn't my fault, guv, it was the other feller made me do it. If there'd been another man, Mikey'd have said so.'

'Maybe he would,' said Shapiro grimly. 'Except—'

It wasn't often that Donovan failed to follow where his chief was leading. But he lost the trail this time. 'Except what?'

Shapiro glowered at him. 'Except that he was never properly cautioned about the consequences of not doing so.'

Chapter Five

The Taylors had a cottage on the Castlemere Canal a mile or so from Chevening village. Even with the directions she'd been given Liz had trouble finding it. She passed the farm lane twice before realizing it was the turning she needed and not just the way to some barn or byre. Leaving the road she drove through the eerie flatness of The Levels with not a house, not a car, not even a tractor in sight.

Then suddenly she was there, a little stand of willows screening the cottage until the glint of water at the end of the lane had already brought her to a halt.

There was no car in front of the house, which might have meant there was no one at home or just that the Taylors hadn't yet replaced the white saloon. Liz rang the bell and waited, and was at length rewarded by footsteps in the hall.

'Mrs Taylor? I don't expect you remember me – I'm Brian Graham's wife, we've met at the school.'

Patricia Taylor nodded, politely enough but without warmth: either she wasn't sure who her visitor was or she didn't care.

Liz pressed on. 'Actually, I'm here in my official

49

capacity, as a Detective Inspector.' She produced her warrant card, mostly from habit. 'About the crash.'

'I made a statement.'

'Yes. I hoped we could talk a bit more about it now the dust's had time to settle.'

Mrs Taylor showed her to a chintzy sitting room that enjoyed the winter sun and a view across the canal to the endless vista of The Levels beyond – a sort of Dutch landscape that made the ordeal of bouncing up a farm track eminently worthwhile. She took a chair and gestured Liz to the sofa. 'I don't know if I can add anything to what I've already said.'

She was a year or two younger than Liz, her nose up against the great watershed of forty. She was dark and erect, with a reserved manner that earlier generations would have considered properly school-marmish. In today's educational climate it set her apart from those of her colleagues who taught in sweatshirts and trainers.

'How are you feeling now?'

Pat Taylor's dark eyes widened as if she considered the inquiry slightly impertinent. Then she seemed to realize it was just part of the process. 'All right, I suppose. Bruised – I've got the marks of the seat-belt printed right across me. Shaken, of course. The hospital said there was no damage done so I suppose I should be grateful. I could be dead. I could be a vegetable!' She heard her voice climbing and fell abruptly silent.

Liz nodded gently. 'I know. It makes you feel so vulnerable, doesn't it? It makes you think you'll never be safe outside your own front door again.' Liz wasn't talking about a car crash but she was talking from personal experience. 'But it does pass. First it fades a little, so it's somehow less intrusive, less disabling. Then you notice that you've gone a whole afternoon without thinking about it, then a whole day. And then it takes its place in history. You don't forget, but you get past it and move on. Thank God it was only the car you lost, not a member of your family.'

Mrs Taylor managed a wan smile. 'I'm sorry. You must think I'm behaving very badly.'

'Don't be silly. You had a brush with death, of course you're shocked. It'll take time to find your feet again. But you must have driven an awful lot of miles when nobody trashed your car, and it's most unlikely anything like it will ever happen to you again.'

'Who was he?' She didn't say who she meant; she didn't have to.

'I don't expect you'd know him. He's only a young lad, but he's got quite a track record. There was a robbery at the garage on Cambridge Road, he may have been involved in that. My sergeant gave chase, and he seems to have been more interested in getting away than winning awards for his driving. You were just very unlucky.'

'Your sergeant,' echoed Mrs Taylor. 'The tall man, who came over to me after the crash?'

'Yes, that's Donovan.'

'He said he couldn't get me out. He said I had to wait.'

'It was the safest thing to do.'

'He got that little thug out of his van!'

'With the van on fire the risk of compounding an injury was irrelevant. If he'd waited for the experts there'd have been only a body to recover.'

'I wish—' She heard herself saying it and stopped. 'No. Sorry. Was he all right?'

'They're both all right, give or take a few cuts and bruises. Now we're trying to establish exactly what happened – just who was responsible for just what.'

Mrs Taylor's eyes flared. 'I hope nobody's saying any of this was my fault! I was already half-way round the roundabout. I heard him coming, I knew he was going too fast, but I thought he'd stop at the broken line. He couldn't have missed seeing me. There was nothing *I* could do – if I'd braked he'd still have hit me.'

'Mrs Taylor, nobody's suggesting you could have done anything more,' Liz said quickly. 'Like you say, he should have stopped at the line. Once he came over it, at that speed, the accident was inevitable. It's just a miracle nobody died.'

'Then I don't understand. What else do you need to ask me?'

Liz went carefully. She didn't want to be accused of putting answers in a witness's mouth, particularly when she was the only witness they had. 'When you saw the van coming at you, did you get a proper look at it?'

'Where else would I be looking?' Mrs Taylor frowned. 'If he's saying it was someone else who hit me, he can think again. It happened quickly, but not so fast that I couldn't see what it was running me down. It was a small red van and it hit me amidships. There was no one else in sight.'

'That's right, Donovan was still coming through the S-bend – the crash had happened by the time he got there. Certainly it was the van that hit you, that isn't disputed.'

'Then what is?'

Liz didn't answer directly. 'It was a two-seater van. Did you see if there was a passenger?'

Her lips made little puzzled shapes as Mrs Taylor considered. 'There was someone else in the van? Someone who didn't get out?'

Again Liz reassured her. 'The van was empty when it blew up. Our Scenes Of Crime Officer would have known if anyone had been left behind – it doesn't matter how fierce the fire, you can always recognize a body. No, the suggestion's been made that someone may have been inside earlier, and we're trying to establish when he left, before the accident or afterwards.'

'Don't call it that,' said Mrs Taylor.

'What?'

'An accident. It wasn't an accident. An accident is something that cannot be predicted or prevented. What happened was the inevitable consequence of deliberate actions. An accident is an accident regard-less of the outcome, but if he'd killed me that boy would have been guilty of manslaughter.'

All right, she taught English, the precise usage of words probably held greater significance for her than for the population at large. It was still odd to insist on something so trivial.

But then, less than forty-eight hours ago this woman was hanging in the straps of her seat-belt as her car rolled down the road like a nine-pin in a bowling alley. She was traumatized, her reactions would be unpredictable for a while. She'd faced death close enough to smell it and nothing would be quite the same again. There were things she would have to relearn, and one was that basically the world was a pretty safe place, there was no need to be afraid all the time; and another was which things mattered and which didn't.

In just a second or two her existence had been turned, quite literally, upside down and all the old certainties had been shaken. There would be times when shaving death in a car crash seemed almost banal; and in the next breath she would burst into tears because there were no chocolate digestives left in the biscuit-tin. In time she would pick up the rhythm of her life once more, but a bad accident is a little like a minor stroke, it creates little gaps in the record, little question marks where none were before.

'So – did you see who was in the van?' prompted Liz gently.

'I saw the driver. I'm not sure I could identify him. His mouth was open and his eyes were staring, but I suppose I looked pretty much the same to him. He had a dark coat on, and a dark woolly hat – his face looked very white between them.' She forced a chuckle. 'I imagine mine did too.'

'What about the passenger? Was there one?'

Mrs Taylor had to think longer about that. 'I'm not sure. I can't picture a second face, not the way I can the driver's, but I couldn't swear there wasn't one. Oh God,' she sighed then, 'it's such a jumble. You'd think it would be the clearest thing in the world, wouldn't you, we were only a few feet apart and I knew he was going to hit me. But I couldn't pick the driver out of a line-up, and I can't even say if he was alone in the van. I'm sorry, Mrs Graham, I'm not being much help, am I?'

Liz smiled. 'I need to know what you remember, not what might have been but then again might not. There are no right answers, only accurate ones. If you say you don't remember, or you're not sure, then I can look for the answers elsewhere. People trying so hard to be helpful that they end up misleading us are the real problem.'

'Didn't your sergeant see who was in the van?'

'Not in the period we're talking about. Never mind, we may find someone else who did – someone crossing the road or driving in the opposite direction. We'll make enquiries.' As she went to leave she added, 'It's just possible that in another day or two you'll have a clearer image of events than you have now. If that happens, if at some point you're pretty sure either that there was someone else in the van or there wasn't, would you give me a call?'

'Yes, of course.' Pat Taylor glanced at her watch. 'I'm sorry but I must go now – I've got a hospital appointment.'

'I'm going back to town, can I give you a lift?'

'Thank you, but no. The taxi's on its way.'

The search party combed every inch of roadside between Kumani's garage and the Chevening round-about, and found nothing. At first they concentrated on the verge which would have been on Mikey's right as he drove. Unsuccessful there, they extended the search to include the left hand verge and as far to the right as a good shot-putter could have lobbed a handgun. Still they found nothing.

Shapiro called them off at midday. Super-intendent Giles wanted his uniforms back for other duties, DC Scobie was needed in court and, estimable as he was in many ways, DC Morgan could not conduct a finger-tip search of three miles of hedgerow on his own.

Donovan ambushed him as he came in. 'Nothing?'

'Sorry, Serg. Did our best.' It sounded like real dismay, but actually Dick Morgan always talked as if someone had spilt ketchup on his cornflakes. It was his Fenland genes, lugubrious and pessimistic: soon it will be autumn and how shall we live through the winter?

'I know. What do you reckon – any point me pushing for another go?'

Morgan thought for a moment then shook his head. 'Somebody beat us to it.'

That was what Donovan thought too. 'No prizes for guessing who. We might have trouble mustering enough people to search for a missing gun but I bet half The Jubilee's been walking up and down that road.' Glencurran, where Donovan came from, was four hundred miles north-west of the Fens but the local character shared the same peaty bleakness. Donovan might have been a square peg in a round hole in Castlemere, but he'd have found no hole at all anywhere else.

He gave a perfunctory tap on Shapiro's door as he went in. 'Bugger-all, then?'

Shapiro eyed him with disfavour. 'I beg your pardon?'

'Sorry, sir. Um – the search of Cambridge Road and Chevening Moss Road appears to have met with no great success, sir. Specifically, the weapon being sought has not proved amenable to discovery. Sir.'

Shapiro sighed. 'Sergeant, one of the few things more alarming than you in a bad mood is you attempting to be funny. Is that the sort of thing that passes for humour in Glencurran?'

'Wouldn't know, sir,' Donovan said woodenly. 'The last man who made a joke there got his head blown off.'

Frank Shapiro, who hailed from the close-knit Jewish community of north London, always thought his people had an odd sense of humour. But if Donovan was at all typical they couldn't hold a candle to an Ulster Catholic.

'I was thinking I might go for a nosy round The Jubilee. If Mikey's dad did organize a Hunt-the-Luger party somebody might let it slip in casual conversation.'

'You mean, with your finger up his nostril?' Shapiro was joking now. Despite appearances – and Donovan could put the fear of God into someone who'd only come to Queen's Street to hand in lost property – he had no history of violence, towards suspects or anyone else.

It wasn't altogether that looks were misleading, more that he knew he could afford no such self-indulgence. Sergeant Bolsover might cuff a lippy youth and everyone would nod and say, That's how it used to be done in the old days, and a lot less trouble we had then too! But Donovan wasn't a fat grandfather with a dozen ancestors in the parish churchyard, and it made a difference. Also, he knew that if he ever started down that route, one day he'd beat the living daylights out of someone. Donovan's temper was like another man's drinking: it was no problem as long as he didn't think he could stop at just one thump.

He looked hurt, but that too was part of the game. 'I mean, in casual conversation. Nice day, how's the pigeons, and by the way who's got Mikey Dickens' stick-up kit?'

'Is anyone in The Jubilee likely to tell you?'

Donovan gave a slow smile. 'There's a couple of people owe me a favour, yeah.'

'And I'd be wiser not asking how?' Shapiro shook his head wearily. 'All right, Sergeant, if you think it's worth a shot go ahead. Try not to start a riot. The reality of life in The Jubilee is that, however close the nearest policeman, there's always a Dickens closer. No one who wants to go on living there can afford to take your side against Mikey.'

'There's also the matter of tribal rivalries,' said Donovan. 'The Dickenses may be top dogs now but there's others snapping at their heels. There's people in The Jubilee would be happy to see one less Dickens around the place. All I have to do is find one, and a nice dark corner to talk to him in.'

Chapter Six

The Jubilee did not entirely deserve its reputation as a hot-bed of crime. Certainly the Dickenses lived there, three generations of them in half a dozen houses scattered among the six streets, and so did their rivals the Walshes. But a lot of decent people without connections to either family lived there too. They minded their own business, stayed off the street if trouble was brewing, and as long as they exercised a little discretion in who they talked to about what nobody bothered them. There were advantages. One was that The Jubilee was virtually a crime-free area, since those responsible for most of the crime elsewhere in Castlemere preferred not to bring work home.

There were six streets but only one way in. Jubilee Terrace was the last turning off Brick Lane before it ran into the dereliction of Cornmarket. Wags in The Ginger Pig reckoned that if you waited till the racing was on the telly and then walled up the junction you'd solve most of Castlemere's problems at a stroke. There was just enough truth in that to make it funny.

The second last turning off Brick Lane, on the other side, was the walkway through to Broad Wharf and Donovan's narrowboat *Tara*. Apart from Martin and Lucy Cole on the *James Brindley*, the denizens of The Jubilee were his nearest neighbours.

He thought about putting Brian Boru on the chain that served as his lead and taking the dog with him. In Brian's company he could walk with impunity into The Jubilee, downtown Beirut or the jaws of hell itself. On the other hand, it was hard to engage people in casual conversation when they kept counting their fingers. He took Brian for a run round Cornmarket, half a mile down the towpath, then left him in *Tara*'s chain locker while he headed for The Jubilee alone.

What he was looking for was a fringe member of the Walsh clan. No one connected with the Dickenses would give him the time of day; neither would anyone without affiliations, for fear of attracting attention. Those associated with the Walsh family would be happy enough to see Mikey get his just deserts and would probably be happy enough to help, but might want to get approval from head office before saying anything. Gang wars had started with less provocation.

So Donovan wasn't looking for an official Walsh spokesman so much as a hanger-on who might talk faster than he thought, who might hear all the gossip mainly because nobody noticed him, and pass it on in the touchingly simple belief that anything that was bad for Dickenses had to be good for Walshes.

Such a man was Billy Dunne, and when Donovan saw the bent little figure shuffling down Coronation Row his heart rose. He faded back into the shadows at the corner of Jubilee Terrace, where a broken light had been awaiting replacement for three years to his knowledge, and waited for the characteristic tap–drag of Billy's progress to reach him.

Billy Dunne may have had his collar felt more times than any man living, even Kevin Tufnall, but never before as he walked round a dark street corner a hundred yards from home. He let out a squawk they could have heard in The Fen Tiger, which was undoubtedly where he was heading now.

It wasn't the most auspicious beginning to a discreet chat. 'Jesus, Billy,' exclaimed Donovan disgustedly, 'have you got a guilty conscience or what?'

'Mr Donovan?' Equal quantities of relief and alarm warred in Billy's creaky voice as he peered into the darkness. He thought at first that he'd been jumped by something nasty, then that it was a policeman, then and finally that being jumped by that particular policeman *was* pretty nasty. He tried frantically to remember if he'd been up to anything Donovan could have found out about.

Donovan had thought he'd keep Billy company as far as The Fen Tiger, where Castlemere's four canals met in a near-subterranean basin near the centre of town. But if Billy Dunne had to talk to a policeman, and he didn't seem to have much option, he preferred to do it in the shadows. He stood his ground nervously. 'Was you looking for me, Mr Donovan?'

'I was,' said Donovan. 'Matter of fact, Billy, I thought you could help me with something.'

The words confirmed Billy's worst fears. When the police asked for your help, without arresting you first, it was the kiss of death to a man in Billy's position. If you couldn't or wouldn't help they never forgot it; if you could and did, everybody you knew crossed you off their Christmas list. Billy replied with a tragic little sigh.

Donovan chuckled. 'Don't sound so worried, I'm not going to get you in trouble. I just wondered what you'd heard about this gun of Mikey Dickens's.'

Those were the magic words that freed Billy's tongue. The muscles of his jaw, that would have clamped tight at the word Walsh, immediately relaxed. He thought he was off the hook. He thought he could get Donovan off his back without calling the fires of hell down on him.

All the same, life had taught Billy Dunne to be cautious. 'Gun, Mr Donovan?'

Donovan's lupine smile was rather wasted in the dark, though Billy shivered anyway, from habit. 'Gun, Billy. The gun he held up Ash Kumani with. The gun he threw away shortly before I caught up with him. The gun his entire bloody family turned out to look for. That gun.'

Billy tried to sound as if he had just this second understood what Donovan was driving at. 'Oh – *that's* what they were doing, is it? I knew there was something going on, I didn't know just what.'

Donovan fought the unreasonable, and unhygienic, urge to kiss him. 'Yeah, that's what it was. They wanted to find Mikey's gun before we did. They did, too. They must have been at it for hours.'

'They were, Mr Donovan. I heard them all setting off about five o'clock yesterday morning – there must have been a dozen cars, maybe more. Then around eight they were back, all laughing and inviting one another in for a drink. Old Roly' – Roland Dickens,

Thelma's eldest and Mikey's father – 'was acting the dog.'

'The dog?' This was one piece of Jubilee argot Donovan hadn't heard before. 'What dog?'

Billy smiled slowly. 'You know, Mr Donovan. The dog that got the cat that got the cream.'

Donovan let him continue on his way. There probably wasn't much he could add, and if Donovan thought of something more to ask he knew where to find him.

So Roly organized the great gun hunt, after he got back from seeing Mikey in the hospital. That figured. If any of the clan had been in a hole it would have been Roly digging them out. The man was an icon to those who mourned the passing of Victorian values, a paterfamilias who had bred copiously and raised his children to follow in his footsteps. Even now they were grown and some were raising children of their own he continued to keep a close eye on all their doings, the rock to which they clung if danger threatened. Admittedly, what they mostly needed his help with was avoiding being locked up on charges ranging from shoplifting to armed robbery. But nothing was too much trouble for this acme of family men: father, grandfather and Godfather.

But knowing who had the gun and finding it were two different things. On what he knew now Donovan could get a search warrant, and strip Roly's house in George Street down to the bricks. And he would find nothing. He might, just, get the warrant extended to cover other properties owned by the Dickens family, and he would find nothing there too.

The gun might already have gone – into the canal

or a landfill site somewhere, or off the stern of a cross-channel ferry on an away day to Calais. If you wanted rid of something as small as a gun, that was easy enough, and if Mikey Dickens had killed someone with the weapon that would surely have been its fate. But he hadn't. The resources of a murder hunt wouldn't be devoted to finding it, and a gun has an intrinsic value in criminal circles: not even the cost of a new one so much as the risks involved in acquiring it. Dealers in unlicensed weapons hazard their freedom and their lives every day, and it makes them paranoid. If they have any doubts about your bona fides they don't just run, they shoot you and then run. Donovan had arrested people buying unlicensed arms who'd been positively relieved to find he was a policeman and not another trigger-happy dealer.

So if the gun could be kept safe until it was wanted again, that's what Roly would do. Send it to ground; and not with another Dickens or a known Dickens associate. It could be anywhere. He could have gone out with a trowel and a plastic bag and buried it in a corner of someone's allotment. Unless Roly could be persuaded to say where, it would never be found.

Donovan was about to leave when he heard the motorbike. There was an extraordinary *déjà vu* moment in which he thought it was his bike and therefore him riding down through The Jubilee; though common sense intervened quickly it didn't quite wipe out the absurd chill of that. Shaking his head to dislodge the sensation – he was an imaginative man, born of an imaginative race; a certain amount of creativity was valuable in a detective but not so much that he found himself wondering if he had his own permission to be riding his own motor-bike – he turned to see where the sound was coming from.

The machine emerged from George Street into the upper part of Jubilee Terrace. There were enough surviving street lights up there to send a constellation of glints and gleams bouncing off the black and chrome of a Kawasaki 400 in show-room condition.

A bike like that didn't belong in The Jubilee. Not because none of the inhabitants could afford it – rob enough garages and you can afford most things – but because if it had belonged there Donovan would have known. If that bike lived anywhere in Castlemere Donovan would have known. He went to the office window at the sound of a bike engine the way other people respond to the sound of a band in the street.

And if it didn't live here, the chances were – this being The Jubilee – it had been stolen. In London, maybe, and brought here in the belief that no one would know. Donovan might not have noticed if someone had come out of George Street wearing the Crown Jewels, but he always noticed bikes.

The rider was dressed like most bikers, in black leathers with a full-face helmet. He wasn't a big man: if Mikey Dickens hadn't been *hors de combat* Donovan might have thought it was him. Except that he rode that bike with a finesse which was not the first quality you associated with Mikey or any of his family. Respect, thought Donovan – for the machine, for what it could do.

All the same, the mere fact of its being here raised enough reasonable suspicion for a conscientious policeman to stop it and seek an explanation. And maybe talk grommits and big ends for a while. As the bike crossed Coronation Row and slowed to turn into Brick Lane Donovan stepped out of the shadows into the middle of the road, one hand up in the prescribed fashion.

The Kawasaki was too well-bred for its brakes to squeal but it kicked a couple of little fish-tails as it came to a halt. Muffled by the tinted perspex, the tirade of abuse from inside the helmet may have lost some of its highlights but Donovan still got 'cretin' and 'bonehead' and (probably) 'sucker'.

'All right, sonny,' he growled, 'you want to tell me about the friend of a friend who didn't at all mind you borrowing his wheels while he was in Benidorm?'

'And another thing,' snarled the rider, unintimidated, throwing off the helmet so that a river of red-gold hair flowed down one black leather shoulder: 'don't call me sonny!'

Donovan didn't believe in love at first sight. If asked he would have said he didn't believe in love; though this was nonsense, all Irishmen are romantics, it's why they write such wonderful songs about all the battles they've lost. But either way, a beautiful girl on a Kawasaki 400 was a dream come true. Donovan felt his jaw drop and closed it. He felt his eyes smart and blinked. Finally he remembered he was still standing in the middle of the road with one hand up and he let it fall. 'Er – hi,' he said inanely.

'I *said*,' repeated the girl, her voice steely with exasperation, 'what do you want that's worth risking both our lives for?'

'I think I was going to make a big mistake,'

admitted Donovan. 'I was going to ask if you'd any right to be riding that bike.'

Even outside the shadow there wasn't a lot of light, but what there was gathered in the pale oval of her face. Enough to show the flash of indignation in her eyes turn first to an appreciation of the compliment and then to amusement. 'That would have been a mistake,' she nodded. Unmuffled by the helmet, her voice had the clear carrying quality of struck crystal. 'Anyway, what business is it of yours?'

His reply was so low she had to ask him to repeat it. 'I'm a policeman!' he said then, loud enough to cause heart attacks all over The Jubilee. 'I'm supposed to challenge anyone acting suspiciously.'

Now the anger had subsided she was rather enjoying his discomfort. 'And I'm Rumpole of the Bailey. What do you mean, acting suspiciously? – I could give lessons on how to ride a motorcycle.'

Donovan didn't doubt it. 'That's what I mean. In The Jubilee, somebody riding carefully on a clean motorbike *is* suspicious. If you want to go unnoticed here, lose that prissy helmet and practise your wheelies.'

The girl laughed. 'My wheelies don't need any practice. I take it you're a biker?'

Donovan did the slow smile. 'Is the Pope a Catholic?'

'What do you ride?'

'Same as yours but the 550.'

The girl nodded. 'I like the power of a big bike but the weight's a problem. The 400's a good compromise – plenty of burn but I can still hold it up in traffic jams.'

'Do you live round here?'

Her head tipped to one side. 'Is that an official inquiry, officer?'

'No.'

'Then no. Castlemere, but not here. I was visiting someone. Why?'

He shrugged in what he hoped was a nonchalant fashion. 'I thought, if you'd got a long ride home, you might like a coffee first. I know a place on the canal, three minutes from here.'

'Well, it isn't *that* long a ride,' she said thoughtfully. 'On the other hand, it's a chilly night. A café, you say?'

Donovan nodded. 'At Mere Basin, where the narrowboats used to tie up. There are still some about. Talk to me nicely and I might show you one.'

Her name was Jade. Some people would have looked for rather more in the way of an introduction but Donovan went for months, sometimes even years, without using his first name and had always found one perfectly adequate.

'How did they know you were going to have green eyes?'

She laughed again, like a crystal fountain. 'How do *you* know I've got green eyes?'

And to be sure, there was nowhere near enough light to tell. But his conviction didn't waver. 'With hair that colour? Of course they're green.'

'The hair colour might have come out of a bottle.'

'Sure it might,' said Donovan. 'And I might be lead tenor in a Welsh miners' choir.'

'You're Irish.'

'And you have green eyes.'

Jade grinned and threw a long leg over the machine. 'Coffee, then. Tell me where to go.'

Donovan didn't need asking twice: he got on behind her, only hoping he wouldn't be flagged down by one of the more reckless PCs for riding without a helmet. But even a PC desperate for arrests would think twice before venturing this far up Brick Lane. In fact they saw no one. Donovan's biggest problem was riding pillion on a bike when he didn't know where to put his hands.

Chapter Seven

Shapiro was unsurprised about Billy Dunne's revelation. Something of the sort had to have happened: if the gun had still been lying by the road on Tuesday his own search would have found it.

'Wherever Roly's hidden it,' said Donovan, 'it won't be at home and it probably won't be in The Jubilee. Can you think of anywhere else?'

Shapiro squinted at him. 'You don't think, Sergeant, that in choosing a safe hiding place for a gun used in an armed robbery, Roly would have it in mind to avoid places known to the local Detective Superintendent?'

Chastened, Donovan nodded. 'So—?'

Shapiro thought. 'The likelihood is that Roly's the only one who knows exactly where that gun is now. He won't tell us, and there's no point putting a tail on him because he has no need to go anywhere near it for the foreseeable future. What does that leave?'

'Guile?' suggested Donovan hopefully. When it came to sneaky, no member of Castlemere's criminal fraternity could hold a candle to its senior detective.

'Trick him? I suppose it's possible. But Roly Dickens is no fool, he'll know we're anxious to get hold of that gun – I don't know what we could do that would make him hand it over.'

Neither did Donovan, but there had to be something. The alternative was that Mikey was going to get away with this. 'Can we get him worried that we might have found it – worried enough to go and check?'

'And follow him there? You'll need a good story. Roly's sharper than he looks: it's no coincidence that he has half The Jubilee under his thumb. Getting him to take your bait may be the easy part. The hard part will be stopping him yanking you into the water and drowning you.'

Donovan was frowning. 'You're not telling me we can't deal with Roly Dickens?'

'Of course not. I'm telling you not to underestimate him. He's a clever, dangerous man and he's fighting for something that matters to him.'

'This is pretty important to me, too,' gritted Donovan.

'I know that. That's why I'm telling you to be careful. He'll make a fool of you if he can; and if he can't he might get serious. I don't want you getting hurt over this.'

Donovan touched a finger to his face. 'Bit late for that, chief.'

Shapiro knew he was wasting his time. Threatening Donovan only made him obdurate. He thought it wouldn't matter; he didn't think he'd get close enough to make Roly angry. 'All right, see what you can do. But don't get so far out on a limb that you don't hear the sound of sawing.'

*

The problem would be convincing Roly that he should be worried. Clearly he would have put the gun where he believed it would be safe: somehow Donovan had to persuade him that the police were closing in on it but there was still time for him to make it safe if he acted at once.

Donovan had an extensive stable of informants, but none of them would be much use to him in this. A man would have to be pretty close to Roly Dickens to know where he'd hidden Mikey's gun, and anyone that close wasn't going to talk to a policeman. Not if he was attached to both kneecaps he wasn't.

He was still fretting about it, and no nearer an answer, when he met Jade after work. They went for a meal, then on to an exhibition at the Town Hall. Two hundred years of the Castlemere Canal in photographs, paintings and artifacts. Jade had seen it advertised and thought Donovan would be interested. But he trailed round behind her like a bored child.

'Well, that went down like a lead balloon,' she growled as they left. 'If there's something you'd rather be doing tonight, don't let me detain you.'

With a guilty start he realized he was squandering his chance with her, and that it mattered to him not to. 'I'm sorry. It's work – I've hit a brick wall and I can't get it out of my head. I'm rotten at keeping my work and my private life separate,' he added honestly. 'Only I don't usually have enough of a private life for it to be a problem.'

Jade gave a little snort, half of impatience, half amusement. Despite his failings there was something about Donovan she couldn't help liking. It might even have been his lack of social skill. There was no polish with him: what you saw was what you got. All right, what she was getting tonight was a rather dreary pre-occupation with his work; but she knew there was more. It wasn't just that he was attracted to her, though she knew he was. Men had liked her before, but she hadn't let them take her for granted. She wasn't quite sure why she was willing to put up with it this time. Presumably, because she thought he was worth it.

She knew now – she'd known last night – it wasn't going to be an easy relationship. They were too alike: impatient, unconventional, fiercely ambitious. Both of them took risks to get what they wanted. Two more cautious people wouldn't have ridden off into the darkness together and spent three hours in a base-ment café that could have been empty for all they knew or cared. For the last half hour it was, except for them and an increasingly irate waiter.

For two pins, she knew, Donovan would have asked her back to his boat when the café closed. For two pins she would have gone. Why? – because a part of her thrived on danger, didn't care if she was being unwise. Trouble she could handle: tame and safe with-ered her. Donovan with his moods and his dark looks and the intensity that radiated from him like a heat made her feel more alive than anything had in some time.

But he hadn't asked her back, and in the end she had too much pride to invite herself. He'd asked to see her again. She'd shrugged, said she'd call him.

As soon as the morning papers arrived she took them to her office, looking for an excuse to make it tonight. When she saw the canal exhibition advertised it was like fate lending a hand. But she waited until lunchtime to call. No need to tell him he'd got under her skin.

So his lack of enthusiasm for what she'd chosen was doubly disappointing. Two truisms occurred to her: one about fish in the sea, and one about flogging a dead horse. 'Do you want to call it a night?'

'No!' The swiftness of his response could only be a compliment, however belated. 'I really am sorry, it was a nice idea, it's just—' He raised one shoulder in an awkward lopsided shrug. 'If you hadn't noticed already, I am to the jolly social whirl what King Herod is to The Mothers' Union.'

She laughed at that, the red hair dancing. *That* was what he did for her that made it worth putting up with the rest: he surprised her, he made her laugh. 'OK, so you want to worry about work. Anything I can help with?'

Donovan gave a rueful grin. 'Not even Rumpole of the Bailey could help me with this. In fact, if Rumpole knew what I was up to he'd get his client discharged without a stain on his character.'

Jade liked him remembering her joke. 'Sergeant!' she exclaimed in mock horror. 'You're not trying to frame someone?'

''Course not.' He sounded outraged; then his eyes slid away and his thin lips sketched a self-deprecating smile. 'But it's not exactly above-board either. I have to convince someone that I know things I don't so he might as well come clean when in fact he'd be better off not doing so. I suppose that's vaguely dishonest but you couldn't call it a frame – he's guilty, I'm just having trouble proving it. God Almighty, I was there

– I *saw* what he did! But he's come up with a pack of
lies that just might be good enough to get him off.
Somehow I have to get him to cooperate in his own
downfall.'

After the exhibition, somehow it seemed natural
to finish up back at *Tara*. Donovan shut out the winter
night and Jade shrugged off her coat and curled into a
chair. Her brow furrowed with thought. 'That's what's
worrying you? If you should do it?'

He shook his head. 'How to do it.'

He didn't set out to tell her everything, but
between explaining the principle and trying not to
sound crooked himself he told her most of it, omitting
only the names. Jade listened in silence. Donovan
couldn't tell what she was thinking.

When he ran out of things to say he got up and
went to one of the big lozenge-shaped windows. Mere
Basin was lit like Santa's Grotto but there were few
lights along Broad Wharf, only a few security bulbs
above the rear entrances of the commercial buildings
on Brick Lane. There were also lights on the *James
Brindley*, but beyond that was darkness. It had started
to rain in the last half hour, a cold sleety rain that
didn't so much run down the glass as slither. Donovan
laid his arms on the sill, dropped his chin on his bony
wrists and watched it.

He was afraid that the next thing he'd hear would
be the door closing as she left. He thought she was
judging him. She hadn't said so. She hadn't said much
at all. Perhaps she thought they still lived in a world
where right triumphed over wrong without a helping
hand. Donovan genuinely saw nothing improper
about tricking Roly, but perhaps it looked different

from the outside. Perhaps someone who'd never met the Dickenses, or anyone like the Dickenses, thought they really were innocent until proven guilty and it really was better that ten guilty men should go free than that one crooked defence should be shown for what it was by a little creative policing.

Listening for the door, he was startled to find Jade standing beside him, her elbows on the same narrow sill. She glanced sidelong at him and smiled. 'Don't look so tragic. It's only a job.'

He thought about that for a moment then shook his head. 'No. It isn't.'

'I wish I could help.'

'You? How can you help?'

His tone stung her. She swung on him, the red hair flying, the green eyes – he'd been right about that – flashing like ice over emeralds. 'Don't be so bloody patronizing! I get around, I hear things. I may even know things that you don't, that you'd give your eye-teeth to know. You don't want my help, fine – but then don't whinge on about how hard your job is!' She stalked away from the window, snatching up her bag.

Another moment and she really would have gone. Donovan didn't know how to stop her. He didn't dare touch her, hadn't the skill with words to talk her round. All he could think of in the time available was to bar her exit. He crossed the saloon in a couple of long-legged strides and put the door at his back. 'Jade—'

'Shift.' She sounded very much as if she meant it.

His voice was low. 'Don't walk out.'

'I'm not walking out, there's nothing to walk out on. I'm just leaving.'

'I'm sorry,' he blurted. He also didn't get much practice at apologizing. 'Whatever – I didn't – I mean, I don't—' It not only wasn't coming out the way he wanted, he wasn't making any sense at all. His hands spread helplessly and then dropped to his sides. 'Don't go.'

'Get out of my way.'

She left him no choice. Right around there persuasion turned into unlawful imprisonment. He stepped aside, opening the door for her as he did. A little flurry of sleet found its way down the companionway.

But Jade stood where she was, her head to one side, eyeing him speculatively. The quick surge of temper had passed but she wasn't ready to forgive him. She waited, expecting him to try again. When he didn't, finally she vented an exasperated sigh. 'Understand one thing, Donovan. I'm nobody's bit of fluff. Don't you dare talk down to me.'

'I'm sorry,' mumbled Donovan. He was still waiting for her to elbow him aside and didn't want to think what it meant that she was still here.

'So why talk to me as if I'm a child? As if I couldn't possibly have anything useful to contribute and it was rather presumptuous to think I might?'

'That isn't—' Donovan shook his head and started again. 'I didn't mean to. I didn't think that – don't think it – didn't mean to suggest it. I'm sorry. I say stupid things sometimes: ask anyone. Things don't come out the way I want them to. People'll tell you it's because I'm Irish but I was never any good at talking to people at home. My brother Padraig, now, he could talk to anyone about anything. I think he got my share of the blarney as well as his own. He said—' He stopped. Under the olive skin Jade saw the colour rising.

'What did he say?'

'He said, I seemed to think it was other people's job to read my silences.'

Slowly Jade smiled. 'I think I'd like your brother. Can I trade you in and have him instead?'

Donovan shook his head. 'He died.'

She put her bag down again and after a moment returned to the sofa. 'Close the door, it's getting cold. I'm sorry about your brother. You miss him, don't you?'

'Yeah. It's – what? – twelve years now, but I still miss him. I wish he was somewhere I could pick up the phone and say, "I've done it again. I met this girl, I really liked her, she even rides bikes. And I blew it."'

Jade's eyes twinkled. 'Was he older than you?'

'Six years older. He was a policeman. He died in a car chase – he thought he was as good a driver as the guy in front, turned out he was wrong.'

'And you followed in his footsteps. Any regrets?'

He shook his head. 'No. There's nothing I'd rather be doing.'

'In spite of the sleepless nights?'

'At least it's something worth losing sleep over.'

She nodded slowly. 'You're right: the important things are worth making sacrifices for.'

Already he was in that position again. There was something he had to ask her, and it might send her heading for the door again. He'd rather have kept her and not known, but he had a duty. The important things were worth making sacrifices for. 'What did you hear?'

She didn't understand. 'What?'

Donovan chewed his lip. 'You said you got about, you heard things. You thought maybe you could help. I could use some help.'

Her green eyes flicked at him and then away. 'Nothing. Probably nothing at all.' She gave an awkward little shrug that contrasted with her usual composure. 'I just meant, in general.'

He knew that wasn't the truth: what he didn't know was what to do about it. 'Last night, in The Jubilee. You said you were visiting. Is that where you heard – whatever?'

There was a dangerous edge on the look she gave him. Some sort of a war seemed to be in progress behind her eyes. He thought it was between staying and going. 'It wasn't a personal call, I was there on business.'

He didn't even know what business she was in. He hadn't asked; he hadn't thought it important. They'd talked about bikes, and canals, and now about his work, and he didn't even know what she did. 'Business?'

'That's right.' Her tone made it clear he wasn't to quiz her. 'Look, Donovan, this isn't something I want to talk about. I'm not a policeman and I'm not a police informant.'

'But I am.' There was battle in Donovan's eyes too, between the need to do his job and the desire not to drive her away. He hated what he was having to do, was scared what it was going to cost him, but he never seriously considered stopping. 'A policeman. I'm investigating a major crime right now. If you've heard anything . . .' He drew breath. 'You said you'd like to help.'

Jade's response was so long coming that he had to draw another breath and hold that instead. He watched her face for the first sign of what she was thinking. If she spat in his eye, that would be a clue.

But she didn't spit in his eye. Finally she managed a slightly wan little smile. 'So I did. All right, Donovan, I'll tell you what I heard. But I won't tell you where I heard it, and I can't vouch for those I heard it from. If you can use it, fine; but you didn't get it from me, all right?'

Donovan nodded. He couldn't believe his luck. She was still here, and she was trying to help him.

'All right. Well, you're not the only man who thinks women are a separate species. A lot of men talk in front of women the way they talk in front of small children, not expecting to be understood. While I was in the parlour of this house, two men were laughing and talking in the kitchen. The door was open, I could hear every word. They were talking about you.'

Whatever he was expecting it wasn't that. 'The police, you mean?'

'You personally. I think: they didn't use your name, but they'd seen you with someone on that corner where you tried to commit suicide under my front wheel ten minutes later so I guess it was you.'

Donovan scowled. He didn't like to think he'd been spotted talking to Billy Dunne, and not only for

Billy's sake. He thought that when he went walkabout at night he was next to invisible. He thought he took the alleycats by surprise. Knowing that the locals had not only spotted him but giggled about it in somebody's kitchen was distressing. 'What did they say?'

'At the time it didn't make any sense to me; but I'm wondering now if it's the same thing you were talking about. The missing gun. Nobody mentioned a gun, but it could have been. They were talking about somebody hiding something.'

Donovan was gazing at her as if she'd sprouted wings. 'Did they say where?'

'No; only that the last time this person was in a place of learning he was still in short trousers. Then they laughed and changed the subject, and at the time it meant nothing to me. Maybe it was nothing to do with your robbery.'

Maybe it wasn't, but Donovan had to believe that it was. He needed an edge, and this was the first glimpse of one he'd had. But he couldn't make sense of it. He thought there was a good chance the men were talking about Roly Dickens hiding Mikey's gun, but what did it mean? A school? There were several schools in Castlemere but none where you could wander in and hide a firearm. Even the Rosedale Academy wasn't that progressive.

He tried to forget about it, at least for this evening. Jade had abandoned all thought of leaving. Her coat lay forgotten over the back of the sofa; later, as the black stove raised the temperature in the saloon, her sweater joined it. Not long after that they were both shedding clothes as if global warming had reached

Castlemere, but neither of them paid any heed to where they landed.

They didn't get as far as the bedroom. Need overwhelmed them and they tangled on the saloon carpet, sweating and grunting like sailors on shore leave, coupling like the first animals hearing the command 'Be fruitful and multiply' from God's own mouth. There was more urgency than grace to it, more intensity than refinement. But it was what they both needed, and if it left them exhausted and bruised from contact with the furniture it also left them replete.

Then Donovan did it again. Having it all – cradling the naked body of a beautiful intelligent girl who rode motorcycles – wasn't enough to keep his mind on the job. It suddenly flashed into his head what the men in the kitchen had been talking about; and he hadn't the sense to keep it there, in his head, until the formalities had been observed. As they gasped the air back into their lungs the first thing he panted was not her name, or veneration of her body or performance. It was, 'The Chemical Street Elementary School!'

Chapter Eight

In his own heart he was sure. Even so he went there
on his way to work on Thursday.

Tucked away behind the gasworks, the black brick
box in Chemical Street was originally built as a work-
house. Minimal changes in the late nineteenth
century equipped it to provide a basic education for
the children of Castlemere's poor, and it survived as
a school until after World War II when the town grew
suddenly ashamed of it and put up a new Infants and
Junior School behind Castle Mount. The Elementary
School served for a time as a technical college, but
demand outstripped its ability to supply and a new
College of Further Education was erected on the ring
road. After brief, unsuccessful incarnations as an
auction room, a carpet warehouse and a discount
furniture store, the building finally fell vacant in the
mid-eighties.

Donovan scaled the high spike fence round what
had been the playground and looked for signs of
recent entry. And signs there were: too many, every
wino, under-age smoker, glue-sniffer and street-
walker in Castlemere must have used the premises
as a base. At first he couldn't imagine how half of
them got over that fence. Then he saw that the side

gate from Viaduct Lane was open, a rusty padlock hanging from a broken chain.

Access to the building was through the broken panel of a door. It would have been a tight squeeze for Roly Dickens but he'd have managed. He'd have headed for the innermost part of the building, to hide the gun away from curious eyes. Donovan moved cautiously into the dim interior, the floor littered with rubble and rubbish, on a quest he increasingly recognized as hopeless. It would take ten men to search this place properly, and even they couldn't be sure that anything they didn't find wasn't there.

But actually he didn't need to find the gun. Roly Dickens knew where it was – all Donovan had to do was make him fetch it. He needed to be confident it was here somewhere, that was all. He wandered the classrooms and corridors, no longer searching for the weapon, groping with his mind for some sense of the aptness of the place. If it was the sort of place Roly would have come. If there was any echo here of him stumbling over these same bricks and blocks and bits of broken furniture.

It felt promising. Donovan might have jumped to the wrong conclusion – if he thought longer he might come up with an alternative – but he doubted it. Chemical Street was a good choice. There was enough illicit but essentially harmless coming and going that nobody would think to report an intruder; but if the gun was found it would be hard to prove who left it here.

There were times when Donovan's gut feelings verged on extrasensory, but this wasn't one of them. Everything pointed to it being the right place, he thought it probably was, but he couldn't be sure. He didn't know whether to tell Shapiro or not.

Then he glanced at his watch and found he'd been here an hour. So he'd have to offer an explanation and, for once, it might as well be the truth.

Shapiro summarized the position. 'We think Roly hid Mikey's gun in the Chemical Street Elementary School. We could search, but we might not find it and even if we did we might not be able to connect it to him. Or we can give Roly a reason to fetch it and pick him up when he does. Suggestions, please – why would Roly Dickens, having successfully hidden the gun that can send Mikey to prison, suddenly decide he'd better get it back?'

Liz didn't have the answer, but she had the template for an answer. 'If leaving it where it is would make things worse for Mikey.'

'Yes, fine,' said Shapiro. 'As in, for example . . .?'

'Suppose we let it be known that we've found a gun – and say something about where that'll make him seriously uneasy without being sure. I know: workmen securing a derelict property behind the gas-works found it. Could be the school, could not. We say we're running tests on it and expect to be able to tie it to the robbery at Kumani's. Then we say we already know it was used in an earlier crime – something nasty, something carrying a life sentence. We can get something suitable off the computer: it doesn't have to be this division, just local enough that Mikey could have been involved. Or maybe it was just the gun that was involved, in the hands of a previous owner.'

The idea firmed in her mind as she followed where it led. 'If Roly does nothing, waits to see if we turn up on his doorstep with a warrant, Mikey could be charged as an accessory to murder. Rather than that, he'd put his hand up for the robbery and explain that he didn't have the gun that long. But if Mikey comes clean over the robbery only to find we were bluffing, we never had the gun, or it was another gun entirely, he'll do time for something he could have walked away from. He needs to know whether we have his gun or not.

'Roly won't be panicked into doing anything pre-cipitate. He'll think it through; he'll want to be damn sure Mikey wasn't involved in a murder; but when he's convinced of that he'll have to check if the gun's where he left it.' Pleased, she sat back, awaiting congratulations.

Shapiro nodded slowly. 'Not bad. A bit more practice and you could be devious for England.'

Her smile revealed dimples. 'Coming from you, sir, I consider that a real compliment.'

They drafted a statement for the local radio, to go out on the evening news. Shapiro chose a post office robbery in Peterborough the previous year in which an elderly woman customer was shot dead. It had to be a real case – Roly would check.

Donovan was worried that he mightn't hear the news. But The Jubilee was full of ears, if Roly missed it himself he'd know all about it within minutes. Sometime between ten and midnight – 'The winos'll

86

give him some cover and Roly isn't going to worry about muggers' – he'd set off for Chemical Street.

'And I'll be right behind him.'

Liz cleared her throat. 'Actually, Sergeant, *I'll* be right behind him. Except for the first couple of minutes. He'll be watching for trouble. So we let him spot you and spend five minutes giving you the slip; with luck he won't see me pick up the tail. I'll follow him to the school, there'll be back-up waiting near by, as soon as he has the gun we arrest him. Unlawful possession and concealing evidence. Then we charge Mikey with the garage robbery; and if we can get Thelma for aiding and abetting we'll have the whole bloody family behind bars.'

Donovan needed to be visible, but not so visible that Roly would suspect. He returned to the corner of Jubilee Terrace: apparently half the Walled City knew he considered it a discreet place to watch them from. A younger, thinner man than Roly might leap over the wall dividing the back yards of Coronation Row from those of Brick Lane; but age and girth were not Roly's only reasons for coming this way. He couldn't lose Donovan until he'd picked him up.

Liz was sitting in her car at the town end of Brick Lane with a Bichon Frise in the passenger seat. She and Bubbles were old friends, they'd done stakeouts before. He belonged to Superintendent Giles's secretary Miss Tunstall and was the perfect excuse for loitering in the street late at night. A man alone might seem suspicious, a woman alone might attract attention, but someone walking a dog was just someone walking a dog. If Roly was on foot she and Bubbles would, well, dog him and he'd think nothing of it. If he was driving they'd follow in the car. Bubbles enjoyed a good car chase.

She didn't know how quickly Roly would respond to the item on the news: somewhere between fifteen minutes and an hour was her best guess but it might take longer, particularly if Mikey wasn't at home. At intervals she checked with Donovan on the radio but The Jubilee was quiet. After an hour Bubbles really did need to go for a walk.

After two hours Liz was pretty sure this wasn't going to work. She called DC Morgan, who was waiting at the school, but he'd seen no one. Even the glue-sniffers seemed to be having the night off. 'We'll give it another hour,' Liz decided, 'but I don't think he's coming.'

Donovan had reached the same conclusion, and was wondering if he should suggest calling it a night or wait for Liz to do so, when he heard footsteps. He'd melted back into the shadows before remembering he wasn't meant to be invisible.

But those weren't Roly's footsteps. The big man was fifty years old and seventeen stone, and he'd never had a light quick step like this. Also, he didn't limp. Donovan waited, listening, and the footsteps reached the corner and stopped.

'Don't mean to disturb you, Mr Donovan.' It was Mikey. Already he'd acquired another of those long, amorphous coats that made him look like a small banshee. 'But my dad says it's a cold old night, and if you're going to be here much longer can we bring you a Thermos?'

*

'They knew. Everything.' It was Friday morning now, but Donovan was still so angry he spat the words. 'Not just that I was watching them: they knew it didn't matter if I was or not. Roly wasn't going anywhere. He didn't have to: he knew Mikey's gun was where he left it. How?'

Liz shrugged. She was tired and dispirited too, but she'd been unsuccessful often enough in the past that she no longer took it personally. 'Maybe we were wrong about the school. Maybe he has it at home. Or maybe he got rid of it permanently.'

'Then what were the men in the kitchen talking about?'

'I don't know,' Liz said irritably. 'Maybe they weren't talking about the gun at all.' She frowned. 'You never did explain how you came to overhear that.'

That was all he'd said – that he'd overheard it. He didn't want to bring Jade into this: partly because of the sense he had that their relationship was valuable and delicate, and just a little bit because he was shy of admitting he had a girlfriend.

The man and woman in this office were the people who knew him best in the world. It wasn't exactly friendship but a professional relationship close enough to mimic it in all the essentials. They knew each other's strengths and frailties. They counted on one another, for their lives if need be. And Donovan knew that if he admitted he was seeing a girl who rode a motorcycle, the Dickens case would go on the back burner while the best detecting minds in Castlemere concentrated on his sex life.

Fortunately he was a fluent liar. Or rather, he was

a successful liar because also he looked shifty when he had nothing to hide. 'I was skulking,' he said defensively. Neither of them would have difficulty believing that. 'I just happened to be in the right place at the right time. Never mind that. Roly Dickens knew about something that was only discussed in this office, and I want to know how.'

Shapiro's eyebrows rocketed. 'Sergeant – are you accusing one of *us* of being in old Roly's pocket?'

That stopped him short. Donovan blinked and then knuckled his eyes. ''Course not. I just – I don't know how it went wrong.'

'Maybe it didn't,' Liz said reasonably. 'Maybe he just didn't take the bait.'

Donovan shook his head. 'You didn't see Mikey. It was like a big joke. Him and the old man had been wetting themselves for two hours, and when they thought I was getting pissed-off enough to go home Mikey came out to share it with me. They knew, the whole thing, and I don't know how if they didn't hear it from someone in Queen's Street.'

Shapiro caught his angry gaze and held it. No facial gymnastics now, just the steady eyes of a man wanting to be quite sure that what he said was understood. 'Donovan, you're suggesting that someone in this building is passing information on an inquiry to a known criminal. That's almost the gravest allegation you can make against a policeman. Do you mean it?'

For a moment the superintendent's tone was enough to silence Donovan. But reflecting on the facts didn't alter them and he nodded. 'Yes. The evidence is there. OK, everything we do doesn't go according to plan. I might have misread the situation. We might have been wrong about who had the gun, where it was, what he'd do if he thought we'd found it. We could have set the whole thing up only to find he'd gone to the pictures. Or there might be something we don't know about that would change drastically how he'd react.

'But it's not just that he didn't jump when we wanted him to. We said Jump and he blew us a raspberry. That's not the thing going off half-cocked: it's sabotage. Roly knew what we were expecting. He knew what we were doing and why. He knew that all he had to do was nothing, and then he was safe enough to let us in on the joke. He *knew*. Somebody told him.'

'All right,' said Shapiro slowly. 'Anyone in particular you want to point the finger at?'

Donovan was uncomfortable but he wasn't going to back down. 'The three of us knew, and Dick Morgan; and the Son of God, and the Station Sergeant.' He was not a religious man: he didn't mean that, just as no sparrow falls unmarked by heaven, so no operation organized at Queen's Street escaped the celestial eye. For reasons now disappearing in the mists of time Superintendent Giles was commonly referred to as the Son of God. 'That's too many to keep a secret. One of us must have said something to someone – in the canteen, in the corridor, in the bog. Anyone in the station could have known.'

'We're not looking for someone who knew, though, are we?' said Liz tersely. 'We're looking for someone who knew, and told Roly Dickens. For a favour or for money. So which of your colleagues do you reckon is in hock to the Dickenses?'

'You're making it sound like it couldn't happen,' Donovan growled, 'and we all know it does happen. There's nothing special about us, it could happen here too. I don't know who. There's nobody I had any doubts about until now. But if we ignore what's happened it'll happen again.'

'So what do you want to do?' asked Shapiro. His broad face remained expressionless. He'd helped Donovan with problems of every kind, professional and personal, in the eight years they'd worked together but he wasn't going to help him with this. If Donovan thought one of his colleagues was an informer he was going to have to prove it. Until then he was on his own.

Out on his own was a place Donovan knew, but that didn't necessarily mean he liked it. People assumed he behaved like this from choice, deliberately taking positions where he could expect no support. He didn't. He didn't enjoy fighting all his battles single-handed, gaining ground a bloody inch at a time and always staring defeat in the face. But that puritan streak insisted that if a cause was right it remained so however few people espoused it, and right was worth fighting for however uphill the struggle. He often wished he could be more flexible, compromise without it feeling like drawing teeth. But he was a prisoner of his own myth, and by now he was so used to being the dissenting minority that he mistrusted anything that seemed too easy.

'God damn it, *I* don't know!' But he wasn't angry with Shapiro, or even himself, so much as a third party he had no way of identifying. 'Roly Dickens is the only one who knows, and he's not going to tell me even if I take a shovel to him.' At the back of his mind he was aware that it might not have been a deliberate treachery so much as somebody saying something to his wife who then said something to her mother who was discussing it with her sister in the queue at Woolworth's . . . That sort of thing happened more than bribery and corruption, and it was unstoppable because nobody ever realized they were the weak spot where the dam started to leak.

'Which you wouldn't dream of doing,' Shapiro said pointedly; and after a moment, reluctantly, Donovan nodded.

''Course not, sir. Figure of speech.'

'Besides which,' murmured Liz, 'you take a shovel to Roly Dickens and he'll wrap it round your neck.'

'OK,' admitted Donovan, 'I can't prove it. But it's happened, and it's cost us time and effort and a couple of good convictions. Worse than that, it's let Roly Dickens get up on his hind legs and crow about putting one over on us. About how his family are fireproof. We can't let the idea get around that there are people in this town that the law doesn't apply to.'

'I know that, Sergeant,' said Shapiro stiffly. 'I may have said as much to you. I may also have mentioned that elephants aren't the only ones with long memories. We'll get them. We'll get Mikey for the garage robbery, and we'll get Roly for concealing the gun. I can't promise it'll be this week or next week, but it doesn't have to be. We'll be here for a while. And this investigation doesn't founder because we haven't got the gun. We'll find someone who saw Mikey alone in the van. Mrs Taylor may be able to help when her head's a bit straighter.'

Liz nodded. 'I'll go and see her again after the weekend. She was still pretty upset when I talked to her before. She'll have calmed down by now, she may have a clearer picture of what she saw.'

'And if she hasn't?' asked Donovan, edgily.

'Then we'll look for someone else,' said Shapiro. 'It was early Sunday evening, there must have been other people on Cambridge Road. If we ask for eye-witnesses there'll be someone who saw Mikey drive off alone. Or maybe I can poke a hole in his story. He's waiting downstairs now.'

Donovan was taken aback. 'You're going to charge him?'

'Certainly not. The obliging little chap's here voluntarily to help catch the wicked criminal who hijacked his van.'

They didn't have irony in Glencurran; even after so long Donovan could miss it if he was preoccupied. 'But – he made that up.'

Liz grinned and Shapiro closed his eyes for a second in despair. 'Sergeant – go find some detecting to do. I'll talk to Mikey. If I can make confetti of his alibi, you'll be the first to know.'

Donovan sniffed. 'If I'm right about the leak, Roly Dickens'll be the first to know.'

After he'd gone Liz said, 'Is he right, do you think – is someone here on more than a nodding acquaintance with the Dickenses?'

Shapiro didn't answer directly. One side of his lived-in face wrinkled up as if he'd sucked a lemon. 'I think he's right about last night – I think they knew what we were up to. Roly knew he had nothing to worry about. That might be because the gun was where it couldn't be found, but we can't discount the possibility that he heard it from someone here. I'd sooner think it was carelessness than corruption, but either way we need to be aware of it. Next move we make stays in this room till it's too late to matter.'

He pushed his chair away from the desk and got up. 'Well, young Dickens and his solicitor are waiting in Interview Room One, and since he's here out of the simple goodness of his heart it would be discourteous of me to keep them any longer.'

Chapter Nine

His brush with death had made a better man of Mikey Dickens. Almost, Shapiro thought sourly, he seemed to be soliciting for some kind of Good Citizen award. Every question he asked, every time he sought a fuller explanation, Mikey's brows knit in concentration and he answered as comprehensively as he could.

Normally that would have pleased the detective: the more complex the lie, the sooner it breaks down. But Shapiro soon realized that although Mikey was saying a lot he was just repeating the same words, and Shapiro had heard them before. Mikey's bladder, the man in the grey coat, the gun: it all sounded terribly familiar. Afraid for his life, Mikey had done what he was told. None of what happened was his fault. He never knew who his passenger was, wouldn't recognize him if they met again.

It wasn't true. Shapiro knew it wasn't true, but that wasn't the point. It *could* be true, and without proof to the contrary Mikey was entitled to the benefit of the doubt. His solicitor was there to remind the superintendent should he chance to forget.

Ms Holloway seemed surprised that Shapiro was still handling this personally. No one was dead, no

one was badly injured: she'd expected that by now
the matter would have been delegated to an inspector.

'I like to keep my hand in, Miss Holloway,' Shapiro
explained affably – carefully pronouncing the vowel
in her title for no better reason than that it seemed
to annoy her. 'New Year's a good chance: it takes a
couple of weeks for business to pick up again after
the holiday.'

She smiled thinly. 'I suppose even criminals like
to spend Christmas with the family.' She said
Christmas to annoy him in return: with a name like
his he wasn't likely to have been at Midnight Mass.

Shapiro replied sunnily, 'Don't we all, Miss Holloway – don't we all?'

He moved on to the missing gun, the posse that
rode out of The Jubilee in the early hours of Monday
morning, and last night's pantomime at the corner of
Jubilee Terrace.

Mikey affected total innocence. He wasn't discharged from the hospital until Tuesday so events in
The Jubilee prior to that were a closed book to him.
He didn't know what became of the gun: he assumed
the robber took it with him. He went out to Donovan
last night because he was afraid he must be getting
cold, and after all, he did owe Mr Donovan his life.
He had no other motive, didn't even know what the
superintendent was getting at. Honest.

Shapiro gave a weary sigh. 'If you'd just stop
saying that, Mikey, people might be more inclined to
believe you.'

Mikey was puzzled. 'What's that, Mr Shapiro?'

'Honest. It's a dead give-away. It's like saying,

97

"You can trust me." It wouldn't occur to anyone who's genuinely trustworthy that they had to say so.'

But Mikey wasn't saying anything more – anything different, rather – and Shapiro didn't want to waste time that he could more profitably use when he had something concrete to put to him. He walked Mikey and his brief as far as the front office. 'I may need to talk to Mr Dickens again. I don't suppose' – he nodded at Mikey's limp – 'he's contemplating a skiing holiday in the near future?'

A glint of humour sparked momentarily in Ms Holloway's green eyes and she tossed the auburn rope of her hair over her shoulder. 'If you can think of anything to ask my client that he hasn't already answered, he will of course be available. To the best of my knowledge he doesn't ski.'

'No?' Shapiro feigned surprise. 'So he'd have no reason to own a ski mask?'

'No indeed,' agreed the solicitor blandly. 'Which is why he doesn't have one.'

'Pity about the van catching fire, wasn't it?' said Shapiro. 'But for that he'd have been able to prove his innocence. If his coat and gloves hadn't been burned, the absence of blood and gun residues on them would have proved that he hadn't handled a gun and hadn't hit my sergeant in the face with it.'

Ms Holloway was nodding. 'Fortunately,' she said calmly, 'my client doesn't have to prove anything.'

They parted there. Shapiro watched them walk down the steps – Mikey's limp becoming positively jaunty – with the composure of a man who'd seen a lot of suspects walk down those steps and had the satisfaction of bringing most of them in again through the back door.

Donovan had been to the chemist. Absent-mindedly scratching with the end of his ballpoint he'd dislodged one of the plasters that was holding his face together, and the station First-Aid box hadn't been replenished since the last punch-up in the cell-block. Mrs Sullivan the chemist's wife fixed him up. Rosa Sullivan was from County Monaghan, Donovan's mid-Ulster accent was the closest she got these days to the sound of home.

Donovan was gingerly patting the little plaster into place when he turned at the foot of the steps and saw them at the top. Everything fell into place with a thump like breeze blocks. He didn't have to work it out, he could see everything he needed to know. He knew now who'd passed information to Roly Dickens. He had.

He'd never asked her second name. If he had he'd have recognized it from Mikey's paperwork. But he'd missed her when she came in here on Tuesday, and a week before that she was still in London. The first time he saw her was on Tuesday night, riding out of The Jubilee on a motorcycle. She must have been seeing Mikey. Jade Holloway was his solicitor.

Donovan froze with one foot on the bottom step, his heart turning to ice. The blood drained from his face and his eyes went fathomless. He said nothing. He waited.

A moment later Jade saw Donovan. She wasn't surprised to see him here, though in a perfect world she'd have timed the revelation better. She drew a quick breath then turned to the young man beside her. 'Mikey, can you make your own way home? I'll talk to you later.'

Mikey nodded. He managed the steps without too much difficulty, but he couldn't manage to pass Donovan without rubbing it in. 'Have you met my brief, Mr Donovan? Fresh up from London – she's been in the Old Bailey and everywhere. Fairly spoils you for old Mr Carfax, doesn't it?'

'Mikey,' said Jade, a touch sharply. 'I'll see you later, all right?'

With a sly little grin he went to leave. But as he drew level Donovan's arm shot out to block his passage. His face was dark with fury and his voice was thick. 'Enjoy it, Mikey. There aren't that many laughs where you're going, this might be the last one you get.'

Mikey contrived to look offended. 'You still think it was me that hit you, don't you? I'm hurt, Mr Donovan, I really am. I explained to Mr Shapiro what happened. I don't know what else I can do.'

Donovan held him with terrible eyes. 'You can go to hell, Mikey, and take your fancy London lawyer with you. I should have left you in the van. I should have let you burn.'

For a split second, before he remembered to do the cocky grin, Mikey looked genuinely shocked. To him this was a game he played with the police. If he lost he'd do his time without much rancour. Along with shimming locks and hot-wiring cars, Roly had taught him to pay for his mistakes. He still hoped to persuade a court that Donovan was mistaken and he too was a victim of the armed robber; but if, inexplicably, they preferred Donovan's version he wouldn't be bitter. He couldn't see why Donovan was turning this into a grudge match.

He gave a little frown. 'Mr Donovan, don't the words "No hard feelings" have *any* meaning for you?' He passed the policeman at a safe distance and limped up Queen's Street into town.

They were left alone, Jade at the top of the steps, Donovan at the bottom. She began, 'It isn't how you think—'

A snort of derision interrupted her. 'It's *exactly* how I think!'

She came down a step towards him. 'I didn't set out to deceive you. You put me in a difficult position. You were trying to entrap my clients. I couldn't pretend I hadn't heard.'

'You lied to me!'

'I didn't lie,' retorted Jade, 'I just didn't tell you I was involved. I didn't ask you to talk about your work; but if I'd stopped you I'd have denied my clients some useful information. They're the ones I owe a duty to.'

'And the men in the kitchen? That wasn't a lie?'

She risked a tiny smile. 'Well, maybe a little one. You backed me into a corner, I had to say something – it was all I could think of at short notice.'

'You made a fool of me! You invented a story to send me off on a wild goose chase, and you let the Dickenses know so they could enjoy it too.'

'I'm sorry, Donovan, I couldn't resist it – you were trying to pull a fast one, I couldn't resist turning the tables on you. All right, that was mean. It was a spur-of-the-moment thing: I was annoyed, I felt you were trying to pressurize me. Later I wished I hadn't done it, but I could only have warned you by identifying myself and I wasn't ready to do that.'

'You could at least have kept quiet about it. I'd still have wasted my evening, but at least I wouldn't have had Mikey laughing in my face!'

Jade gave an elegant little shrug. She still seemed to think it was funny, was surprised he hadn't seen the joke by now. 'I thought I'd better. *I* knew you weren't going to do any harm watching half the night for someone who wasn't going anywhere. But there are some hot-heads in The Jubilee, so I'm told, I didn't want one of them thumping you.'

'You set me up!'

'I didn't set you up.' The corner of her mouth twitched. 'I just let you set yourself up. Donovan, if you're going to play games with people you mustn't be surprised if they try to win.'

'Nothing the Dickenses do surprises me,' spat Donovan. 'But I talked to you as a friend. OK, that was stupid. But you didn't have to sell me to the highest bidder.'

'Don't be so melodramatic,' she said dismissively. 'You made a mistake. You were indiscreet, and you paid for it. Perhaps I should have told you who I was when we first met. Perhaps you should have asked. But you didn't, and by the time it mattered I had good reason not to. Yes, I betrayed your trust. If I hadn't I'd have betrayed that of a client. I'm sorry, Donovan, but the bottom line is, if the information was sensitive you should have kept it to yourself.'

She took another step towards him. This time he backed away. He said in his teeth, 'I never was a great judge of character.'

Jade ignored that. 'This doesn't have to change things between us. You won't make the same mistake again.'

He actually panted in astonishment. The thought of resuming intimacy with a woman who'd auctioned his integrity was inconceivable to him.

Nominally a Catholic, in fact Donovan didn't have what it took to be a Christian at all. He never forgave and forgot. Occasionally he forgave; eventually he forgot; but his instinct was to carry a grudge until it could be redeemed. It was why he couldn't accept that this time Mikey Dickens might get off scot-free.

In the same way he couldn't imagine putting aside his grievance against Jade Holloway, either for affection or carnal need. Inside her body he'd lost himself. The sheer power of the experience had stripped away his defences. He wasn't a man who made friends or took lovers easily. There was nothing casual about him: to Donovan a personal relationship meant commitment, and by the time he was ready for that he was open to being hurt. He mightn't have called it love but he'd felt something fierce and extraordinary, and he'd thought she had too. Knowing she'd laughed about him with his enemies struck him to the soul.

'Damn right I won't! Christ Almighty, that is absolutely one mistake I won't make again. Not change things? You used me. You came to my bed, we made—' He couldn't have said it before, he certainly couldn't say it now. 'Then you waited for me to roll over and stabbed me in the back.

'You know it can't end here? I have to tell my chief. I've been accusing half Queen's Street of bubbling: I can't keep quiet now I know it was me. I guess my chief will want a word with yours.'

'Tell Shapiro by all means,' she said off-handedly. 'If he wants to talk to Mr Carfax he can do. I have no doubt Mr Carfax will back me. Who I sleep with is none of their concern. The only issue is what I did with information gained in a personal conversation, and I have no doubt that what I did was right. The one who behaved inappropriately was you. You talked about things you had no business mentioning outside these walls.

'You want to tell Shapiro that you're so smitten by the sight of a naked woman that you'll tell her any-thing? Go ahead, it's probably something he needs to know. You think I betrayed you, and maybe I did. But first you betrayed him.'

Donovan rocked as if she'd slapped his face. It was true: that was the hard thing. She'd used him, but the real and original act of treachery was his. And he'd been so involved he hadn't even realized what he was doing.

It was the one thing with which he'd always con-soled himself. He made mistakes, he got things wrong, but he clung to the thought that everyone knew that, when the chips were down, Donovan could be counted on. Now it turned out even that was an illusion. He was like a stray dog: show him a bit of kindness and he'd do anything for you.

His lip curled, but his contempt now was entirely for himself. 'You hear about it, don't you? – men with good jobs, men with families, losing everything for a woman. And you think, By God, that must have been some woman, that he gave up all he had for her. But

104

it's not like that, is it? It isn't passion, just stupidity –
not seeing soon enough where it's leading. A man
who leaves himself that vulnerable deserves to lose
everything. Not for being wicked: for being that
stupid. For not knowing there are two kinds of
whores, and the honest ones only want money.'

If they'd been alone she'd have hit him for that.
But they were on the front steps of a police station,
they were already attracting curious glances, if this
went on much longer explanations would be required.
Her slim hands fisted at her sides, her lips tight, Jade
stalked past the hurt and bitter man at the foot of the
steps, pausing just long enough to deliver a parting
shot.

'It's time you grew up, Donovan. The real world
doesn't abide by playground rules. Success is what
you're measured by: if you want a piece of that you'll
have to shake off this idea that other people would
rather lose than take advantage of your naivety.'

Donovan stood immobile at the bottom of the
steps, one hand on the brass rail, his eyes hollow,
wondering where on earth to find the courage to go
upstairs and make the confession he knew he had to
make.

Liz was passing through the front office when her
attention was drawn to the scene by WPC Wilson. 'Do
you think he needs help?'

Liz watched for a moment on the monitor,
chewing her lip. It looked personal. On the other
hand, a stand-up fight on the steps of a police station
between a Detective Sergeant and the legal representative of a man accused of assaulting him could hardly
be considered a private matter. She was opening the

door when Ms Holloway made it easier by walking away. When Donovan still didn't move Liz went down to him.

The first he knew that she was there was her scent. He could never be sure if it was a perfume she used or just the lingering aroma of horse feed. With a watercolour label and a name like 'Summer Meadow' it would cost £20 a bottle; as horse and pony nuts it would sell for £6 a sack.

He looked up quickly, defensively. Her eyes were concerned. 'Donovan? What's wrong?'

He drew a ragged breath. 'Can we go upstairs? I've got something to tell you. You're not going to *believe* how stupid I've been.'

Chapter Ten

Shapiro listened with more composure than Donovan spoke. In thirty years on the job he'd seen it all before. He'd seen good coppers leave the rails for love, for money, for the hell of it. He'd known them go to bed with defendants' wives, daughters, mistresses, and on one memorable occasion the defendant himself. A defence solicitor might have been a new departure but it was only a variation on the theme.

'And you didn't know who she was until just now?'

'No. She was riding a motorbike when I met her.' He seemed to think that explained everything.

'And she didn't quiz you about the case?'

Without looking up Donovan shook his head. 'She didn't have to. I couldn't have said any more if she'd laced my cocoa with truth serum. I didn't think I was compromising the investigation, but together with what she already knew of course I was. I knew *somebody'd* got a big mouth: it never occurred to me it was me.' He filled his lungs and raised his eyes. 'There's no need to start disciplinary proceedings, unless you want to. You can have my resignation.'

Shapiro raised an eyebrow. 'Is that what you want?'

Donovan's eyes flared. 'You're joking! I just – don't see any alternative.'

Shapiro sighed. 'Don't be so theatrical, Sergeant. Yes, you've made an idiot of yourself. Yes, you've wasted everybody's time. And yes, you'll take a bit of stick over it in the canteen – for a week, or however long it takes for the next poor soul to cock up. It isn't a resigning matter. It isn't even a disciplinary matter. You've set the record straight, we know what went wrong, we know it won't happen again – that's it. Go, and sin no more.'

'But—' Donovan couldn't believe it was over. 'Mikey Dickens is going to get away with armed robbery because of me!'

'Maybe he is, maybe he isn't,' said Shapiro calmly. 'It's too soon to say. You can take the blame if it makes you feel any better, but since we don't hand out medals every time we get a conviction I don't see why you should do public penance for this. You made a mistake; all right, you made a stupid mistake. I can cope with honest mistakes, even stupid ones, as long as I know about them. If you'd taken money from her, or if talking was the price of getting her into bed, you'd have been an ex-policeman by now. But with all your failings, Sergeant, I've never had cause to doubt your honesty and that's worth a lot. You're forgiven, Donovan.

'But if you want to pay them back, go find someone who saw Mikey driving up Cambridge Road alone on Sunday evening. It's quite true: success is the best revenge.'

Donovan had walked in here thinking he'd trashed his career, and he was going to leave with

108

hardly a stain on his character. He looked as if a puff of wind would knock him off his feet. He mumbled thickly, 'I won't let you down again. And I will get Mikey Dickens. Maybe not for this, but somewhere and sometime, and the smartest London lawyer money can buy won't do him any good.'

Shapiro nodded tolerantly and let him go; only murmuring after him, 'It's not the smart ones you have to watch for, it's the pretty ones.'

Liz shook her head knowingly. 'It's the ones on motorcycles.'

When they were alone Shapiro laced his fingers over his chest and regarded her speculatively. 'Was I right? Or should I have given him a hard time?'

She shook her head again. She had her hair down today and it danced on her shoulder in a mass of fair curls. 'I don't think anything you could say would hammer the lesson home any harder. That's one mistake he's never going to make again. My guess is the next woman he wants to sleep with will have to fill in a questionnaire.' Her face split in a grin. 'It's a pity, really. I find it enormously cheering that even Donovan can make a fool of himself over a girl.'

Beyond Broad Wharf the towpath ran east for half a mile before turning up the northern spur of the canal, now derelict. Before the railway came the area between the waterways was a centre of the forage trade: hay and grain grown on the water-meadows of the River Arrow went by barge to feed carriage horses and dray horses all across the south-east. It was still called Cornmarket, though it had been wasteland for a generation.

Sergeant Bolsover, who was born in Castlemere, remembered when this was the town's industrial estate, home to numerous factories and extensive railway yards. Shapiro remembered the yards closing in favour of a passenger halt across town, and the factories either closing or moving out to the new ring road. By the time Donovan came it was just a thousand acres of rubble, emptier and more desolate the further east you went. Youngsters held mountain bike trials there; people walked their dogs there, as long as they could be home by nightfall; people abandoned their clapped-out cars and defunct settees there.

People who'd spotted the name on a map were devastated by the reality and couldn't imagine why it hadn't been redeveloped. But Castlemere had shrunk, in size and in population, since Cornmarket was the beating heart of its commercial success a hundred years ago. It wasn't redeveloped because it wasn't needed.

A small community of tramps and dossers lived there, in homes made by stretching plastic or tarpaulin between the remaining bits of masonry. Their social focus was a great bonfire that burned for most of the year in a ring of discarded furniture. Keeping it fed was the main reason Cornmarket hadn't disappeared under a sea of detritus long ago, because the town's refuse collectors would only come here under protest and armed guard.

Fenland winters are bitterly cold: anyone with anywhere else to go had gone months back. Those who still had some family may have spent the long summer evenings abusing them from the comfort of an overstuffed settee in front of the bonfire; but by the middle of October the memory of their sins was fading and as the frosts deepened vacancies appeared on the settees. Others, who had no families or whose families wouldn't have them back, headed for the milder climate of the big city and took a cardboard box behind King's Cross station till spring. Only those with no alternative remained at Cornmarket throughout the iron-hard winter, huddled together like puppies in a crate to share the meagre warmth of their wasted and rancid bodies.

Such a one was Desmond Jannery, age thirty-two going on fifty, one time actor, one time chicken shed mucker-out, long time nothing at all; hobbies – cider, cheap wine and methylated spirits. Desmond had family, he even had family not far from here, but they'd long given up on him – and no one who wasn't there while they were still trying has any right to criticize. He tried wintering in London once but found the pace hectic and decided, like George V, that he didn't much care for abroad. He had no ambitions left, not even rock-bottom ones like getting through the next night. Each dawn he woke with a sense of disappointment.

Once or twice he'd summoned the strength of purpose to make an end, saved up enough cider to drink himself into a stupor and lain down unprotected on the bare ground to let the cold leach away his life unnoticed while he slept. But each time another derelict had seen, and solicitously tucked a blanket around him, and he had woken to another chill dawn and a day without promise. He'd given up on suicide now. It seemed to be something else he was no good at.

It was the dog that woke him. Desmond liked dogs, even this one with its mantrap jaws and unforgiving eyes. Its name appeared to be Brian You Bastard. It came by here most nights, and often paused in the pool of warmth around the fire, the red glow revealing the hard framework of muscle and sinew so that for a moment it appeared not a real dog but some epic statue, an heroic dog of bronze. Then it lifted its leg against the settee and broke the spell.

Tonight, though, the dog had other things on its mind. It stood silhouetted by the fire and stared at him, so intently that Desmond was willing to believe the stare alone had woken him. He looked round but saw no one else astir. The fire was burning low: he threw some wood on to it. His feet were numb with cold and he got up to stomp the life back into them. He didn't know what time it was but clearly it was late, probably after midnight. The dog bounded past him into the encircling dark. On an impulse, taking a brand from the fire he followed.

Even with his alfresco torch he almost didn't see the figure on the ground. It was clad in black and lying motionless, face down on the frozen ground, just a darker shadow in the shadow of a broken wall.

Desmond's first thought was that it was a fellow sojourner – somehow they never quite thought of one another as friends – who'd had too successful a day's begging for his own good; or maybe, as Desmond had himself before now, saved up enough strong cider to see him on his way. When it happened to him Desmond had thought it no kindness to drag him back. Now he found he could not just turn and walk away. He bent down, holding the brand close, and shook the figure by a thin shoulder. 'Hello there?'

There was no reply; and then he saw why not, and that there was unlikely to be however hard he shook. The torch he held cast only a dim red light but it was enough to pick up the gleam of blood in the tangled hair.

No one committed suicide by hitting himself over the head. A broken skull meant violence and that, even in the fringe society to which Desmond Jannery belonged, meant calling the police. It would be a difficult time for all of them but there was no alternative. The man might not be dead. Desmond couldn't go back to the fire and let someone else discover him in the morning if there was even a slim chance that he was still alive.

He took a deep breath, meaning to rouse the camp. But as he turned he almost collided with a man standing behind him: a tall string-thin figure as dark as the one on the ground. Desmond raised his brand, more for protection than illumination, but there was enough light at such close quarters for him to see and, after a moment, recognize the man's face.

Startled as he was he leaned forward, peering. 'Is that you, Mr Donovan?'

II

Chapter One

At one in the morning The Jubilee was as dark and eerily quiet as a disused stage-set. No lights showed in the front parlours; even the upstairs windows were black. They kept regular hours in the six streets: those whose trade required the cover of darkness were away pursuing it while the day-shift were tucked up in their beds. Even the local cats were staying home tonight.

Liz parked in front of the house in George Street and looked up at its narrow frontage, three windows and a door, wondering how three generations of Dickenses managed to live in such close proximity. Perhaps it was bigger than it appeared; also, the three generations were now represented by just three people. Thelma was a widow, Roly's wife left him years ago and only his youngest child remained at home. Fifteen years ago he must have been putting them to bed with a shoe-horn.

It was tempting to linger in the frosty peace of the street, but there was a difficult job to do and it was better to get on with it. There were no bells in the Victorian front doors – when she rapped the iron knocker it was like cannon-fire ricocheting between the brick frontages.

She expected Roly to come down, but when the hall light came on and the door opened it was his mother standing there in her dressing-gown, her thin grey hair plaited into a cord, a peevish expression on her sleep-wrinkled face. She may have recognized Liz's car from her bedroom window. She'd certainly seen it often enough.

But her expression changed as she took in Liz's. She may not have known why the Inspector was here but she knew it wasn't to arrest anyone. 'What's happened?'

'I'm sorry to get you up, Thelma. It's Mikey. Is Roly at home?'

'He's asleep. Shall I get him? What's Mikey done?'

'I think you should wake him,' said Liz. 'There's been – an accident. Mikey's in the hospital.'

When Thelma woke him with the news Roly Dickens threw on whatever clothes were nearest and hurried down. The effect was of a badly wrapped parcel. He was a big man, in every direction, and the combination of a sweatshirt that barely made it down to his middle with a pair of those special builder's trousers that barely made it over his hips was not entirely becoming.

'Accident? What kind of accident? Is he hurt?'

At the same time there was something rather touching about Roly Dickens as a sartorial disaster area, simply because it wasn't his normal way of dressing. The man had a certain style. Whatever he wore for work, he turned up for court appearances in a three-piece suit. He polished his shoes and matched his tie to his breast-pocket handkerchief. The fact that he came before Liz in such disarray now said clearer than words that even if Mikey struck the rest of the world as one scant evolutionary step above the wood-louse his father cared about him. The heavy face, unshaven jowls blue and bristly, twisted with anxiety and there was fear in the bloodhound eyes.

In the second before she answered Liz felt it like a physical pang that this was something whose direct equivalent she would never experience. If she'd married a man who turned out like Mikey Dickens she'd have divorced him; if she bought a horse that shifty and unreliable she'd have it shot. But your children were part of you, and remained so however unsatisfactory you found each other; and most parents, like Roly, found they had no option but to love them pretty much as they were. She wondered if Mikey had known how lucky he was that there was one person in the world who loved him enough for news of his misfortune to cause such distress. She hoped so; because it sounded as if what Mikey didn't know yesterday wouldn't trouble him in the future.

'He has a head injury,' she said. 'It's serious, but he's in hospital and they have enormous expertise at dealing with these things. I'll drive you there. By the time we arrive the doctors'll maybe have a clearer picture.'

Thelma was going to get dressed and come too but Roly wanted her at home. 'Get on the phone, tell the family what's happened. Tell them I'll be in touch when I know more.'

As he squeezed his bulk into the car he said, 'What kind of an accident?'

Liz could have lied, she could have fudged; both seemed crueller than giving him all the bad news at once. 'Actually, Mr Dickens, we think Mikey was attacked. He was found half an hour ago by one of the Cornmarket dossers. He'd been beaten up.'

Dickens stared at her in disbelief. 'Some dosser broke Mikey's head?'

Liz was quick to scotch that. 'No, we don't think so. The dosser found him, that's all. He'd been lying there for some time already: if he hadn't been found he'd have been all night and he wouldn't have survived.' It was important that Roly understood that before he organized a lynch-mob.

Mikey was in theatre. While Roly sat hunched in a corner, repeatedly checking his watch as the slow minutes passed, Liz talked to the casualty registrar.

'He was beaten up?'

'He *was* beaten up,' agreed Dr Morrison. 'But it wasn't a fight that got out of hand, or even a systematic beating that went too far. Someone tried to kill him. Eighty per cent of the effort expended went into smashing his head. There are other injuries but they're almost incidental. They were probably done after he was unconscious.'

Liz stared at him. 'They fractured his skull and *then* gave him a drubbing? Why would anyone do that? – and anyway, what makes you think so?'

Dr Morrison looked tired. 'Why is more your business than mine, Inspector. Maybe to disguise the real purpose of the attack – make it look like a fight instead of an execution? What makes me think so is the angle the blows landed at. Apart from the one that stove in the back of his skull – which was probably the first because he was vertical then and horizontal thereafter – that boy didn't move from the beginning of the attack until it ended. Even broken bones don't stop you thrashing about on the ground: you'd expect the injuries to reflect different degrees of force arriving from different directions but they don't. He just lay there and took it. I don't think he knew it was going on.'

Liz was trying to visualize what happened. 'So he was on his feet when somebody hit him from behind, laying him out cold. But they didn't walk away then – they continued hitting him, about the head with enthusiasm and in a rather more desultory way about the body. How long for – seconds, minutes?'

'That depends on how many they were. One man would have taken minutes to do that much damage, and that's not allowing for a break to get his breath back. More of them could do it quicker.'

Liz pondered. 'You said that, apart from that first blow, they all arrived with similar force from the same direction. Does that sound like several men at work?'

Morrison thought, then shook his head. 'No, it doesn't. In fact, most of those injuries were inflicted by someone standing in the same place. So the likelihood is there was just one assailant.'

'What did he use?'

'Probably a baseball bat or a pick-axe handle – something long, wooden and without corners. The first blow was full strength, just as hard as he could make it. The boy dropped like a stone, and while he was lying face down on the ground the assailant stood over him and hit him again and again. Maybe a couple of dozen times in all. Mostly he worked on the head. He didn't plan on Michael Dickens waking up.'

The only place Mikey got his full name was on charge sheets: it quite surprised Liz to hear somebody call him that. 'And will he?'

Morrison didn't answer at once. His gaze strayed to Roly, still huddled oblivious in his corner. 'Inspector Graham, you've seen enough assaults and road accidents to know that, this early in the game, our best guess is exactly that – a guess. People with head injuries surprise us more often than not. They surprise us by dying when they should recover and by living when they should die. They surprise us by being totally incapacitated by a relatively minor injury, and by overcoming the loss of a substantial part of their brain. I bet on horses but I wouldn't bet on the prognosis for a brain injury.'

He sucked in a slow breath. 'That said, we'd get more on the EEG from an earthworm. The machines are all that's keeping him alive. That's all right, a lot of head trauma cases owe their eventual recovery to the fact that a ventilator kept them going for the critical first three days. But this boy? He might not die; but if he was my son I'd be hoping he would.'

As soon as Scenes of Crime took over at Cornmarket Shapiro took Donovan back to Queen's Street. They needed to talk, possibly at length, certainly without interruption. His first instinct was to adjourn to *Tara* which was closer. On reflection, though, this was a conversation that would be better conducted in the office. He wasn't sure what was going to come of it,

but if Donovan's explanation was not satisfactory –
and perhaps more importantly if it was – he didn't
want the record to look as if it had emerged from a
cosy chat rather than a formal interview. Everything
that had happened so far and everything that happened from now on would be subject to scrutiny. It
was important that nothing he did made it look as
if different rules applied when a police officer was
involved.

Donovan was slow to realize that this was more
than a debriefing. He hadn't been much use at the
scene but that was understandable. Stumbling
without warning on a murderous assault isn't the
same as investigating one, and Shapiro was not surprised that his sergeant, who'd seen almost
everything the job had to offer, was somewhat
shocked.

Fifteen hours earlier Mikey Dickens had been a
thorn in his flesh, the source of professional indignity
and personal humiliation. If the devil had appeared
in a puff of smoke and offered to do Donovan one
untraceable favour, the striking down of Mikey
Dickens with the smug grin still on his face would
have been tops. Finding him in his blood in the rubble
of Cornmarket, a bit of human detritus as broken up
as the rest of the rubbish, must have been like having
an unworthy birthday wish granted. No wonder he
looked shocked; guilty, even.

As long, Shapiro thought grimly, as that was the
only reason. 'All right,' he said, 'tell me again.
Everything.'

Donovan nodded compliance. 'It was a bit after
midnight. I couldn't sleep. I was still – yeah, OK, I

was still too angry. I thought I'd walk it off. I got the dog and set off down the towpath.

'I didn't see a soul till we reached Cornmarket. Then I could see the bonfire, and the dog silhouetted against it. I headed that way, but by the time I reached the fire he'd gone. Then I saw movement by those tumbledown walls where the Inland Navigation offices used to be. I didn't want to call him and wake every dosser in Castlemere so I went to get him. But when I got there this guy Desmond was standing staring at something on the ground, and it was Mikey.

'My first thought was Desmond had floored him. But that made no sense: any dosser would run a mile from any Dickens, and if he didn't he wouldn't have got the better of him. Mikey might be a little runt but he's a runt with street-fighting in his blood.

'I wasn't carrying' – he meant a mobile phone, not a gun – 'so I hared up on to Brick Lane and woke the first house I came to. You know the rest: by the time I got back to Cornmarket the area car was arriving and the ambulance was right behind it.' He drew breath. 'What about Mikey?'

Shapiro grimaced. 'He made it to hospital alive, they took him straight to theatre. He's in a bad way, but just how bad they won't know for a day or two.' He changed tack a little. 'From the blood on the ground SOCO reckoned he'd been there twenty minutes – possibly a little less, allowing for the cold. Would you have been out that long?'

Donovan thought. 'Probably about that. It's half a mile from *Tara* to the start of Cornmarket, a bit further to the fire. I walk it in about ten minutes in daylight. It's slower in the dark, plus I was in no hurry – I wasn't going anywhere, I just needed the fresh air.'

'So if whoever did this came back along the towpath, you should have seen him.'

'If SOCO's right about the time, yes. Even hurrying he couldn't have passed *Tara* before I left.'

'And you saw no one.'

'Not till I saw Desmond. So the guy left by Brick Lane; so either he had a car or he hadn't far to go. Someone who'd just left a Dickens for dead wouldn't choose to walk past The Jubilee, not if he had a choice.'

Shapiro frowned. 'You think someone from The Jubilee did this?'

Donovan shrugged. 'I don't know. Walshes and Dickenses trade the odd black eye, but most of the time a sort of armed truce suits both lots. This is an invitation to Armaggeddon. If it was a Walsh we're going to have war in The Jubilee.'

Shapiro scowled. 'Then we'd better find out who did it before things deteriorate that far.' He straightened behind his desk. 'You'll understand, Sergeant, that I have to ask you this. Are you responsible for the attack on Mikey Dickens?'

Donovan let out a snort that was half a laugh. 'You're kidding!' Only then, when Shapiro's face didn't dissolve in its wry crumpled grin, did he realize the superintendent was serious. 'You're not kidding. Dear God, you mean it! You think I maybe smashed Mikey's head with a baseball bat.'

'Is that what it was?' asked Shapiro softly. 'A baseball bat?'

'I don't know,' grated Donovan, 'I wasn't there. I

found him – no, Desmond Jannery found him, I arrived right after that. He'd been on the ground twenty minutes before I got there.'

'We both know,' Shapiro murmured, 'that the first man to see the victim dead was quite often the last one to see him alive. That's why I have to ask, and you have to answer as clearly as you can, as often as it takes, in as much detail as necessary to show that it was just an unfortunate coincidence that you were there when Mikey was found.'

'It was a coincidence all right.' Donovan's voice rose dangerously. 'I don't know how unfortunate it was. If I hadn't been there Desmond would still have been gawping at him, wondering what the hell to do, half an hour later, and another half hour would have seen Mikey on the substitutes' bench at the Pearly Gates. Now, there's people enough in this town would agree that was the height of misfortune. But I thought we took the view, at least officially, that all human life is worth preserving.'

'Don't take that tone with me, Sergeant,' snapped Shapiro. 'We're talking in my office because for now I'm prepared to treat you as a witness rather than a suspect. Any time I can't get a straight answer from you that can change, and we'll finish this in an interview room with the tape running. Is that clear?'

Donovan was on his feet, leaning forward over his fists on the desk. 'What's clear, sir, is that I've worked for you for eight years and you *still* don't know if you can trust me!'

Getting older and fatter had not yet deprived Shapiro of a surprising turn of speed when it was called for. He shot out of his chair and faced the younger man nose to nose. 'That depends what you mean by trust. I would trust you with my life, Donovan. I would not necessarily trust you to keep your temper in the face of provocation from some pushy little low-life.'

'And what? Wait till he turned his back before stoving his head in? Then beat him up some more while he was unconscious on the ground? Jesus Christ, is that what you think of me?'

It was late, they were both tired and stressed, in another moment Shapiro might have said something he would have regretted. He sank back into his chair. 'Of course not. But for a second, forget it's you and look at the facts. The boy made a fool of you. He knocked you down, you had to risk your life to rescue him, then he wormed off the hook thanks to someone you confided in. Only yesterday morning the three of you were involved in an altercation on the steps of this police station. You said things then that could be interpreted as threats.'

'But—'

Shapiro waved him to silence. 'I know: they weren't meant that way. But you must see that now we have to go over what's been said and done with a magnifying glass. It's not enough that I don't believe you capable of a sustained attack on a helpless man. To an objective outsider it might seem a reasonable hypothesis. I have to be able to show I considered it and had good reason to dismiss it. Do you understand?'

At a cerebral level Donovan did. Caesar's wife wasn't the only one who had to be above suspicion: police officers who found that intrusive had to look round for work where the presumption of innocence applied. There must be half a dozen people in Castlemere with as good a reason for flattening Mikey Dickens, but all of them were entitled to be assumed innocent unless evidence of their guilt could be found. It might be unfair that the same indulgence didn't extend to the investigating officers, but at a rational level he accepted the necessity.

The problem was, too much of Donovan's thinking came not from his head but from his heart. He knew, and so did those around him, that too often emotion coloured his judgement. There were times when it hindered his efficiency as a detective.

'Yeah,' he said at last, thinly. 'Of course I do.' One long hand sketched an apology in the air. 'It's just . . . You flog your guts out for a job, you even risk your life, God damn it; and sure, everybody's glad of a result, you're the boys next time the Assistant Chief Constable's passing through; still, that's what you're paid for, isn't it? And then something like this comes up, and everything you've done somehow gets forgotten. We've always had our doubts about Donovan – he's got a temper, he's got a bad mouth, it was only a matter of time before they got him in deep shit. Evidence? – well no, maybe not; but there's no smoke without fire. And after eight years that . . .'

'Hurts?' Shapiro offered softly. 'I know, Donovan – I remember.'

'Yeah.' Donovan forced a rough little laugh. 'That really *was* stupid. I mean, *I* could believe I might dump on a suspect, but how could anyone think you had? That's like accusing Mother Teresa of white slaving.'

Shapiro squinted down his nose. 'I'll take that as a compliment, shall I? Listen. I'm not doing this because I don't believe you, I'm doing it because it's required of me. You'll put up with it for the same reason. And after that we'll go out and find who really did flatten Mikey. Yes?'

Donovan nodded. 'Yes. Sir.'

Chapter Two

No one in Brick Lane heard a car entering or leaving Cornmarket. No one in Cambridge Road saw Mikey's van racing away from Kumani's forecourt. Donovan spent Saturday afternoon going door to door and getting nowhere, and Sunday evening he went back to stop traffic near the garage in the hope of finding someone who only passed that way once a week. He found a couple of people who visited relatives for Sunday tea but neither of them had seen Mikey's van.

On Monday morning Liz visited Mrs Taylor again. She took Donovan with her. 'She's the one person we know saw that van at a time when, according to Mikey, there were two people in it. She'll be calmer now, maybe her memory's clearer. If she can say for sure that the driver was on his own, that's one less thing to worry about.'

Donovan was still feeling under siege or he wouldn't have taken offence at that. 'Yeah,' he growled, 'once we're sure whether I'm lying about the hijacker we can concentrate on whether I beat the suspect's head in.'

Liz thought of herself as a patient woman. It wasn't altogether true, but she thought it. But when Donovan was in this mood a little of him went a long way. 'Donovan, stop feeling so bloody sorry for yourself! There's a nineteen-year-old boy in the hospital who looks like a steamroller's been over him, and the likelihood is he's never going to tell us who was responsible. We have to find out. The fact that you and the victim weren't on speaking terms is immaterial; so is the inarguable fact that Mikey Dickens is a thief, a liar and a general waste of space. Nobody had the right to do that to him, and unless we want him to do it again next time someone annoys him we'd better get him found.'

Liz was driving, and when she turned into Chevening Moss Road Donovan felt a quiver of disquiet. He must have been this way a thousand times, without any problems until eight days ago; now he expected trouble round every twist of the lane. Mainly to avoid thinking about it he said, 'This baseball bat or whatever. Do you reckon he took it home with him?'

Every available officer had been drafted for a systematic combing of Cornmarket that lasted most of the weekend. It was no more successful than the search for Mikey's gun. It was beginning to look as if the assailant had held on to it. But so much of the sprawling wasteland was littered with bits of discarded wood that it could have passed unrecognized with twice as many people searching. On top of which, the more nights that passed without finding it, the greater the chance that Desmond Jannery or one of his friends would gather it, all unknowing, and throw it on the fire.

'We're not having a lot of luck, are we?' said Liz. 'I gather your enquiries were just about as profitable.'

He sniffed morosely. 'The three monkeys are a bunch of blabbermouths compared with this lot. Brick Lane I can understand, maybe Roly warned them off, but Cambridge Road? I don't think his influence stretches much beyond the round of the armour-plated bread van.'

Liz gave an appreciative little chuckle. 'It's just the combination of the time and the place. Tea-time on a Sunday in the middle of winter there were never going to be many people about; and this side of Kumani's the houses are bigger and further off the road so nobody would see much through the window. As for Brick Lane, I don't know. Would Roly stop them talking to you? He's got a better reason than anyone for finding out who did this.'

Donovan was so used to thinking of the Dickenses as enemies he needed reminding that this time they shared a common cause. 'Maybe he thinks he knows,' he grunted.

'If he blames you he didn't say anything to me about it. And why would he? – apart from Castle-mere's finest Roly Dickens knows you as well as anyone in town, if you'd been prone to thumping lippy kids he'd have heard about it before now. All the same, stay away from him. What Roly knows on a rational level and how he might react to finding you on his doorstep might be two different things. We don't want an incident. Mikey's head could be the least of it if tempers fray in The Jubilee.'

Donovan was confused. 'Then we should concentrate on finding whoever attacked him. Nailing his crooked defence to a charge he's never going to be fit to answer can wait.'

'If I knew where to look for Mikey's attacker I would,' said Liz. 'I don't. So let's press on with what we have a chance of tidying up, if only to clear the decks for if SOCO come up with something useful.'

'You mean, when.'

'Of course I do,' she agreed.

Two sharp turns and Chevening roundabout came into view. Despite the cold of the day Donovan felt a sweat break out under his clothes. 'Do you want me to talk to Mrs Taylor?'

Liz shook her head. 'No, I'll talk to her. I want you there mostly as a memory-jogger. Accidents do queer things to the mental processes. If you're hurt enough, or scared enough, the mind can block it all out. If she still doesn't remember, you may be able to talk her through it when nobody else could. Just seeing you will take her straight back there; with luck the details will follow.'

Donovan had no difficulty believing it. Being here was certainly bringing it back for him. The wreckage was gone now, even the burnt-out digger, but there was a big charred mark on the road that would serve as a reminder until Chevening reached the top of the road-works waiting list around the turn of the millenium. He could have died here, and that black mark have been his only memorial. There were those, he thought sourly, who'd consider a nasty stain in the road the most fitting one he could have.

Liz parked by the canal. 'Stay here, I'll give you a call if I need you. Seeing you might come as a bit of a shock, I don't want to spring it on her without warning.'

'You don't need to explain,' Donovan said mournfully, 'I've heard it before. Mostly when I was of an age for meeting girlfriends' mothers.'

Liz chuckled. 'And now you're all grown up you don't get to meet their mothers?'

'Now I'm all grown up,' growled Donovan, 'I don't even meet the girls.'

Liz rang the bell, and when there was no reply rang again. Pat Taylor answered with her hair tied up in a scarf, a brush in her hand and a smear of distemper on her cheek. 'Oh, Inspector Graham. Come in. You've caught me decorating. Can you wait five minutes while I finish and get clean?'

'Of course.' Rather than waiting in the sitting room she followed Mrs Taylor back upstairs.

'My doctor suggested I take a few more days off work, but just sitting was driving me crazy. I'm going back tomorrow. As long as I don't try to move too quickly I'm all right.'

'How are the aches and pains?'

Mrs Taylor gave a taut smile. 'Oh – settling down. Some of the bruises are pretty spectacular, but I can get out of my chair now without planning it like a military manoeuvre. When I've finished this I'm going to risk a good soak in the bath. So far I've got by on showers, but it's not the same.'

Liz was a wallower too. 'Leave your phone within reach so if you get stuck I can come and haul you out.'

She watched Pat Taylor finish the undercoat. It had been a child's room, with some kind of a mural. It seemed a shame to cover it up, but Taylor junior had probably drawn the line at waking up in Noah's

Ark one more year. Since he could now be old enough
to vote, perhaps he had a point.

'There.' Mrs Taylor left her head-scarf and coverall
in the bedroom and firmly closed the door on them.
'Now, what can I do for you?'

'I wondered if you'd thought any more about the
acci— About the crash.'

Mrs Taylor's glance was sharp. 'I've thought about
nothing else.'

Liz nodded her understanding. 'I know: the flash-
backs are the worst part. But they do stop. Be patient,
it'll pass.'

It was in Pat Taylor's eyes that she found the
advice extraneous if not impertinent. Liz wondered if
she'd been away that week last summer when the
only topic of conversation in town was the rape of its
senior policewoman. 'I do know what I'm talking
about,' she could have said, 'it isn't just a quote from
the Victim Support handbook.' But she didn't. Mrs
Taylor might have found it helpful if she'd remembered but not if she had to be reminded. Besides, it
smacked too much of competitive suffering: 'You
think *you've* had a rough time . . .?' She let it go.

'In that case,' she said, 'are you any clearer about
who was in the van?'

Mrs Taylor was fiddling with the ornaments on
the table. They didn't need arranging: it was displacement activity. As was the decorating, Liz supposed. 'I
don't understand why it matters,' she said. 'You can't
hold a passenger responsible for what happened.'

'Not what happened to you, no,' agreed Liz. 'But
we've got two different accounts of the earlier incident, the robbery at the garage, one from the driver

and one from Detective Sergeant Donovan. Who's right depends on whether there was a passenger in the van.'

'You mean, the boy who hit me and your sergeant are telling different stories, and you don't know who to believe?'

Put like that, Liz understood her puzzlement. 'Anyone can make a mistake,' she said lamely. 'The problem is, Donovan's so convinced he's right he's nailed his credibility to it. If we can get independent confirmation it'll spare him a lot of hassle and possibly some real trouble. So, can you help?'

The pause was almost long enough for Liz to say it again. Then Mrs Taylor turned to her. 'Yes.'

Donovan was like a lemming, irresistibly drawn to water. When the front door of the cottage opened he was half-way down the stone steps to the canal and the two boats moored there. One was a small motorboat, the other an elegant old-fashioned rowing skiff.

He turned at the sound of the door and saw the women on the threshold. For a second his eyes met Pat Taylor's before she backed into the house. 'I'm sorry, I don't want to talk to him. It's – too soon.'

'I understand,' said Liz. 'Thanks for your help.' She walked back to the car.

Donovan met her there. His eyes were wary. 'Well?'

'Get in the car. We're finished here.'

'Don't you want me to talk to her?'

'She won't talk to you. Says it's still too painful.'

He frowned. 'It's my fault Mikey turned her car over?'

'Of course not. But it brings it all back, and she's not ready to deal with it yet.'

'But if she doesn't remember—?'

'Ah.' Liz got in behind the wheel and waited for him to get in too before she explained. 'She does remember. She says she remembers quite clearly now. When she realized the crash was inevitable, there was nothing she could do to avoid it, she looked at the van and she didn't look away until it hit her. She has no doubt what she saw.'

'Which was?'

Liz took a deep breath. 'You were wrong. She saw two faces behind the windscreen. She couldn't identify either of them - she couldn't even be sure they were both young men - but she's adamant there were two.'

'This is crazy!' snarled Donovan. 'Thugs don't hijack other thugs! They hijack taxi drivers and clerks and women doing their shopping. Mikey Dickens getting hijacked is like two suicide bombers catching the same plane and blowing one another up!'

Liz shrugged. 'I grant you it's a long shot. But rank outsiders do sometimes win the Grand National, and even Mikey Dickens can be the random victim of violent crime.'

'Twice?' said Donovan incredulously.

'OK, maybe not,' said Liz, considering. 'What if the hijacking was indeed random - Mikey just happened to stop the van in the wrong place at the wrong time. Suppose, though, he knew the man - they move in the same circles, it's not unlikely. He knows

Mikey's going to be questioned, starts worrying that he might talk if the alternative is going down himself. So he waylays Mikey at Cornmarket for a pre-emptive strike. A hijacker who was known to him would have an even better motive than you for going after Mikey with a baseball bat.'

That shut Donovan up, at least for a moment. One of the two smartest people he knew had sent him looking for someone who saw Mikey alone in his van, the other thought it might be better if there was a hijacker. Donovan no longer knew what was best. He just knew what he believed, which was that the man who hit him was the same man he dragged out of the burning wreckage in Chevening a few minutes later. He couldn't prove it. But he was there, he knew what happened.

He gritted his teeth. 'It was Mikey in the garage. It was Mikey who hit me.'

It was like arguing with a child who thought the more times you repeated something the truer it became. All out of patience Liz snapped, 'You can't possibly know that. He was masked and muffled up from head to toe. Ash Kumani saw him for longer than you did, and knows him just about as well, and he wasn't sure if it was Mikey or not. Even you can be wrong, Donovan. Even you.'

''Course I can,' he shot back. 'But I've no reason to lie, and Mikey has.'

'And Mrs Taylor?'

'If I can be wrong, I'm damn sure she can.'

'Then who attacked Mikey? If there was no second man scared of being fingered?'

Donovan had his mouth open to answer but no

answer came. '*I* don't know. What was he doing that night? Maybe he was up to no good again. Maybe this time it misfired.'

Liz kept one eye on the road and regarded him askance with the other. 'You mean, he tried to mug one of the Chicago White Sox?'

He had the grace to admit it was improbable. He even found himself wondering if she could be right, if he'd done Mikey an injustice. But not for long. 'So why did Roly have everyone out before dawn on Monday if it wasn't Mikey's gun they were looking for? And how did he know where to look?'

That was a valid point. If Billy Dunne was telling the truth the gun had to be Mikey's. 'Then suppose there *were* two of them, but they were in it together. Mikey did the driving, his friend did the hold-up. When one got caught and the other got away they fell out and the friend shut him up. Does that work?'

'No,' said Donovan stubbornly. 'If Mikey was only the driver, why wasn't he in the van when I took the keys? He couldn't have been *that* desperate for a leak.'

That was true too. It would also take a fairly optimistic armed robber to hold up a garage and *then* start looking for a getaway vehicle. 'We haven't got it right yet, have we?' sighed Liz. 'But there must be a connection between the robbery and the assault. Let's try and work it backwards: if we knew what happened to Mikey at Cornmarket maybe we'd understand more about the robbery.'

'Who do we ask?'

'You could try Desmond and his mates again. They might remember some more detail by now. Specifically, they might remember hearing a car. It's a fair step from town, so if he was on foot he probably is local.'

'OK. And you?'

'I'll talk to Roly again, see if he'll put me on to Mikey's friends. He won't be keen, but with Mikey on life support maybe he'll force himself. If I can find out who Mikey was with that evening, maybe I can find out what he was doing at Cornmarket. Was he taken there, did he go there to meet someone, is it where his mates hang out when there's nothing better to do? But it was a cold night, they weren't sitting on a wall passing reefers and dirty pictures. He must have had some reason to be there at midnight.'

Donovan kept a diplomatic silence. Even before he had the dog he often went out at night to wander through the silent dereliction along the canal. But Mikey had never struck him as the sort of man who needed solitude to still the turbulence of mind and breast stirred up by a hard day's work.

It was after one. 'Drop me off at home, will you,' said Donovan, 'I'll take Brian for a run.'

As always, Liz did a mental double-take before the image of the dog that was definitely not a pit bull terrier supplanted that of her husband in her mind. 'Er – why *do* you call him Brian?'

'Brian Boru,' said Donovan, 'High King of Ireland.'

That explained it. Liz smiled. 'I think mine's named after the snail in *The Magic Roundabout.*'

Chapter Three

Liz returned to the house in George Street. Again it was Thelma who answered the door. She looked worn out. Two months ago she was in front of the Magistrates for handling stolen goods – 'It's me age, Your Worships, me eyes are going. When the constable told me it was a Cartier watch and the jewels were real, of course I knew *then* nobody got it with petrol coupons.' The way she looked now, the least sentimental of Crown Prosecutors would be embarrassed about proceeding against her.

She was seventy-one – Liz knew from the charge sheets. Two months ago she was a spritely energetic seventy-one, the sort of old lady whose wrinkled skin and thinning hair hid a frame of iron and a heart like a steam hammer. As long as there was fuel for the fire – in her case a nice bit of cheque fraud or demanding with menaces – it would keep thumping long after nobler hearts had given up the ghost.

But the business with Mikey had taken all her reserves, left her grey, shrunken and frail. When she saw who was at the door she turned away, leaving it open, and returned to her chair and the sort of daytime television she'd always been too busy scheming to watch before.

'Is there any news?' asked Liz.

Without looking round Thelma shook her head. 'No change. They say it's still early days but I don't know. He doesn't look to me like there's anyone at home.'

'I'm so sorry,' said Liz, and meant it. 'How's Roly bearing up?'

'I haven't seen much of him,' said Thelma. 'He just comes home to change his clothes. I don't think he's eaten properly since it happened.' She glanced over her shoulder. 'He's at the hospital now, if you're wanting him.'

'I'll tell you what I really want. I want the bastard who did this.' It was a token of the respect she enjoyed in this least law-abiding of homes that Thelma accepted she meant that too. 'I'm going to need some help with Mikey's movements on Friday night.'

Thelma might be drained, sapped by worry and lack of sleep until she hardly knew what time of day it was, but while there was breath left in her she wasn't going to miss the subtext to that. The eye was still shrew-sharp. 'You want me to tell you who he was with? What they were doing?'

Liz took a chair and leaned close. 'I'm investigating an attempted murder, I'm not interested in any little sidelines Mikey and his mates were pursuing. Even if I was, even if Mikey was up to no good, it could be a long time before I could charge him. That's not what I'm after.'

At length Thelma looked up again from the television. 'What do you want from me?'

Liz breathed softly. 'I need to know who he was with that evening, where they went, what time they split up. I need names.' She knew that, in The Jubilee, people would part with blood and even a minor extremity before they'd part with names.

For a moment it seemed she'd asked too much. 'I'm not giving you names!' exclaimed the old woman, horrified.

Disappointed, Liz straightened up. 'Then—?'

'But I'll talk to his friends myself. If any of them was with him, and if they're prepared to tell you about it, they'll contact you.'

'And if they aren't prepared to talk about it?'

'Well,' said Thelma pensively, 'I can't be sure but I think probably Roly will want them to reconsider.'

So there were two ways Liz might discover who Mikey spent his last evening with: if they called her, or if they turned up in the same ward at Castle General.

'Thanks, Thelma.' She touched the older woman's arm. It felt like a dry stick through her cardigan. 'Tell Roly I'm doing my best.'

She almost made it out of the house without the thing she'd been waiting for coming up. But Thelma followed her into the hall. 'I heard Mr Donovan was there when Mikey was found.'

Liz wasn't going to lie, and she thought it would do more harm than good to hedge round it. 'That's right. He was out walking that dog of his. It was the dog that found him.'

Thelma nodded and said nothing more. Liz left wondering if she'd doused a fire or poured petrol on it.

*

Donovan put off visiting Desmond Jannery and his dosser friends until first thing Tuesday morning. Afternoons they were away begging; by evening they were mostly drunk.

Trying to get a coherent picture of their movements the night Mikey came to grief was like juggling with mercury. Their accounts varied so wildly, from person to person and from one telling to the next, that if he hadn't seen them there himself Donovan would have thought they were curled up in a Salvation Army hostel at the relevant time and were making the whole thing up.

Desmond had the clearest recollection. He remembered seeing the dog, following it and finding the injured boy among the rubble of the broken walls. He remembered seeing Donovan there. He didn't remember, as a woman called Sophie did, a giant silver snake slithering in from The Levels. He hadn't noticed the UFO which landed near the abandoned railway carriages or the space-suited alien who'd travelled from a world beyond the orbit of Pluto for the purpose of appearing to a man called Wicksy.

But though he thought about it again, he also hadn't seen a car or a man wandering around Cornmarket with a baseball bat. He hadn't even seen Mikey earlier on, when he was still vertical.

The Scenes of Crime Officer had confirmed, from the blood spatter pattern on the brickwork, that the attack took place where Mikey was found so either he met his attacker there or they went there together. It seemed likely that some sort of conversation or argument passed between them before Mikey succumbed to the assault. But no one heard anything.

Desmond and Sophie, and probably also Wicksy unless he was behind Venus at the critical moment, were dozing round their fire only a hundred metres away while somebody hammered a teenage boy into the dirt, and he couldn't have had more privacy if he'd jumped Mikey in thick fog in the middle of The Levels. Even now they'd got over the excitement, and were neither too drunk nor too sober to make sense, the closest Donovan had to witnesses seemed to have heard and seen nothing at all.

'I heard a car.'

Donovan started at the voice close behind him. He'd thought there were just the four of them. He'd taken the black heap at the end of the settee for a bin bag. 'Who are you?'

'I'm Leslie.'

Donovan didn't think he'd forgotten but he checked his notes just in case. 'You were here Friday night? You didn't make a statement.'

'I slept through it,' said Leslie regretfully. 'Finding him, the police cars, the ambulance – the lot.'

'And the spaceship?' asked Wicksy, appalled.

'The lot,' Leslie said.

Donovan looked doubtful. 'Then, when did you hear the car?'

'*Before* I went to sleep,' Leslie said contemptuously. 'Of course.'

Of course. 'Which would have been about when?'

'Five to twelve,' said Leslie confidently. 'I listen to the midnight news on my transistor, then I go to sleep. I heard the car just before the news came on.'

'This was Friday night–Saturday morning?'

'Every night,' said Leslie firmly.

'So, going up to twelve on Friday night you heard a car.' Donovan wasn't convinced but he was so desperate for someone to know something he'd have followed it up if Grandma Walsh had seen it in the tea-leaves. 'Driving through or did it stop?'

'It stopped. It came from that direction and stopped just about there.' The little man was pointing confidently.

Donovan let go of the breath he was holding in a weary sigh. 'Yeah. Right, Leslie, I'll bear that in mind.' There was no car. There was no road for it to have come up. He was pointing at the canal.

Demoralized, Donovan walked home along the towpath with Brian bounding ahead of him. He almost hoped someone would speak to him for the pleasure of snarling back; but he saw only a couple of kids fishing off the quay and someone messing about in a boat off the *James Brindley*'s stern. Donovan didn't mind talking to people with boats, but as he looked to see who it was the outboard engine caught and it chugged away, towing a silver wake eastward up the canal.

Brian had found a stick. Though he was definitely not a pit bull terrier, there wasn't much Golden Retriever in him either. Mostly it was bloody-mindedness that made him fetch: however often Donovan could throw something away Brian could bring it back, and the crosser Donovan got the more the satisfaction the dog got out of it. Once, in exasperation, Donovan tried to end the game by lobbing it in the canal. He spent the rest of the evening in the close confines of *Tara*'s saloon with a stinking wet dog smirking at him over a slimy stick.

The stick looked like something the kids might have been playing with but nobody seemed to want it back. Donovan didn't want it either. He threw it away. Brian brought it back. He threw it away again; Brian brought it back. He went to throw it away again—

An invisible mule kicked him hard under the heart, and his jaw dropped and he just stood holding the thing, his long fingers wrapped around a grip cobbled out of electrical tape, his eyes caught, as if on a nail, by the splintered and grimy end, bruised by fresh fang-marks, stained with something like tar.

When he finally got a measure of control over himself, oblivious to the dog's requests which were fast turning to threats, he whispered, 'Oh shit.'

Even the preliminary tests took a little while. But knowing what they would reveal eased the tension. Mikey Dickens's blood at one end of the stave, Donovan's fingerprints at the other.

This time they talked in the interview room. It might have been a matter of form – Shapiro was determined to do nothing that smacked of favouritism, if he had to mill Donovan down to a fine grey powder to prove that all avenues had been explored he would do it – but then again, it might not. Nothing in the superintendent's manner suggested this wasn't for real.

'You didn't see it before the dog brought it to you?'

'No.'

'So you don't know where he found it.'

'No.'

'Could he have brought it all the way from Cornmarket?'

'No. I'd have seen if he had.'

'So he picked it up on the towpath. When was the last time you noticed he didn't have it?'

Donovan gave a giant shrug. 'Jesus, I don't know! You don't, do you – you don't notice that somebody *hasn't* got something. But we must have been pretty well back at the boat: if he'd found it much earlier he'd have wanted it throwing.'

Shapiro nodded, expressionless. 'So you're telling me this weapon that was used to beat Mikey Dickens within an inch of his life was lying round in the immediate vicinity of your boat.'

Donovan raked thin fingers through his hair. It needed cutting again. It always needed cutting. 'I suppose it must have been. But if you want to know how it got there, I've no idea.'

'Could it have been there since Friday night?'

'How would I know? I suppose so. I suppose whoever hit Mikey came back up the towpath and threw it away there.'

'You've had Brian out since then, though. Wouldn't he have found it before if it was there?'

'I expect so. Yes.'

'So, having made his getaway, with the weapon either in his possession or secreted somewhere we couldn't find it despite an extensive search, the assailant came back to move it to where it would be found. And not just by anyone: by the detective most closely involved in the case.'

'Sounds crazy, doesn't it?' admitted Donovan. 'But yes, that has to be what happened.'

Shapiro waited for him to elaborate. When he didn't the superintendent gave a little grimace. 'What do you suppose it is? Apart from the thing that beat Mikey's head in?'

'A baseball bat?'

'You thought it would be a baseball bat, didn't you? Why – is there a lot of baseball played round here?'

'*I* don't know!'

'Then why assume that's what was used? Not a pickaxe handle, that you can buy in any hardware shop, or a bit of two-by-four, but a baseball bat?'

'Because that's what they use back home!' exclaimed Donovan. 'There's only one baseball team in the Six Counties, but they sell hundreds of the bloody things every year. It's the ideal tool for the job. After all, with one minor difference, it's what a baseball bat was designed to do.'

'What difference?'

Donovan sniffed. 'The ball's a bit smaller than a man's head.'

Shapiro said nothing for a few moments. Donovan shuffled under his gaze.

'If you were using it to play baseball, or beat a man's head in, you'd hold it by the narrow end. Where the tape was,' the superintendent said then. 'If you were throwing it for a dog, though, it wouldn't much matter how you held it. Odd, then, that your prints ended up in the same place.'

Donovan was worried enough to start fighting back. 'Yeah, isn't that odd? The only part of a beat-up old bat that's smooth enough to carry a print, and it ends up carrying mine. You'd almost think that was planned, wouldn't you? You'd almost think someone deliberately wound some new electrical tape round this crappy old bat specifically so that whoever handled it next would leave their prints on it. That he then left the thing where the dog could hardly miss it in the sure expectation that I'd have it in my hands before it occurred to me what it was. As frames go it's not exactly sophisticated, is it?'

Shapiro cocked an eyebrow. 'Sophisticated enough that you can't prove that's what happened.'

'Wouldn't be much point framing me if I could,' grated Donovan.

'All right.' He tried to give even crooks a fair hearing, he wasn't going to deny the same courtesy to his sergeant. 'Why you? Just because you and Mikey were involved in a rather public battle of wits and the last thing you said to him, before witnesses, could have been a threat? But Mikey must have other enemies, any one of whom would be an easier target – any one of whom we'd have been happy to charge. So *why* you? Why any policeman? Why was he so determined it should be you that he held on to a weapon he should have got rid of and four days later returned to the scene of the crime in order to leave it where your dog would find it? Who hates you that much, Donovan?'

Donovan glowered at him. 'How long have you got?'

Frank Shapiro was a man with a healthy respect for instinct. It was no substitute for evidence, but it had helped too often in the search for evidence for him to ignore a good gut feeling. His instinct said Donovan didn't do this. He could have done. He was in the right area at the right time; he had a motive, he had a temper, and now the weapon had his prints on it. Shapiro couldn't ignore all that. But he felt Donovan was telling the truth, that he was being set up for this. Why and by whom were questions to which, as yet, he had no answer.

The alternative was to believe Donovan capable of premeditated and sustained brutality. If Mikey had stormed into Queen's Street with a black eye Shapiro just might have believed it. There *was* a fury in Donovan, the fact that he kept it under strict control didn't preclude the possibility that one day, with enough provocation, it could momentarily slip its leash. But this wasn't a momentary loss of temper. This was deliberate, cold-blooded even. And after doing it he'd have had to do the rest – lie, lay this false trail and then feign bewilderment. None of it was impossible. But if he'd done all that then Donovan wasn't the man Shapiro had taken him for.

And that, in part, was the problem. Shapiro had a lot invested in Donovan's innocence. Eight years of trust, of commitment, of mutual reliance. Eight years of standing up for him when it would have been easier to go along with the general view that Donovan was a grenade with the pin out. If he'd been wrong about that he'd been badly wrong and Mikey Dickens had paid the price. What concerned Shapiro now was the danger of wanting to believe in Donovan too much.

He breathed steadily for a moment, formulating what he wanted to say. 'All right, Sergeant, this is the situation. If you were anybody else and the best defence you could offer was that somebody was framing you, I'd be deeply sceptical but I wouldn't be ready to arrest you. I'd ask you to remain available for further interviews, and I'd show you out.

'There are two differences between you and everyone else. One is that we've known each other a long time and I don't think this is your style. The other is that you're a police officer. Anyone else would be entitled to the benefit of any doubt going, and to get on with his plumbing or road mending or door-to-door brush selling until I could make a case against him.

'But a policeman under suspicion of a serious offence can't go on as if nothing has happened. You know that, we all do. So I'm sending you home. Don't take it personally: with luck we'll sort it out by the weekend, in which case it was just a few days' extra holiday, nothing more. No, *don't* argue, Donovan,' he said quickly, seeing the resentment rising in the younger man's face, 'there's no alternative. I have to ask for your Warrant card.'

'You believe it!' exclaimed Donovan, and his eyes were angry and incredulous. 'Somebody who can't decide if he hates me or Mikey most tried to kill him and frame me, and you believe it.'

'I didn't say that,' snapped Shapiro, exasperated. 'I most specifically *did not* say that.'

'Well anyway, you think it's possible.'

'I didn't even say that. I said it had to be investigated. I said you were relieved of duty until it was sorted. For you – as for me and for all of us – it isn't enough just to say you've been framed. You have to prove it.

'Go home, Donovan, do some thinking. If you're

152

being set up, who's behind it? It has to be someone you know – take the dog for a walk and give it some thought. No,' he added then, '*don't* take the dog for a walk. The way your luck's going he'd probably come back with your signed confession.'

There were too many years and too many culture differences between them for a common sense of humour. Donovan had to be concentrating to know when Shapiro was making a joke and right now he was too upset. In his eyes there was no acknowledgement that there might be a wry side to this. They were bitter, and hurt, and afraid. His voice was low. 'You didn't have to say If. And you could have said We.' He left the room so quickly it almost looked as if he was running away.

Which meant that by the time Shapiro had worked out the meaning of that cryptic farewell it was too late to explain or apologize. He'd meant, *If* it was a set-up; and *We* have to prove it.

His heart blazing sulphurously within him, ignoring everyone he met on the stairs and in the corridor, Donovan stalked out to the yard and punched life into his motorbike. He had no idea where he was going as he swung out through the gate, only that he was going to set a land speed record for getting there.

Chapter Four

Liz took an early lunch on Tuesday and went home in the hope that Brian would have done the same. Her heart lifted at the sight of his car in the drive.

People who reckoned to know about men and women were puzzled by the success of their marriage. They had nothing in common. Liz was an energetic ambitous career-woman who'd already punched through many of the invisible barriers raised between her and where she wanted to be. A few remained, but having proved herself as a Detective Inspector she was now due promotion and a squad of her own. From there, given her ability and strength of purpose, the sky was the limit and no glass ceiling would stop her. Superintendent – ACC – maybe even Chief Constable, depending on how much she wanted it, how hard she worked, where the breaks came. She'd done well already, and would do better.

Brian was head of Castle High's art department mainly because he was now the oldest teacher working in it. He had no desire for his own school so saw no point scrambling for a deputy headship: he was happier doing what he did well than over-stretching himself with something bigger and expected to stay at this level until he retired. Unless

Liz's job took them away from Castlemere, in which case he might have to settle for less. That too he could face with equanimity. Equanimity was his middle name.

He was forty-four now and his hair was going fast; but he was spared the anxiety that his good-looking wife might be drawn to a more attractive man by the knowledge that when they first got together twelve years ago he was already nudging middle-age, his hair was already looking impermanent and the kindest epithet applied to him was usually 'homely'. If Liz had wanted a handsome, vital, exciting partner she'd never have married him. Brian Graham took considerable consolation from the fact that, unless he became an alcoholic or caught leprosy, time was unlikely to much diminish the Adonis factor in his case.

They didn't share the same interests. Liz spent her leisure time riding, kept her mare Polly in the backyard. Brian liked visiting museums and galleries. Liz enjoyed a good steak; Brian was a non-obnoxious vegetarian. Brian liked culture-vulture holidays in Greece; Liz rather fancied white-water rafting. It had to be love: there was nothing else keeping them together.

'Will whatever you're doing split in half?' she called as she let herself in.

''Course it will,' he replied nobly from the kitchen. 'A jug of wine, half a spinach rissole and thou – what more could even Omar Khayyam ask?'

They ate from trays in front of the living-room fire, enjoying the unexpected bonus of one another's company. When there was a shit-fan interface at

Queen's Street they could go days without sharing a meal.

'Pat Taylor was back at school this morning,' said Brian, diplomatically ignoring the tomato sauce Liz was wielding so liberally. 'She says she's better, but she still looks a bit drawn.'

'An accident knocks the stuffing out of you,' said Liz. 'Even when it doesn't actually, a really close call leaves you feeling desperately mortal. Most of the time that's something we know at the back of our minds without really acknowledging. I suppose by the time you've been bowled down the road by a van hitting you at sixty miles an hour you're feeling about as mortal as you ever want to. Maybe someone who's had to be cut out of her car is doing pretty well to be back at work nine days later and only a little drawn.'

'To be honest,' said Brian, 'she was a bit drawn before. Problems at home. She and the husband – Clifford, you met him at the school fête – have split up.'

'She really isn't having much luck, is she?' Liz remembered Clifford Taylor, who ran the bottle stall next door to her white elephants, well enough to be surprised. 'He didn't strike me as the type.'

'What type?'

'The bimbo-chasing type. You know: "Dear heaven, my wife's nearly forty, if I don't replace her with a newer model people might notice I'm forty-five."'

Brian chuckled. 'I don't think bimbos were involved. I don't know what the problem was – I don't actually *know* anything – but the staff-room gossip reckons it was more of a growing apart. Wanting different things. Clifford moved out before Christmas. Edwards in Physics, who plays squash with him, says he's taken a flat in one of those big Victorian houses in Rosedale Avenue.'

'I wonder if he knows about the accident.'

'I expect so. Clifford's a decent sort, he won't have severed all communications. If she needs help, he'll be there for her.'

'Except with the decorating,' grinned Liz. For an art teacher, Brian was notoriously bad with more paint than you could put on a palette.

When the phone went Brian let her answer it. The chances of it being for him were too long.

Liz came back with an odd expression, forked up the last of her rissole and pulled her coat on. 'I have an assignation,' she said. 'With someone who wishes to remain amominous but was with Mikey Dickens the night he was attacked.'

They met at the house in George Street. Thelma answered the door. Before she went through into the parlour Liz said quietly, 'Thanks for this, Mrs Dickens.'

Mikey's grandmother shrugged. 'I want to know what happened. You're my best chance of finding out.'

Liz nodded slowly. 'I understand that. But – you will leave it to me to deal with, won't you? Even if it turns out to be – well, someone you know.'

'Walshes,' said Thelma baldly. 'It won't be. They wouldn't be that stupid.'

'But if they were?'

'Mrs Graham, I'm too old for going out late at

night with a violin case under my arm. If you can find whoever knocked seven bells out of our Mikey, I'm happy for you to deal with it. But I'll tell you now, his father won't be. Nothing you say and nothing I say will make him feel differently. You figure out who did this, you'd best collar him fast. Or find some excuse to bang Roly up for a day or two. There'll be blood on the streets else.'

Inside, a nervous young man screwed round on the sofa when she opened the door. He was about Mikey's age: spots and the pale shadow of a moustache he shaved about once a week, mostly for the practice. Liz took a moment to put a name to him. Barker – Vinnie Barker. No form to speak of: a couple of convictions for joy-riding but round here that was the minimum necessary if you wanted people to talk to you.

'I want to remain amominous,' he said again.

'That's fine, Vinnie,' said Liz ingenuously. 'What can you tell me about Friday night?'

He'd been expecting an argument about his anonymity; relieved, he relaxed a little. 'I'm only here 'cos Mikey's gran said so. I don't grass on no one for nothing.'

'You know who hit Mikey?'

He shook his head. 'No.'

'Then you're not grassing, are you?'

'Er – no,' he agreed after a moment. He sounded a shade disappointed. 'Then what—?'

It was like talking to an idiot child. Compared with Vinnie, Mikey Dickens was a Napoleon of crime. Liz hung on to her patience. 'You may be the last person who was with Mikey before he was attacked.

You can tell me what time you were together, where you were, whether he had any plans for later. The more I know about his movements Friday evening the closer I get to whoever put him in the hospital.'

'We weren't doing nothing,' said Vinnie defensively. 'Just hanging out.'

'Hanging out where?'

'Down The Fen Tiger.'

'About closing time?' Vinnie nodded. 'Helping people out of the car-park?' Liz was being kind. What they were doing, as she very well knew, was playing Car-Park Vigilante. You targeted someone who was over the alcohol limit and offered to guide him out of the car-park. It didn't matter if there was enough room to three-point-turn an articulated lorry, if he didn't want you making an anonymous – amominous – phonecall to the police he'd accept your assistance, however grudgingly, and hand over a five pound note. If he was well over the limit he'd produce a tenner.

'What happened then?'

'Nothing. About half eleven I said I was heading home. It was freezing, my mum doesn't like me sitting on the bollards when it's cold, I might get a chill.'

Liz wanted to scream. 'So you parted about eleven-thirty. Do you know what Mikey was going to do then? Was he heading home too?'

Vinnie shook his head. 'He said he'd got somebody to see first. He said he'd head up the towpath and go home from there.'

Hope quickened under Liz's breastbone. Finally they were getting somewhere. 'He was meeting someone at Cornmarket? Did he give you a name?'

'Nah. Just—' He stopped.

'What?'

'Nothing.'

It wasn't true. She'd come back to that later. 'So at eleven thirty he was fine, he was heading up the towpath and he was going to meet someone. That was the last you saw of him?' Vinnie nodded. 'Was he worried about this meeting or looking forward to it?'

'He wasn't expecting to get beat up, if that's what you mean!'

'But it wasn't a friend he was going to see.'

'Hardly.'

Liz leaned forward in her chair. 'You know who it was, don't you? Mikey told you who he was going to see. Tell me. Right now it's all you can do for Mikey: tell me who he was meeting.' Still the youth hesitated. 'It doesn't mean that person beat him up. Mikey may never have got there. Or they might have talked and then separated, and Mikey was attacked after that. But until I talk to this person the suspicion has to be that he's responsible. If you're trying to protect him, for whatever reason, think about this. You can keep his name from me, all I can do is charge you with withholding evidence. But Mikey's dad can take you apart.'

Vinnie wriggled unhappily but all three of them knew it was true. When he looked to Thelma to deny it she looked away. His hands spread helplessly on the sofa cushions. 'I don't want no trouble. Mikey's gran asked me to help' – from his tone Liz guessed Thelma's request had been almost as hard to refuse as Roly's would be – 'but I don't really *know* nothing.

I know what Mikey told me, that's all. If I tell you what Mikey said I'm going to have you on my case, and if I don't I'm going to have his dad. None of this is my fault,' he whined, 'I don't see why it all comes down to who's going to dump on me!'

Liz didn't understand. 'Vinnie – why do you think I'm going to dump on you? All I want is the truth. Tell me who Mikey was expecting to meet and we'll all be happy.'

'Wanna bet?' said Vinnie Barker glumly.

Shapiro had sandwiches at his desk, and after that he rested his head on his hand and shut his eyes for a moment. It was a puzzle to him that, when his phone went a minute later, half an hour had passed.

'DI Graham for you, sir,' said the switchboard.

By the time she came on he'd had time to work out what day it was and get the blood flowing in his fingers again. 'Liz? What's up? Where are you?'

'I'm on my way in,' she said, 'I'll be there in five minutes. I wanted to make sure you'd be there.'

There was something very odd about the pitch of her voice that was explained neither by the cell-phone signal nor his own post-prandial doziness. 'Has something happened?'

'Yes,' she replied briefly, and made no attempt to elaborate. 'Where's Donovan?'

'I sent him home,' said Shapiro. 'After the business with the bat I didn't feel I had any option. You need back-up? – I can get Morgan for you.'

'No, I don't need back-up. But I think you should get Donovan in again. Oh God, Frank, I don't know how to say this. But I found a friend of Mikey's that he spent Friday evening with. They parted a bit before midnight because Mikey had to meet someone at Cornmarket.'

Shapiro's voice was wooden. 'Go on.'

'He didn't call Donovan by name but I don't know who else he could have meant. He said The Filth wanted to talk to him again, and he hoped it would be as entertaining as last time.'

Chapter Five

'There's no sign of him at the boat,' said Liz, flopping on to Shapiro's chair, 'the bike's gone and his phone's switched off. But the dog's still on *Tara* so he'll have to be back by tonight. I left a note for him to call when he gets in.'

'What will you tell him?' asked Shapiro.

Liz threw him a hunted look. 'That we need to talk. That there've been developments.'

'Will you tell him what?'

'Not till he's safely in here, no.'

Shapiro elevated an eyebrow. 'You think he'll make a dash for the nearest port?'

'Of course not,' she said shortly. But she didn't know what to expect instead, and however Donovan reacted it would be easier managed inside the police station.

'Liz – honestly – do you think he did it?'

She almost said, 'Of course not,' again; but that would have been her heart talking and she needed to focus on the facts. 'Frank, I don't know. Vinnie Barker wasn't lying, it was too much like pulling teeth getting it out of him. But Vinnie telling the truth doesn't necessarily mean Donovan's lying. He and Mikey may have met and parted, or they may never have met. But a meeting was planned, and I'm desperately worried that Donovan didn't see fit to tell us about it.'

'So you *do* think he did it.'

'No,' she demurred, 'I'm not saying that. But he'd better have a bloody good explanation for keeping quiet about it even when Mikey turned up half-dead. All right, he wanted it off the record: that I can buy. He wanted to mark Mikey's card without being constrained by the Police and Criminal Evidence Act. Inappropriate but understandable. He was angry and he was hurt. Maybe he meant only to give Mikey a piece of his mind. Maybe he came back with his lip, and Donovan lost his temper and—'

'And?'

'And hit him.'

'Having first asked him to turn round?'

He could have asked but Mikey would hardly have obliged. 'Maybe he waited till Mikey went to leave.'

'At which point Donovan produced a baseball bat he happened to have handy and smashed Mikey across the back of the head? And went on hitting him after he was down? That's not a temper tantrum, Liz, it's attempted murder.'

They regarded each other for some time without speaking; then Liz shook her head. 'It doesn't work, does it? However angry he was, I can't see Donovan planning it like that. Going equipped. He might hit out with his fists, if Mikey had been knocked down and cracked his skull I could accept it. But not that Donovan planned it, and not that he waited till Mikey turned his back.'

'So you *don't* believe he did it.'

She was tired of doing all the work. 'Never mind

what I believe. Do *you* think he could have done it? Like that – the way it was done?'

Shapiro was silent, clearly thinking. Liz found that more shocking than almost anything he could have said. They were talking about a colleague, a man with whom they shared a close professional relationship, and Shapiro was wondering whether he'd plotted the murder of a nineteen-year-old boy. In a way, it hardly mattered what he decided now. Liz was glad Donovan wasn't there to mark that hesitation.

Shapiro came at his answer tangentially. 'I've been in this job too long to think only certain people commit crimes. In the right circumstances, any of us can do just about anything. The question is not whether Donovan could do this, but in what circum- stances would he do it? To save his own life or someone else's? – of course, it wouldn't even be a crime. For money? – no. That I wouldn't believe. But in a state of utter rage, because Mikey had made such a fool of him he'd thought he had to quit a job that means everything to him? Liz, I'd give my right arm – I may actually mean that – to be able to say no. But the truth is, I don't know either.'

His gaze left her and wandered round the office, finding the framed photographs of his children on the windowsill. David had taken the one of the girls; probably Shapiro had taken the one of David, because he was scowling as if he was doing it wrong. 'I've a lot of time for Donovan. He drives me mad, I never get through a week without shouting at him in a thoroughly unseemly fashion, but in a real emer- gency there's only you that I'd rather have beside me. Despite that shifty tinker façade, I've always thought

I could count on him. I've trusted him, and he's never betrayed that trust. Until maybe now.

'And now I don't know if I misjudged him; or if he's changed; or if he was just pushed too damned hard this one time, and he's ruined Mikey's life and his own because of it. Is it my fault? Did I give him too much rope? – because that was how he got his best results. But I owed him better. Should I have realized he needed closer supervision, that something like this could happen if he got too far out on his own? If you make people think it's results that matter, isn't it your fault when they start thinking that any means are acceptable?'

Liz's hand crossed the desk and closed on his wrist. He wasn't a bony man, but in his tension she could feel the bone and the tendons knotted over it. 'Frank, that's nonsense. Nobody could have had a better teacher or a steadier guide. Nobody else could have made a detective of Donovan, would have put up with him long enough to see the potential. If he has gone off the rails – and we don't know that yet, we're worried and we may be making too many assumptions – it's not your fault.'

He appreciated her saying it, even if he wasn't convinced. 'It's just – such a pity,' he stumbled. 'He's a good copper in so many ways. And then something like this happens and even those of us who know that can't rule out the possibility that he did exactly what it looks he did.'

'Anyone can be framed.'

Shapiro shook his head. 'For a frame to work it not only has to be possible, it has to be credible. It has to be more convincing than the truth. Someone could say *you* beat Mikey Dickens's head in, but people would think it was a sick joke. Say the same thing about Donovan and you have to take the suggestion seriously. That may not be fair, but it's a reflection of the fact that you and he are different types of people. He gets angry and you don't.'

'Of course I get angry,' snapped Liz, proving it. 'The main difference between Donovan and me is that he *shows* it and I don't. You said anyone could do anything in the right circumstances: well, I could have beaten Mikey. All I had to do was take him by surprise. And I'd have got away with it because I'd have more sense than to threaten him beforehand. Donovan's tragedy is that, in a world where the opposite is the norm, he's a better man on the inside than he seems on the surface.'

Shapiro's expression surprised her. The pain in his face had given way to a sombre smile. 'Correct me if I'm wrong,' he said. 'But I think we're both saying we could see this happening, just, if Donovan momentarily lost control of his temper; but not if he had to plan it and arm himself first. Yes?'

Liz drew in a long breath and released it before answering. 'Yes.'

'Then he didn't do it, and he is being framed.'

'But then, why didn't he tell us about the meeting?'

'Tell you what,' said Shapiro. 'When we get him in here, I'll ask him.'

Liz didn't miss the significance of that. 'You want to talk to him yourself?'

'It's probably better. One way or another he's

made a damn fool of himself, he'll probably find it easier to confess to me than to you.'

That was part of it. Liz thought the other part was sparing her an interview that would leave a legacy of resentment. If, when everything was known, Donovan still had both his liberty and his job, the fences between him and his superintendent would be easier to mend.

'What do you want me to do?'

Shapiro said pensively, 'I wonder if Vinnie Barker knows the other man in the van.'

Liz frowned. 'Why would he?'

'If he was a genuine hijacker he probably doesn't. But if he was a partner, maybe he does. Vinnie must know most of Mikey's friends. Now he's started talking you might be able to get him to say more.'

'Maybe,' Liz said doubtfully. 'I don't see how that helps Donovan.'

'Actually,' said Shapiro, peering down his nose in gentle reproof, 'clearing Sergeant Donovan of a crime he may in fact have committed is not the primary function of this department. I don't propose to put everything else on hold until we know whether Donovan actually brained Mikey or only thought about it.'

Liz ducked her head, chastened.

'Though to be honest,' admitted Shapiro, 'it might help Donovan too. We can guess why he wanted this meeting with Mikey – to warn him off. That's why Donovan went to Cornmarket; but why did Mikey go? Donovan's twice his size, and he must have suspected it could get physical. But he not only went, at night and alone, he dropped his guard long enough to get decked. After the week he'd given Donovan I can't believe he'd make that mistake. Why risk it? – it wasn't an official request. What did he stand to gain?'

Liz shut her eyes for a moment. That was why he had Superintendent on his door while she had Inspector on hers. The way he thought reminded her of one of those before-the-tigers acts in a travelling circus, where someone kept plates spinning on top of canes. She'd never known anyone who could keep so many ideas in play at one time. 'But he told Vinnie—'

'He was going to meet The Filth – I know. At least, that's what Vinnie thought he said. Suppose he actually said he was meeting someone *about* The Filth? This partner of his, that he robbed the garage with – maybe he wanted to discuss keeping us off their backs. Mikey would have met his mate at midnight in Cornmarket. And the man who robbed Mr Kumani at gunpoint, and pistol-whipped Donovan, is a prime suspect for taking the back of his head off with a baseball bat.'

'Donovan won't have it that there was a second man.'

Shapiro frowned. 'Mrs Taylor saw one. Didn't she?'

'Donovan thinks she's mistaken.'

The superintendent squinted. 'She'd better *not* be mistaken. Mikey having a partner might be his best chance of staying out of prison.'

Liz was about to leave when the phone rang. Answering it, Shapiro waved her back to her seat. It was the Scenes of Crime Officer calling in from the Forensic Science Laboratory.

'Something a little odd turned up, sir, I thought you'd want to know.'

'Nothing cheers my heart more, Sergeant Tripp, than something a little odd turning up.'

Shapiro came from a race that used words, that played with them, that wove little patterns with them and took pleasure in their faceted meanings. Sergeant Tripp, on the other hand, was a Fenlander, with roots as deep as the peat, for whom words were a burden. He used them sparingly and stuck to the same ones whenever possible. He was irritated by the mere existence of the word 'shovel' when 'spade' was good enough for any purpose. He kept waiting for Shapiro to say something that made sense.

Shapiro sighed. 'What did you find, Sergeant?'

'This bat thing. It's certainly what was used in the attack – the blood and hair on it match the victim's. And the fingerprints on the electrical tape are DS Donovan's; but we were expecting that too.'

'What *weren't* you expecting?'

SOCO thought he was being rushed. Shapiro could hear him putting the brakes on: his voice came slower and more sonorous than ever. 'We did a full surface examination. There were no more prints, the surface is too rough, but we took random samples from the grime in the cracks in case there was anything useful there.'

'And was there?'

'No,' said Sergeant Tripp with heavy satisfaction. 'So then I wondered if there was anything under the tape. It's quite new, I wondered if it had been put there to hide something.'

Shapiro hardly dared ask. 'Had it?'

'No,' said Tripp again. 'But we found another print on the sticky side. A partial oblique of a right thumb, a bit blurry but good enough to say what it wasn't. It wasn't DS Donovan's. In fact, I don't think it was a man's print at all. I think that tape was stuck on by a woman.'

Shapiro went on regarding his inspector thoughtfully for a couple of minutes after he put down the phone. 'Vinnie Barker,' he said at last. 'Little chap, is he? Mikey's size or smaller?'

She shook her head. 'No, he's a good bit bigger than Mikey. Almost everybody is.'

'No, not everybody,' said Shapiro. 'Just men. We're looking for someone with a dainty right thumb: a boy or a woman.'

As Liz thought about it, things which had refused to fit started looking like they might. The armed robber in the garage, so small and slight Donovan was convinced it was Mikey: that could have been a woman. A woman with a baseball bat and enough determination could have inflicted Mikey's injuries; and he might have been readier to turn his back on her than on another man. He would have had no reservations about meeting her alone at night. 'A girl put Mikey in the hospital?'

'Well, that's rather a leap of faith,' said Shapiro. 'Though it's possible. But there's a girl involved somewhere. Whoever actually wielded the bat, between the assault on Mikey and the thing turning up at Broad Wharf a woman wound electrical tape on to it specifically to hold Donovan's prints. If she didn't attack Mikey she knows who did.'

'How do we find her?'

'They're trying the print against the database right now. We may get lucky – it's probably good enough for an ID if it's on record. If not, we'll have to start with girls who know Mikey Dickens well enough to ask him for a moonlight rendezvous.'

'Shouldn't be difficult,' said Liz. 'Most girls who kissed a frog that turned into Mikey would kiss it again.'

Shapiro grinned. 'It's something else you could try on Vinnie. Is there a girl in their circle of friends who wouldn't mind getting her hands dirty? He might know her as a girlfriend of Mikey's, in which case she may have done the robbery with him, thought he was going to give her away and shut him up. Or she may be a friend of this partner of his, in which case her involvement is probably rather more fringe. But she's the one whose print we've got: if we find her we can tie her to this, and if there's anyone closer she'll give him up. Finding her's the key. Lean on Vinnie. Try Thelma too – if she's Mikey's friend she's probably been to the house.'

Liz said doubtfully, 'I'm not sure Women's Lib got as far as The Jubilee. It's a male-dominated society. Roly wouldn't take a woman as a partner, not because he thinks there's anything wrong with armed robbery as a profession but because he reckons a woman's place is in the home. Mikey's a younger generation but it'll take more than one to change attitudes that much. It's my guess the print belongs to a gangster's moll rather than another gangster.'

Shapiro couldn't fault her reasoning. He nodded. 'Whoever she is, find her. We need her.'

Chapter Six

By the time Liz got to Vinnie Barker's house he'd gone out for the evening. Liz didn't explain what she wanted or say when she'd be back, leaving his sullen sister to suppose it was just another bit of police harassment such as residents of The Jubilee were well used to. It was not impossible, Liz thought, that his desire for amominity was based mostly on a fear of his family's reaction to him helping the police. Vinnie was the black sheep of the Barker household: he was fifteen before he made his debut at the Juvenile Court and he'd never yet done anything they could boast about to the neighbours.

Instead of going home then Liz returned to Queen's Street, hoping Donovan would have called. He hadn't; but while she was debating her next move someone called on his behalf.

'I'm Martin Cole, Mrs Graham – my wife and I have the *James Brindley*, we're Donovan's next-door neighbours.'

They had met, in passing. 'Of course, Mr Cole. What can I do for you?'

'I've just found your note,' he said, 'asking Donovan to call in. Thing is, I don't think he'll be back tonight. That's what I was doing on *Tara* – he asked me to feed his dog.'

'Oh – right,' said Liz. 'Well, thanks for letting me know. I'd have been sitting here half the night otherwise.'

'I left the note where he'd see it when he does get back,' Cole volunteered. 'But he could be gone a while. He said could he phone if he needed Brian seeing to tomorrow, and I said sure.'

'If he does phone, let him know I'm looking for him.'

There was nothing more to do at the office. She went home and fed her own Brian. Admittedly, she fed her horse first.

'Bit of gossip for you,' said Brian as they ate. 'We think we've worked out what the problem was between the Taylors. Kids. Apparently she was keener than him.'

'Don't they have children?' Liz was remembering the mural on the bedroom wall.

'No. They've been trying for years. Fertility clinics: every time Pat read of something new she wanted to try it. Clifford thought ten years was enough, that if they didn't settle for what they'd got soon they wouldn't have anything at all. Which is how it ended up. Pat said she'd have a better chance with AID anyway, and Clifford left.'

Liz winced. 'Bloody hell. The messes people get themselves into! These clinics have a lot to answer for, you know. For every happy couple they present with a squawking bundle all of their very own they send away a lot more with their pockets lighter, their hopes dashed and the best years of their lives squandered. I'm not sure the successes are worth prolonging the agony for everyone else.'

'Yes,' said Brian reasonably, 'but then you don't want a child. You might feel differently if you did.'

'There are lots of things I do want and can't have,' she countered. 'Robert Redford for one. Success and recognition for another.'

'You *are* successful,' said Brian, surprised. It was characteristic of their relationship that he saw Robert Redford as no particular threat.

'For a woman,' she countered. 'For a woman detective I've been very successful. Or lucky, depending on who you ask. But if I'd been a man I'd have been a chief superintendent by now. I'd have done Bramshill, I'd have been fast-tracked and I'd be looking for an ACC post somewhere. We all have our frustrations, Brian, the only way to avoid them is to have no ambition. But you have to be able to swallow the disappointments and get on with life. Or you're not going to have any life worth living.'

'I suppose she's no choice now,' said Brian. 'Pat, I mean. Whatever chance remained, I guess it went when Clifford did.'

'When I was at the house,' said Liz, 'she was re-decorating a bedroom. A nursery. I thought she must have finished with it – the kids were old enough to want something more grown-up now. But that wasn't it, was it? She was kissing her hopes goodbye.'

'She asked after Donovan,' said Brian.

'Did she?' It took Liz a moment to think why. 'Maybe she's feeling a bit guilty. I took him along when I went to see her but she wouldn't talk to him.'

'Why not?'

'Painful memories, I suppose. The last time she saw him she was very, very scared.'

'That wasn't his fault.'

'She doesn't think it was. It's more – If somebody tried drowning you in champagne you wouldn't blame Dom Perignon. But you still wouldn't fancy champagne for a while.'

Much later the phone went again; again it was Martin Cole. But he sounded quite different: troubled and tense. 'Mrs Graham, I don't know what's going on at *Tara* but something is. There's a crowd gathered on the wharf, and the dog's going spare. I think—' He stopped then, abruptly. When he came back his voice had risen half an octave. 'They're chucking bricks through his windows! Should I try and stop it?'

'No,' said Liz sharply. 'Don't even stick your head outside. I'll have a car there in three minutes, until then you stay inside and keep the curtains drawn. Clear?' She rang off and called Queen's Street.

By the time she reached Broad Wharf there was nothing left to see, only a few stones dropped on the quay by people who hadn't got the chance to heave them before the police turned up. A couple of arrests had been made but PC Stark reckoned they'd caught the slowest ones rather than the ring-leaders. All the glass along *Tara*'s port side was broken. When Liz stepped on to the deck she could feel a quiver in the steel hull from the frenzy of the great dog in the chain locker.

The couple from the *James Brindley* came over as she was pondering what to do. Lucy Cole was a tiny, waif-like woman in her mid-twenties who wore long skirts and illustrated children's books. 'He can't stay here now. What if they come back?'

Privately Liz thought Brian Boru was more than a match for any mob that wasn't armed with bazookas, and anyway she wasn't going to be the one to open the door. 'What do you suggest?'

'We'll take him home with us,' decided Lucy. She might have been talking about a stray kitten rather than five stone of teeth and muscles.

Liz was going to protest but Martin Cole shook his head. 'Everything on four legs adores Lucy. She treats them like pets so that's how they behave. She's had a meaningful relationship with a wharf-rat before now.'

As they spoke the barking stopped as if a tap had been turned and Lucy emerged from the chain-locker with the great black dog gambolling and fawning at her heels. 'Poor boy,' she murmured, and his tongue fell out the side of his face.

Liz shook her head in wonder, and Jim Stark grinned. 'Donovan always says he's an old softy really.'

'That might be what Donovan says,' said Liz, 'but you'll notice that what he uses for a lead is a length of chain you could tow this barge with.'

It was too late to get a glazier out. Stark arranged to make *Tara* secure with plywood while Liz went round to Shapiro's house.

Following the divorce he'd moved into a terrace of old stone cottages behind the castle. They had mullioned windows and little porches, and narrow front gardens down to a gate in the picket fence.

She'd phoned ahead so he was waiting for her, wrapped in a tartan wool dressing-gown like one of

Lucy Cole's illustrations. 'I don't like the way this is shaping up.'

'That's why I thought I'd better get you out of bed.'

It wasn't the most serious incident of public disorder either had ever dealt with. But more important than a few broken windows on a narrowboat were the implications.

'They're blaming Donovan for what happened to Mikey.'

Liz shrugged. 'Somebody's gone to a lot of trouble to make sure they do. They'd have to be pretty dim not to have put it together by now.'

'Who was behind it? Vinnie Barker?'

'No way. He probably went along with it – that's probably where he was when I went to his house, out with his mates gathering missiles and Dutch courage – but it wouldn't occur to him to organize something like that.'

'Roly, then.'

'According to his mum he's spending all his time at the hospital. More likely friends of his, out to show some solidarity.'

'By heaving bricks through Donovan's windows.'

Liz grimaced. 'That may not be what they went there for. I think we should be glad Donovan wasn't home tonight.'

'He can't ride his bike round East Anglia forever. Tomorrow or the next day he'll be back, and he'll walk into a lot of bad feeling he's not expecting. Maybe I should put the number of the bike on the wire so anyone seeing him can warn him what's happened. He doesn't have to go home, particularly if he knows the dog's being cared for; he can go straight to Queen's Street.'

'Do you really think they'd take a swing at him?'

Shapiro gave a tartan shrug. 'They didn't find those bricks lying around on Broad Wharf, they armed themselves before they went. When they were still expecting to find him on board.'

'Then they think he's guilty.'

'It's a reasonable conclusion. On the evidence we have, the question is why *we* don't believe he's guilty.'

'But we don't,' said Liz. 'Do we?'

'It's getting harder,' admitted Shapiro. 'But even if you forget that this is a man we know, that we don't think would behave that way, you're left with two good arguments against. All the things that don't fit, and all the things that fit too well.'

'What if we're wrong?' asked Liz softly.

'If we're wrong, I will throw every book I possess at him, starting with Archbold and proceeding in diminishing order of size to *The Politician's Guide to Ethics*.'

Donovan rode through the dark and the intermittent flare of headlights until the gauge showed he was low on petrol. He found an all-night garage and then rode some more. The miles and the hours hummed past. At some point the traffic thinned to a hard core of long-distance lorries and the occasional utility vehicle; sometime after that he started seeing milkmen. He had only a vague idea where he was. The silent villages hardly impinged on his consciousness, and even small towns came and went in a handful of junctions where nothing challenged his right of way. He wouldn't have been amazed to see either Brighton Pavilion or Blackpool Tower twinkling at him out of the night.

It wasn't that he was going anywhere. It wasn't even that he needed time to think; in fact, riding his bike was an antidote to the unproductive merry-go-round thinking that swamped his head. At home, trying to read, trying to watch television, trying to catch up on the maintenance that was a constant factor in owning an elderly boat, so worried that nothing from outside the claustrophobic triangle of Broad Wharf, The Jubilee and Cornmarket could reach him, so full of resentment he wanted to fight with the very people – the only people – who could help, the hours would have dragged and each one brought him closer to an indiscretion that would finally nail the lid on his career. On the open road they flew by, and if he achieved nothing for all the miles he covered at least he wasn't making things worse.

By degrees, though, the darkness, the cold and the freedom from thought instilled the beginnings of calm in his mind, and calm was a foundation on which useful things could be constructed. He found himself considering, with a detachment he had not been capable of before, whether this flight into the dark – which had been necessary and therapeutic when he embarked on it – hadn't by now achieved all it was going to. He had never fled his enemies in the past and would not have people think he was running away now. On top of which, the only place any of this could be resolved was back in Castlemere.

He had friends there as well as enemies; and even if he hadn't, he had work to do there.

The first time he saw a signpost to anywhere he recognized, he turned for home.

Chapter Seven

Early in the New Year six-thirty in the morning seems like the middle of the night. It's pitch black and the coldest part of the day. Even in built-up areas the streets are virtually empty, and the curtained windows of the houses are dark. At six-thirty this January morning in Castle Place it was as if the Martians had landed, and the only person who hadn't been told was Muriel Watkins.

Mrs Watkins owned the paper shop. Over the door it said 'Paper Chase' but throughout Castlemere it was known as Muriel's. The only thing that had been there longer was the castle. Mrs Watkins was sixty-three now, and had bought the shop before she was thirty. She still opened seven days a week at seven o'clock, which meant arriving at six-thirty in order to take in the deliveries, sort the orders and organize the paper rounds.

As the first person up and about in Castle Place, Mrs Watkins had seen some things in her time. She had picked her way over snoring drunks in her doorway. She had crabbed in sideways to avoid noticing cars with the front seats reclined bouncing up and down beside the kerb. She had found unwanted dogs tied to her railings, and unwanted curries plastered across her glass.

She had never before found an armed robber waiting patiently for her to open up.

Her first thought was that he was a dosser who'd slept in her doorway, though with only an anorak and a woolly hat for protection the icy tiles should have stolen the life from him during the night. Then she thought he might be an early customer. 'I don't really open for half an hour,' she said; then, relenting, 'But if there's something particular you need—?'

There was, but it wasn't something she sold. As she unlocked the door he followed her inside, and when she turned to serve him she met the blank stare of a gun.

Mrs Watkins had never been held up before. Paper Chase wasn't the sort of high turnover business that attracted thieves; not ambitious ones, anyway. Perhaps it was the sort of business that novice robbers cut their teeth on. Taken aback as she was, Mrs Watkins could hardly fail to notice how the gun shook in the gloved hand.

'Empty the till!' said the man, and his teeth chattered with cold and nerves.

Muriel Watkins eyed him in disbelief. 'It's six-thirty in the morning. There's nothing in the till.'

'What?' It simply hadn't occurred to him that robbing a shop first thing in the morning he was unlikely to get more than enough loose coins to change the first ten pound note. He had to think quickly. 'Then open the safe.'

'I don't have a safe.'

Kevin Tufnall, for it was he, felt sweat break out

under the pulled-down brim of his woolly hat and wiped the back of a hand across his brow, coming within an ace of shooting himself in the eye. It was vital not to panic. All right, armed robbery was a new departure for him, but how difficult could it be? Luck had presented him with a weapon to use – as he understood it, you pointed it at people and they did as you said. They didn't, particularly if they were little old ladies with grey hair scraped into a bun, stand there looking you up and down as if you were something the cat dragged in.

He looked round desperately. Paper Chase was a tobacconist as well as a paper shop: his eye lit with relief on the shelves of cigarettes. There was a ready market for those, wasn't there? 'All right. All right. I'll take the smokes. Put them in a bag.'

Mrs Watkins knew that no one with any sense argued with a man pointing a gun. So what if she lost a few hundred pounds worth of tobacco? – that was what insurance was for. No one would expect her to have a go at an armed robber. She was sixty-three and five-foot-one, and a stiff breeze made her tack across Castle Place like a sailing dinghy. She was the perfect muggee, except for one thing. The small spare frame of Muriel Watkins contained the heart of a lion, and a bad-tempered lion at that. Her very eyebrows bristled. 'Certainly not. And you can stop waving that thing in my face as well!'

What happened next depended on who you asked. According to Kevin, she leapt on him like a fury, snatched the gun and flung it across the shop, then beat him about the head with her bony little fists. According to Muriel, she knocked the weapon aside and Kevin dropped it, and as he went to recover it he banged his forehead on the edge of the counter. Either way, the great paper shop robbery ended with the robber sitting on the floor nursing his head while the robbee phoned the police.

When Liz heard there'd been a stick-up in Castle Place and the perpetrator had been arrested, her first thought was that Mikey's accomplice was going solo. Her hopes soared. Armed robbery was not so common a crime in Castlemere that the odds were absurdly long. If he was also responsible for Mikey's present condition and she could charge him, she could get word to The Jubilee and Donovan could come home.

All that evaporated when she saw the name on the charge sheet. 'Kevin Tufnall? He's doing armed robberies now?'

'Not very well,' said the Custody Officer. 'Muriel Watkins beat him up.'

The facts of the case were simple enough, and except for precisely how he was disarmed Kevin did not dispute them. Liz thought he was glad to be off the street and in a warm cell. What did concern her was the gun.

'Where did you get it, Kevin? You've never carried a gun before.'

'I found it.'

It wasn't a very original defence. What was novel about it was that, this time, it was probably true. Kevin hadn't the money to buy it or the nerve to steal it. 'Found it where?'

Kevin gave her a hunted look. 'Don't tell him.'

'Tell who?' She wasn't trying to trap him, she was genuinely having trouble following this conversation.

'I didn't steal it, I only borrowed it. I was going to put it back before he wanted it again. Only now—' There was no point in finishing the sentence. Clearly the gun would not be put back now.

'Whose is it, Kevin? Where did you find it?'

Kevin heaved a vast lugubrious sigh. 'That garage in Brick Lane. Where he keeps tools and stuff. Where he used to keep that dog. It was sleeting down, I was that bloody cold, and he hadn't locked up properly and I thought I'd get in out of the weather. I knew he didn't keep the dog there no more. There was some dust-sheets and things and I was going to sleep there. Then I thought' – the eyes came up, shiftily – 'there might be something to eat, so I had a bit of a look round. And I found that.'

He hadn't been looking for something to eat, he'd been looking for something to sell. What he'd found was something that would help him steal something to sell.

Liz still didn't know what garage he was talking about, though she was plainly supposed to. Had the gun been secreted on a Dickens property after all? Had Roly double-thought them and put it where they'd assume he'd have more sense than to put it? 'Which garage, Kevin? The lock-ups in Brick Lane? Which one – who rents it?'

Kevin couldn't decide if she was being dim or devious. His whipped-dog gaze took on a faintly irritated cast. 'He shouldn't have had that, Mrs Graham. You're not supposed to have them, not unless they've been Issued. And even if it was, it shouldn't have been left lying around in a garage where anyone could find it.'

'Anyone capable of breaking in, anyway,' amended Liz absent-mindedly. 'Kevin – who exactly are we talking about? You're right, it shouldn't have been lying around in a garage, but whose garage in particular should it not have been lying around in?'

He was going to answer, he was just working up to it; but before he got there Liz knew what he was going to say. The garage – the tools – the dog that wasn't there any more – the gun that should have been Issued . . . He wasn't talking about Roly Dickens. He was talking about—

'Donovan's?'

Half-way through conveying this latest bit of bad news Liz realized Shapiro wasn't reading the same things into it that she was. It was nothing he said, just the expression on his face at different points. He wasn't worried enough. At times he seemed grimly amused.

She frowned. 'What? What have you spotted that I've missed?'

He had the grace to look faintly apologetic. 'Sorry. But isn't it stretching probability a bit thin to blame Donovan for every crime in town?'

'I'm not!' She blinked. 'Am I? I'm not saying he held up Muriel's – I'm saying Kevin Tufnall did it, using the gun he found in Donovan's lock-up. And he's right, Donovan has no business keeping a gun there. Or anywhere else, come to that.'

'What makes you think it's Donovan's?'

Her eyebrows lowered suspiciously. 'What makes *you* think it isn't?'

'You only think it might be because you also think he might have hit Mikey with a baseball bat. But if he had a gun we knew nothing about, why did he need the bat at all?'

'You think Kevin's lying? Frank, I don't think Kevin Tufnall has the mental capacity to lie.'

'On the contrary, I'm sure he found the gun where he said he did – rooting around in Donovan's garage. Which wasn't locked properly. Does that sound like Donovan?'

He kept the motorbike in there, and the national collection of sprockets. 'Not really,' admitted Liz. 'But then, nor do some of the other things he may have done recently.'

'Fair enough. So let's think about it. If the gun *isn't* Donovan's, who do you think it might belong to?'

Her eyes widened. 'Mikey?'

'And who might have put it there?'

'Roly?'

'And why?'

'Because it's the last place in town we'd think of looking for it!'

Shapiro smiled. 'That's my girl. And that's why Kevin was able to get into the garage: Roly forced the lock first. This gun – I imagine it was pretty well hidden? – he wouldn't want Donovan spotting it while he was doing an oil change or something.'

Liz nodded cautiously. 'It was in a biscuit tin at the back of a cupboard behind a stack of old biking magazines. Kevin only got it out because he thought it might still have some biscuits in it.'

'We'll have to see what Forensics come up with. But if, as I hope, it still has Donovan's blood on the muzzle end, it's the one used in the robbery. Now, I suppose it's just about possible that Donovan picked himself off Kumani's floor, hurried out to his bike and caught up with the van in time to see Mikey, or his mate if he had one, sling it out of the window. Then he stopped and hunted for it – and it was dark, remember, and it probably ended up in the long grass or the ditch – and after he found it he got back on his bike and caught up with the van *again* in time to see the immediate aftermath of the crash in Chevening. But if I went to the Crown Prosecutor with a story like that he'd laugh in my face. It isn't enough that it could just about have happened, with a following wind and a great dollop of luck. If it isn't what *would* happen then it isn't what *did* happen.'

Liz was still trying to work out what having Mikey's gun meant. They'd looked so hard for it, then resigned themselves to not finding it, now she couldn't quite remember what they wanted it for. Oh yes: tying Mikey to the robbery. It seemed a bit academic now. 'Maybe they'll turn up some fingerprints. If Mikey's are on it he was at least a willing partner.'

'Maybe we'll get lucky and find someone else's too. Roly's, perhaps, though I don't hold out much hope – I can't see an old pro like him handling it without gloves. We may have a better chance of getting something from Mikey's partner.'

'If he had one.'

'If he had one,' agreed Shapiro. 'But think about it: they're two young men, or just possibly a young man and a girl, planning their first armed robbery. This may be the first gun of their own that they've had: it's the most natural thing in the world that they'd be passing it between them, admiring it, getting the feel of it; pretending to shoot one another, for pity's sake. It would get their prints all over it. All right, so they'd wipe it down afterwards. But there are a lot of surfaces to a gun, if we're lucky they put on a couple more prints than they got off.' He sucked in a deep breath. 'And if we're unlucky—' He stopped.

Liz raised an interrogative eyebrow. 'If we're unlucky?'

'If we're unlucky, we'll find one of Donovan's.'

Chapter Eight

It was a little after eight when Donovan came off the motorway at the Castlemere exit. Apart from an hour at an all-night transport café, where he'd fallen asleep over a pot of coffee and nobody'd fancied being the one to to wake him, he'd been riding all night. Despite his leathers he was chilled to the bone. He needed a hot breakfast and a hot bath.

But the other thing he needed, which was a sense of perspective on what was happening to him, seemed somehow to have crept up on him unnoticed during the dark hours. He no longer resented Shapiro's decision to suspend him, saw that he had little choice. He hadn't the heart to go on hating Mikey either: whatever he'd done he'd paid for. And if he wasn't ready to extend the same indulgence to Mikey's solicitor, still felt both used and abused over that, he was within striking distance of seeing the funny side of it. He'd been made a fool of by a clever, unscrupulous woman: that wasn't high tragedy so much as farce. He'd get over it.

He'd get over all of this. Perhaps right now he couldn't see the way through, but there had to be an explanation and Shapiro would find it. None of this was random. Someone wanted to destroy him, wanted it enough to sacrifice another man in the process. That wasn't a casual dislike: it was deep and personal, and it came from somewhere. Somewhere there was some record of how he'd occasioned that much anger, and Shapiro would find it. Donovan believed that absolutely. He had to.

He found himself thinking about Mikey. Mikey wasn't worried about what was going on. Mikey was unlikely to worry about anything ever again. Presumably, whoever did this could have done it the other way round, could have split Donovan's skull and framed Mikey for it. In a very real sense, therefore, it was a privilege to be the one doing the worrying. Almost, Donovan felt a sense of obligation to Mikey Dickens.

Which must have been why he turned on to the ring road instead of heading into town, and two minutes later was parking the bike in the Staff Only part of the Castle General car-park.

He knew his way round this hospital better than some of the staff. The Intensive Care Unit was at the back of the building, on the first floor. No one challenged him: they recognized him, assumed he had business here. His disgrace was not yet a matter of public knowledge.

They had Mikey in the corner. He knew it was Mikey only because of the name on the graph. His head and most of his face were swathed in bandages; there were pads over both eyes. One arm and both hands were in plaster, and there was a cage under the sheet covering his legs. Between the dressings, where Mikey himself was visible, great splotches of multi-coloured bruising spread like a sunset across his arms, shoulders and ribs. He lay on his back in the middle of the high hospital bed as if he hadn't so much as twitched since they put him there. A forest of metal had grown up about his head, stands carrying drips and monitors and ventilating apparatus. He was dwarfed by it all. There wasn't a lot of Mikey Dickens at the best of times: now he looked like a battered child.

There was a chair by the bed. Donovan hooked it out with a foot, dropped on to it half sideways – as if he didn't want to look he was staying long. As if he didn't want to be mistaken for a relative or a friend, or anyone to whom Mikey's condition was of particular moment. But apart from the ward sister who nodded at him, no one was taking any notice. Nobody cared what Donovan was feeling.

Freed of the need to feign disinterest, Donovan finally looked at the injured youth not with a policeman's eyes, gauging the degrees of damage, toying with the unworthy thought that he'd brought this on himself, but with ordinary common humanity. This was a nineteen-year-old boy, and someone had taken away all of his life that was worthy of the name. All right, Mikey Dickens was never going to be a great violinist, a creator of beautiful or important things, even a decent hard-working husband and father. But he'd been vital, quick and sharp-witted, and now there was only the slow pulse of the bulb in the ventilator to say he belonged up here rather than down in the morgue. The only valuable thing about Mikey – the uniqueness of his personality – was gone, stolen, squandered, and the enormity of that crime struck Donovan as if for the first time. A breath of a sigh escaped him and he gave a weary, incredulous shake of the head.

The ward sister was at his elbow. 'You're not hoping to question him today, are you?'

Donovan twitched her a sombre smile. 'You reckon I'd be better coming back tomorrow?'

'I doubt it. Or next week either.'

'He's not going to make it, is he?'

With relatives she was more circumspect. Policemen counted almost as honorary staff – except when it came to parking spaces – and she could afford to be honest. But the regret was genuine. 'I don't think so. Not the way you mean. The equipment may keep him ticking over but I don't think it's going to bring him back.'

'How long do you wait?' asked Donovan. 'Before turning it off?'

'That's something the doctors will decide in consultation with the relatives. His father's been here almost since he was brought in, I think he knows what the position is. The only real question is whether they wait a week or two, a month or two, or longer.'

'Roly's a realist,' said Donovan. His tone of voice rather surprised him: it sounded like respect. 'He won't want the kid lying around like this once there's no hope left.'

'No,' she agreed. 'Well, we're not quite there yet. Miracles do happen – actually, more than you might think. Maybe young Mikey's got one coming.' She found a bit of bare skin on his arm and gave it an encouraging pat.

After she had gone about her business Donovan continued looking at the wreckage of Mikey Dickens with a compassion that had nothing to do with self-interest. If Mikey woke up, and brought with him some recollection of the events of that night – why he went to Cornmarket, who he met there – he could very much simplify the task facing Castlemere CID. If he could only remember bits of it he would still be the best witness they had. But that wasn't what Donovan was thinking. He was sorry. He was sorry for the mess Mikey had made of his life when he had it, and sorry he'd never now get the chance to do better.

A little while later the sister came back, and for a surreal moment thought the policeman was bent over the bed praying. She was surprised but rather touched. Of course, he was Irish and perhaps that made a difference. But moving closer she realized her mistake. He wasn't praying: he'd folded his arms on the edge of Mikey's bed, lowered his head on to them and fallen asleep.

The gun came back from Forensics with as good a report as Shapiro could have wished. There was tissue and O-rhesus-negative blood residues on the left-hand rim of the muzzle; as if a right-hander had used it as a club. Mikey Dickens was right-handed; Detective Sergeant Donovan had O-negative blood.

Apart from those microscopic traces the gun had been wiped clean. There were no prints on the grip or the barrel. But Sergeant Tripp wasn't born yesterday. Some jobs are awkward with gloves on, and loading a revolver is one. He'd dusted the caps of the unused bullets. He'd got several partial thumbprints, two of them good enough to use in evidence. They matched those filed under the name of Michael Dickens.

'So Mikey loaded the gun,' said Liz. 'So he wasn't hijacked. He was at least an equal partner.'

'Or Donovan was right all along and he was on his own.'

'Not according to Mrs Taylor.'

'I know. But look. It was Mikey's gun, he loaded it. He drove his van to Kumani's garage, and when Donovan walked in there was someone small enough to be Mikey wielding the gun and nobody in the van. Pat Taylor is the only one who says someone else was involved.'

'You're saying she was mistaken?'

'It's possible. After all, she didn't remember this passenger until you spoke to her on Monday. When you asked her last Tuesday she didn't know.'

Liz shrugged. 'Some time passed. She calmed down, was able to think more clearly.'

'All right,' nodded Shapiro slowly, 'so there was a passenger. Probably. But not a hijacker: now we can prove Mikey was in on the robbery.'

Liz squinted at him. 'But that isn't the issue, is it? – it never was and it isn't now. We always knew Mikey was lying, all that's changed is that now we can prove it. But it's a big jump from him having a partner to him having a partner who beat his head in and set Donovan up to take the blame!'

'But unless Donovan really is responsible, somebody did exactly that. If Donovan was a total stranger instead of someone we reckon to know, I still wouldn't believe he'd done everything he'd have had to for this to work. Not because he couldn't, but because there was no need for half of it. The baseball bat: he could have left it at the scene or he could have disposed of it. But why on earth would he pretend to find it four days later?'

She had no answer to that. 'What do we know for sure? – what do we have actual evidence for? We know Mikey was in on the robbery. We know he was driving the van when it crashed. We know that the gun had already been ditched, and that somebody found it and put it in Donovan's lock-up.

'We know that, five days later, Mikey went to Cornmarket in the middle of the night and somebody beat his head in with a baseball bat. We know Donovan was on the scene shortly afterwards, and four days later it was him who found the weapon. We know someone with small hands had put insulating tape around the handle.'

'I can't imagine any circumstances in which Donovan would have asked someone else to do that.'

Neither could Liz. 'He'd have done it himself if he thought it necessary. He couldn't afford for anyone else to know what he was up to.'

'Unless it was purely to mislead us,' Shapiro said reluctantly. 'You could get a mystery print inside your sticky tape if you wanted it there. The girl next door – Lucy Cole? If he said he'd managed to stick the end of his roll down and could she get a fingernail under it, she'd have obliged and never given it another thought. Her prints won't be on record anywhere, but they'd be just enough to cast doubt on Donovan as a suspect. I'm not saying he did that,' he added hastily, 'only that he could have done.'

'Could have, might have, would have, wouldn't,'

grumbled Liz. 'It's like trying to eat spaghetti with a spoon. What about the gun? Mikey loaded it, Donovan was hit with it, it wasn't found at the scene of the crash but it turned up in his lock-up. Could Donovan have put it there?'

'No,' decided Shapiro. 'He went straight from Chevening to the hospital, even if he'd acquired it somehow he couldn't have held on to it. Besides, we're pretty sure Roly's search party found it. That's what Billy Dunne said, and Mikey wouldn't have been so cock-sure if it hadn't been safe.'

'All right; so Roly had it. And looking for a safe place to hide it he broke into Donovan's garage and put it at the back of a cupboard. He wiped it down first, but he didn't think to wipe the bullets. He thought it could be months before it turned up, and when it did there'd be nothing connecting it to him or to Mikey. That, and for a bit of a laugh, is why Roly hid it there. Now suppose Donovan had somehow both acquired the gun and held on to it. Would *he* have hidden it there?'

Again Shapiro shook his head. 'Last place. If he attacked Mikey he did the rest as a smokescreen, to suggest an alternative scenario. But if he was a suspect we'd search his boat and his garage. If Kevin Tufnall hadn't got there first we'd have found the gun and Donovan would have been sunk.'

'And it was another risk he didn't need to take,' said Liz. 'He didn't need the gun. He didn't use it on Mikey and he didn't produce it as evidence against him, even when we were desperate to find it. He could have avoided that whole nonsense about the school, that left him with more egg on his face than a Chipperfields' clown. That he was ready to resign over. Do you believe he let Jade Holloway humiliate him when he had Mikey's gun in his possession? – because I don't.'

'No,' agreed Shapiro, 'I'm satisfied Roly planted the gun on him. But Roly has no interest in framing him. Roly wants the real assailant, not a convincing substitute.'

'But either Donovan did it or he *is* being framed,' said Liz. 'There are a lot of problems with him doing it. So suppose he didn't: then someone else did, and that's who's framing him. It isn't Roly; probably it's this partner of Mikey's, who either is a girl or has a girlfriend who helps out with the fiddly bits. Vinnie Barker has a sister, but Vinnie Barker has no reason and more sense than to take on the Dickenses.'

Shapiro was off on one of his lateral thinking exercises. 'We're assuming this was done by someone who hates Mikey; and so clearly it was. But he or she also hates Donovan. It would have been much easier to frame one of the dossers – any of them could have done it and not even remember. But it had to be Donovan, even if that meant the assailant hanging on to the weapon until he could be sure Donovan would find it. Why? Why did he not only want a scapegoat, but want Donovan as a scapegoat?'

'Because he – or she – has unfinished business with him? Maybe it *is* a woman, and the grudge is personal.' Her eyes sharpened on Shapiro's face. 'Frank, we know a woman who might want to hurt Donovan. Who knows Mikey well enough that he'd be happy to meet her somewhere quiet, and who has the physical fitness and the mental application to

do what was done. Jade Holloway. Mikey's brief;
Donovan's Nemesis.'

For once she'd got there first. Shapiro's eyes
widened and his jaw dropped, like a man doing 'flab-
bergasted' for Charades. His voice was a stunned
whisper. 'God in heaven, Liz, you're not seriously
suggesting that the boy's solicitor beat his head in?'

Though she'd made it, the proposition had also
come as a shock to Liz. 'I don't know. Why not? All
we know about her is that she's a ruthless cow. And
that she and Donovan had a very public, very savage
bust-up on the steps outside. And she sent Mikey
away telling him she'd see him later. What if she did?
Frank, what if she did?'

They were prevented from following it much
further by a call from the switchboard. 'About your
alert for DS Donovan's motorbike. We've just had a
sighting of it.'

'Excellent,' said Shapiro. 'How far did the silly sod
get?'

Even over the phone WPC Wilson maintained a
straight face. 'Don't know, sir. But now the bike's in
the hospital car-park.'

'Our hospital – Castle General?' He wasn't
expecting that.

'Yes, sir. PC Stark spotted it. He's gone to find DS
Donovan now.'

'What's he doing in the hospital?' frowned Shapiro
when he'd put the phone down.

'Visiting Mikey?'

'I can't think what else. But then, I wouldn't have
thought of that.'

Liz returned to her own office, struggling with

the idea of Jade Holloway as prime suspect. All her instincts told her it wasn't possible; but the plain fact was, on what they knew right now, it was. One way or another, even at the risk of alienating half the legal profession in Castlemere, they would have to follow it up.

She was still pondering how, half an hour later, when Shapiro tapped and came inside, shrugging on his overcoat. His face was troubled. 'I'm going to the hospital. We can't find Donovan. The staff on ICU saw him there earlier, but not since about nine o'clock. Stark's checked everywhere he could think of and there's no sign of him.'

Liz stared. 'And the bike's still in the car-park?'

'That's what's bothering me,' admitted Shapiro. 'I suppose it might have broken down or something.'

'The way he looks after it? Besides, if it wouldn't start he'd strip it down on the spot and fix it; and if he couldn't fix it he'd push it away. Every joy-rider in Castlemere knows the hospital car-park is the best place to get your wheels. Donovan knows that too. If the bike's still there, Donovan's still there.'

'But where? And why?'

III

Chapter One

Donovan woke to a grip like a Sumo wrestler's at the back of his neck and the prick of a blade at his jugular. Surprise and fear – because if he didn't know what was going on he was fairly sure it was nothing good – convulsed through him and then he froze, breathing lightly through parted teeth, not grabbing for the hand or the blade, not driving an elbow into the ribs of whoever was standing behind him, not shouting for help or doing anything else that could get him killed. He knew only two things about the man behind him, and even that was one more than necessary. The first was that with hands like the grabs on a dock-side crane this was a big man, and the second was that he meant business. Donovan kept very still and very quiet, and offered no reason for even a big, serious man armed with a sharp blade to cut his throat.

Another moment and he'd have worked out where he was, whose bed he'd fallen asleep on the edge of and therefore who the big man with the knife was. But Roly Dickens saved him the trouble. He leaned close over Donovan's bent body and murmured in his ear, and the voice, heavy and fruity as a Christmas pudding, was unmistakable. 'And now, Mr Donovan, you and me are going for a little walk while we discuss some things.'

If there'd been anyone close enough to help Donovan would have risked raising the alarm – after all, if a man had to get his throat cut he couldn't find a better place. He did not, he definitely did not, want to go anywhere with Roly Dickens.

There were things about Roly that an open-minded person could respect, even admire; but there were more that would scare him shitless.

At Queen's Street they used the cypher ODC – ordinary decent criminal – to describe those who made a career of burglary and the like, who pitted their wits and skills against those of the police and took the consequences calmly if they lost. They didn't carry guns because they'd rather do time than risk killing someone. They didn't hurt old ladies or children, or anyone else if they could avoid it. It was just a job. They were working men: they didn't do drugs, keep high-class prostitutes or order hits over their mobile phones. If a madder-than-average Home Secretary had decided to disband the police they'd have been as worried as anyone else. A man who works nights needs to know there's somewhere his family can turn in an emergency.

But nobody who knew Roly Dickens genuinely considered him an ODC. Roly didn't dislike hurting people: Roly rather enjoyed it. Not just anyone, but anyone who posed a challenge to him. Donovan had seen what happened to people who got in Roly's bad books: they ended up on sticks, or avoiding mirrors, or trying to teach their guide dogs to shoplift. If Roly thought he might be to blame for Mikey's condition, the last thing Donovan wanted was a long talk with Roly somewhere quiet.

But Roly had left him no choice. He'd waited, watching Donovan sleep, until the ward staff were occupied elsewhere. It was just the two of them now, and half a dozen people in various depths of coma, and if he'd decided to gut Donovan on the sister's desk no one would have intervened.

But he had something else in mind. He hauled Donovan to his feet and away from Mikey's bed, walking him out into the corridor. He draped one long arm amiably over Donovan's shoulder and even if they'd passed anyone it would not have been apparent that by this means Roly Dickens was keeping the blade of a purloined scalpel against the carotid artery behind Donovan's jaw.

Roly had lived in this building for four days, he knew his way around. He avoided the passenger lift which was in regular use and steered his captive instead to a utility lift in a little-used corner of the first floor.

While they waited for the doors to open Donovan risked speaking. 'You're making a mistake, Roly.'

'We'll see,' said Roly stolidly.

'Whatever you've heard, I'm not responsible for what happened to Mikey.'

'Shut it.' The pin-prick pressure of the blade firmed to the tiny burning sensation of parting skin. Donovan shut it.

The lift came, the doors opened, the steel box was empty. The two men stepped inside, and to all intents and purposes disappeared.

*

At the end of another hour Shapiro was as sure as he could be that Donovan had left the hospital. He'd had the bathrooms checked, and the side-wards. He'd had the nurses make sure they hadn't acquired an extra patient when no one was looking: if Donovan had been riding all night an empty bed might have tempted him. He checked the waiting areas, the cafeteria, the domestic and managerial offices, even those operating theatres which were not in use.

He wasn't entirely sure what he was looking for. Donovan might just be brooding the time away; he might have fallen asleep somewhere; he might have been waylayed and be lying injured behind a locked door. It had not escaped Shapiro's notice that, with Mikey in residence, his family and friends were much in evidence, and these were the same people who had gone to Broad Wharf armed with bricks. Shapiro had the mortuary staff check their trays against a list of who should be there, in case some wag had thought that the best place to hide a tree was in a forest.

But they found nothing. Not Donovan, alive, dead or something in between. No sign of what had happened to him. The last sighting had been in ICU at around nine when the ward sister saw him buckled fast asleep over Mikey's bed and resisted the urge to move him on. Next time she looked he was gone. She assumed he'd woken up and gone home.

And perhaps he had; or at least, set off for home. But he hadn't got as far as his bike, which was still attracting acid looks in the staff car-park.

Queen's Street was strangely quiet. Everyone there

was trying to get on with some work and listening for the phone.

Liz too had wondered if Donovan had run into the Dickenses. But in spite of what happened at Broad Wharf she was not convinced that they would have snatched a detective sergeant in a public place. It might happen in gangland areas of London but not in Castlemere. Crime here was played by a set of rules, and one was that you out-witted the police or out-ran them, you didn't declare war on them. The Dickenses and the Walshes might break one another's legs with joyful abandon, but they'd think long and hard before manhandling a police officer.

But the rule-book may have gone out of the window when Mikey got his head beaten in with a weapon which, by the time it was found, had Donovan's prints all over it. Nothing the boy's father might do after that could be considered wholly rational. A jury would accept that, even if he was wrong about Donovan, he had thought this was the man who maimed his child. The longer Donovan was missing, the more likely it was that someone was holding him, and she could only think of one man with a reason. Liz was afraid for Donovan's safety, for his life, and afraid for all of them in the storm that was looming.

She tried to put it out of her mind and think about something else. Jade Holloway, for instance. Sooner or later she was going to have to grasp that nettle: she might well come away with a nasty rash but that wasn't a good enough reason for avoiding it. If Holloway was involved, the quicker Liz found out the better. Wherever he or she was, finding Mikey's assailant was the best service she could render Donovan right now.

If the woman had been anyone other than Mikey's brief she'd have been in for questioning before now. But it wasn't absurdly improbable: people who spend too much time with criminals, and this could apply equally to defence counsel as to police officers, ran the risk of absorbing their morality. It took a keen imagination to envisage Jade Holloway taking a baseball bat to her client's head, but solicitors are human too – if Mikey was capable of driving someone to murderous rage, why not her? Maybe she'd felt as strongly about what she and Donovan had, that Mikey's antics had put an end to, as Donovan had. Maybe he made one smart remark too many and . . .

Ruefully, Liz acknowledged that it was an outside chance. But maybe she didn't know everything. Maybe it was time she found out a bit more about Ms Holloway, starting with where she was on Friday night.

A clerk went to ask if she was available. After five minutes, which was almost but not quite long enough for Liz to start insisting, she was shown into one of the offices, all leather and wood panelling, of Carfax and Browne.

Jade Holloway was dressed as Liz had seen her before, in a sharp business suit with her hair tied back, the epitome of disciplined chic. Liz tried to imagine how she'd appeared to Donovan, in motorcycling leathers with all that red hair tossing wildly about her face and the green eyes of a feral cat. Of course she'd bowled him over. She'd have knocked a more practised womanizer than Donovan for six.

Her voice was low, controlled. 'If this is about Detective Sergeant Donovan—'

'It's not,' Liz interrupted shortly. 'It's about your client, Mikey Dickens.'

Jade stared at her. 'What's happened to him now?'

'Nothing more. I'm still trying to work out what happened to him on Friday night. Who he went to Cornmarket to meet. We think it may have been a woman. When you sent him home you said you'd see him later.'

The solicitor had been present at too many police interviews to be intimidated by this one. She considered before answering. 'That's right. I called at his house on my way home after work. About six o'clock. What passed between us is, of course, privileged information.'

'Then what did you do?'

'I told you: I went home.'

'Did you go out again later?'

Jade was regarding her with cool disdain. 'You realize, Inspector Graham, that if I decline to answer your questions you have no grounds on which to proceed?'

'Perhaps not; but I'd have every reason to wonder why. What does a respectable family solicitor get up to on a Friday night that she can't talk about even to a police officer investigating an attempted murder?'

The smile that tilted the blood-red lips didn't reach the cat's eyes. 'In fact, nothing at all. I was home all evening.'

'Can anyone confirm that?'

'I'm afraid not. I was alone. My last relationship had just ended; or hadn't you heard?'

Liz hung on to her patience. 'I'd heard. When Donovan left you he came to me to explain what had happened. He was going to resign. We talked him out of it.'

'Resign?' Jade sounded taken aback, as if she hadn't anticipated that. 'Because—?'

'Because you passed on things he had no business telling you. You said he was naive, and you were right. But he deserved better than that. You hurt him.'

'I hurt him?' The green eyes flashed. 'He called me a whore!'

Liz refrained from commenting. 'So you were angry with him. Angry enough to want to hurt him some more?'

Jade wasn't sure now what she was being accused of. Her gaze grew wary. 'Angry, yes. Sufficiently angry to do something about it? – no. I thought I'd done enough.'

So did Liz. But she also thought the woman was probably telling the truth. If she'd had anything much to hide she'd have fallen back on her rights before now; after all, she knew them inside out. 'So you know nothing about the attack on Mikey or the subsequent attempt to implicate Detective Sergeant Donovan?'

Jade shook her head. Her voice was low. 'A frame. Is that how you're describing it?'

'You mean, you think he did it?' Liz found herself fighting a thoroughly unprofessional desire to slap the other woman's face. 'You think you mattered to him so much that losing you drove him over the edge? Don't flatter yourself!'

'You didn't see his face.'

Liz was staggered by her impertinence. 'Ms Holloway, I have worked with Donovan for three years now. I've seen him angry, and scared, and desperate. I've seen him in pain; I've seen him bleed. Don't presume to tell me I don't know what he's capable of.'

The younger woman dipped her gaze in what might have been an apology. 'All right. If you say it isn't possible I'll believe you. Gladly: I've been worried that he might really have done it, and he might have done it at least in part because of me. I'd much sooner think that I have an inflated idea of what our relationship meant to him.'

As she talked Liz began to understand what it was about Jade Holloway that Donovan had responded to. She was a good-looking woman, but that was the smaller part of it. And there was the fact that she was a biker. But there was also a directness about her that would appeal to a man who put a premium on honesty. He'd thought she was someone who'd always be straight with him. Her deception had been devastating.

'Look,' said Jade, 'if there's any way I can help I'd like to. For Mikey's sake, and for Donovan's. We were angry with one another, but I don't want to see him take the rap for something he didn't do. If he isn't to blame for what happened to Mikey I hope you'll prove it. You say you're looking for a woman. You think Mikey was attacked by a woman?'

'It's possible,' said Liz guardedly. 'It's probably more likely that the woman was the assailant's accomplice. But we have a small sized fingerprint, and it occurred to me . . .' She petered out, a little embarrassed. Put into words it sounded pretty silly.

Jade smiled again. This time there was some warmth in it. 'I understand. But it isn't mine, and I can prove it. Why don't I stop by Queen's Street and give you a set of my prints? For elimination purposes.'

Liz nodded a gracious acceptance. 'I'd appreciate it. I appreciate your co-operation.'

'Inspector,' said the other woman, 'I realize I'm not Flavour of the Month at Queen's Street right now. I'm sorry about that. What I did was probably a misjudgement. I'd quite like the chance to tell Donovan that in person, but if he isn't there when I call – or if he's too busy to see me – I'd be glad if you'd tell him for me.'

Liz stared at her. But of course there was no way Jade could know what was going on. Roly might need her to know afterwards but not in advance. 'Ms Holloway, Donovan's missing. We've found his bike, we can't find him. There's a possibility – I wouldn't put it any higher than that – that the Dickenses have got him.'

She watched comprehension grow in the cat-green eyes, and with it a concern Jade couldn't possibly have feigned. Her voice cracked with fear. 'You have to find him. They'll crucify him!'

'We're doing our best,' said Liz. 'We've got people looking for him and for Roly. Until one of them's spotted there's 'not much more we can do. Which is why I thought I'd come here and annoy you – to take my mind off . . .' She didn't finish. 'Anyway, thanks for your help. It was always a bit imaginative, I just felt I had to be sure before binning it. It made a certain amount of sense. It was a girl's print on the weapon: if the passenger in Mikey's car was also a girl, obviously she knows everything that happened. It was mostly wishful thinking that she might be someone we already know about.'

Jade's eyes were still full of the image of Donovan in Roly's hands. She shook her head, partly to clear it. 'But Inspector, there wasn't— ' She stopped.

It didn't matter. If she'd finished the sentence she couldn't have made it any clearer. Liz's eyes opened wide. 'There wasn't anyone in the van with Mikey?'

It had been a mistake on the solicitor's part; not an important one, because the chances of Mikey needing that defence again were remote, but still, a legal representative who lets vital secrets slip while conversing with the police is about as much use as . . . well, as a detective who blabs to his suspect's brief. Colour rose through Jade's ivory cheeks. 'Shit!'

Then, collecting herself: 'I didn't say that, Inspector. If you want to put words in my mouth feel free, but don't expect me to confirm that that was in fact what I was about to say.'

But there was no doubt in Liz's mind. Jade Holloway knew – of course she did – that that plank of Mikey's defence was rotten, and shock had thrown her off her guard just long enough to admit it. There was no passenger. There was no partner who might have required Mikey's silence.

If there was no passenger, why did Mrs Taylor say there was?

Mrs Taylor was back at school now. Liz headed back to her car; but before she got there another brass plate on the wall caught her eye. Birdsall, Taylor and

Nesbitt, Accountants. Perhaps Clifford Taylor could cast some light on the mystery of the crime victim who lied to assist the perpetrator.

Taylor was much as Liz remembered him, a pleasant man, quiet of manner and open of countenance. He didn't react defensively, demanding she explain herself – which was just as well because she couldn't have done.

He took her to his office, but this wasn't a social call and he didn't waste time on small-talk. They'd been on first-name terms at the fête but this was a different sort of occasion. 'How can I help you, Inspector Graham?'

'To be honest, Mr Taylor, I'm not sure you can. But I'm a little worried about your wife. You know she was involved in a car crash ten days ago?' Taylor nodded, his eyes attentive. 'The car was a write-off. Mrs Taylor seemed to come out of it all right, but I've seen her a couple of times since and she still seems badly shaken up. And some of the things she's telling us – well, don't seem a very accurate representation of what happened. I suppose what I'm asking is, how reliable a witness should we consider her? Is she someone who'd be so upset by an incident like this that she could produce a sort of false memory of it?' She gave a little wry grin. 'Answer in two hundred words or less, using one side of the paper only.'

He returned her smile, but gave her question several moments' thought before responding. 'You know that we're separated.'

'You still know her better than anyone else.'

'I expect so. Pat isn't the biggest extrovert in the world: we were together almost twenty years and I still wouldn't claim to know everything about her. But it doesn't surprise me if she's – gone off the rails a bit. I don't mean to be unkind, but she tends to look for conspiracies. She always has to blame someone. Is that what she's doing – trying to blame someone who doesn't deserve it?'

He could hardly have got closer if he'd been trawling around inside her head. 'It's possible. And that would make sense to you?'

Taylor shrugged. He was a big squarish man, with freckles and sandy hair that had once been red and would soon be grey. 'It was something like that we split up over. She was dissatisfied with her life. That had to be someone's fault too: in this case, mine.'

'Have you spoken to her since the accident?'

'I haven't seen her since I moved out before Christmas. That's not my choice: she put me out of her life and doesn't want me back in.' He flushed. 'I'm sorry, that sounded spiteful. I suppose I'm trying to explain why I've stayed away. It's not that I don't care.'

'I understand that. I don't mean to suggest you should be doing more for her: I was worried that maybe I should.' That was true, though not the whole truth. Liz took a deep breath. 'This really will sound impertinent, but it just might be relevant so – can I ask what it was that split you up?'

Taylor couldn't imagine what bearing that might have on investigating a car accident, but he was a middle-aged middle-class professional, it didn't occur to him to refuse to answer a police officer's question.

'She wanted a baby,' he said. 'Desperately. She's thirty-eight now, which means the chances are fading fast anyway. We went to a fertility clinic for ten years and never even got close. I said it was time to stop, she didn't want to. She said it could still happen; I felt we were throwing good money after bad. We had two good salaries coming in, and a big part of it was going straight to the Feyd Clinic. I didn't begrudge it when there still seemed to be some hope. I came to begrudge it when we had nothing to show for it after ten years. We argued, we both dug our heels in and she told me to leave. By then I was glad to go. I couldn't take the recrimination any longer.' He met Liz's gaze a shade defiantly. 'Does that tell you what you need to know?'

In fact it told her little that was new. Shapiro said those were the most useful interviews; when you were asking questions to which you already had the answers. They added little to your knowledge but increased your understanding enormously.

'I'm grateful for your frankness,' she said. 'We're having problems with several aspects of the case and Mrs Taylor's attitude is one. This helps. It's the double grieving thing, isn't it, where somebody copes magnificently with a death in the family only to fall apart six months later when the corgi gets run over. I wonder if that's what happened to Pat. She lost her marriage, and her last hope of a longed-for baby; when she lost the car as well it was the last straw. She isn't this upset by the crash: she's dealing with ten years of disappointment.'

'Is that my fault?' It wasn't a challenge: he genuinely wanted her opinion.

'Of course not,' Liz said firmly. 'Sooner or later

she was going to have to face it. Time, tide and a woman's body-clock wait for no man.'

'She was so – angry.'

'She was after the crash,' nodded Liz. 'That was what bothered me. Most people who walk away from a bad accident are euphoric, amazed at their own survival. But Mrs Taylor wanted to lay the blame. She wouldn't let me call it an accident. She was even angry with my sergeant, who was first on the scene: for causing the accident, for leaving her while he helped the other driver, who knows? Of course, it makes more sense if she was angry before the crash. She probably thought that one man running her off the road and another leaving her upside down was just par for the course.' She stopped abruptly then, afraid that she might have offended him. 'I'm sorry . . . '

Taylor smiled wryly. 'You're right, I don't think she has much of an opinion of men just now. That's how she is: she takes things personally, cares too much. If she'd been able to keep a sense of proportion I think we'd have been all right. But it mattered too much to her, and it drove out all the things that mattered less. Like being happy together.'

There wasn't much more they could say. Either Liz asked now the question no one else could answer or she left with it unasked. She was a professional: she'd asked all sorts of people all sorts of questions, often at the worst possible times. She'd learned the knack of distancing herself from the hurt it not infrequently caused.

'Mr Taylor, this is going to sound dreadful. But we've been discussing how your wife feels, and why she feels that way, and I will understand if it's led her to do something that would normally be considered irresponsible. What I need to know is whether her anger has a vindictive side? Can you see her doing something – unkind, let's say, and unfair – to avenge herself on someone she believed had harmed her?'

He didn't answer right away. Liz saw reluctance in his eyes but also recognition. Finally he sighed. 'Yes.'

Liz breathed steadily for a moment. 'I think so too.'

'What do you think she's done?'

'Oh, nothing too awful. I think she lied about how many people were in the van that hit her, and I think she did it to make trouble for my sergeant. His account of what happened hinged on the driver being the only occupant of the van. But Mrs Taylor said she saw two faces. It undermined DS Donovan's credibility; it was part of why he was taken off the case. We believed Mrs Taylor because we thought she had no reason to lie. But maybe she had after all. She thought Donovan let her down. Maybe in her current state of mind that seemed reason enough.'

Chapter Two

Shapiro went alone into The Jubilee. He gave a little thought first to whether a show of force or an appeal for reason was most likely to succeed, decided that he'd lose more than he stood to gain by throwing his weight around. If the moment came when he thought Donovan's safety required him to search every room, cellar and outhouse in the six streets, somehow he'd find the manpower and the authority to do it. But he judged that moment had not yet come. If this could be caught at the silly-buggers stage, before Donovan or anyone else got hurt and while any charges could be kept to the minimum, the ill-feeling afterwards would be less of a problem.

He didn't expect Roly to be at home, and he wasn't. Thelma answered the door. Neither of them wanted to hold this conversation on the step: she asked him inside.

He couldn't be sure how much she knew: probably some of it but not all. She knew about the vigilantes at the wharf last night. She knew, and seemed relieved, that they hadn't got what they went for. She didn't seem to know until Shapiro told her that they might have got it this morning.

'The last time anyone saw DS Donovan was about

nine o'clock this morning when he visited Mikey in the hospital. He was there for a while, then he disappeared. But he didn't leave the way he came – his motorbike's still in the car-park.'

Thelma didn't insult his intelligence by asking what this had to do with her. She said, 'Roly hasn't been home for twenty-four hours.'

Shapiro nodded slowly. 'So far as you know, would he have been at the hospital around nine this morning?'

'So far as I know, he's been there for the last four days, except for a few hours here and there. He hasn't slept at home since it happened.'

'I've had people looking,' said Shapiro. 'He doesn't seem to be there now.'

Thelma Dickens had used up all the emotion she could muster. Now she seemed drained, utterly weary, too exhausted to worry any more about either her grandson or her son. 'That's your answer, then.'

'You think he'd do that? Kidnap a police officer?'

The thin shoulders shrugged inside her cardigan. 'Mr Shapiro, nobody knows for sure what somebody else is capable of. If you'd asked me a month ago if Roly would do GBH on a policeman I'd have thought you'd been drinking. If I'd asked you a month ago if your sergeant would beat the living daylights out of a nineteen-year-old boy you'd have thought the same about me.

'In the normal way of things it's not Roly's style. He may not be Citizen of the Year material, but he's not a fool. But now his youngest son's lying in the hospital and the chances are he'll only leave it in a box. And that wasn't an accident, or even something that got out of hand. It was deliberate – intentional. Somebody meant to beat Mikey to death.

'And the only name anybody's come up with so far is Mr Donovan's. Mrs Graham said she didn't think he'd done it, and unless you've found out who actually did it that's about as far as you can go too. We started off by believing her. But things have happened since to make us wonder. Can you tell me they haven't made you wonder too?'

Shapiro wouldn't lie to her. 'We wondered. We looked into it. Mrs Dickens, I can't tell you yet who attacked Mikey but I don't believe it was Detective Sergeant Donovan. There are too many things that don't fit. He said someone was framing him, and that's what it looks like. Plus, this isn't *his* style.

'What I can tell you is that we now have the gun used in the garage robbery. It makes a nonsense of Mikey's defence. We can prove that Mikey was no innocent bystander but in fact carried out that robbery. I hope one day he'll be fit to stand trial for it.'

'From your mouth to God's ear,' murmured Thelma; which rather surprised Shapiro, who hadn't heard that since he was last in Golders Green.

'I also hope, very much, that Roly isn't going to be in the court next door on charges arising out of today's events. Or that if he is, we're talking unlawful imprisonment not murder. There's not much either of us can do to improve Mikey's chances, but together we may be able to help both your son and my sergeant. What do you think?'

She didn't have to think. 'If I knew where they were I'd tell you. I don't; and I don't know anything else that might help you find them.'

Shapiro believed her. 'All right. Then, if Roly gets in touch will you let me know?'

That she did give a moment's thought; then she nodded. 'If you'll promise me – promise, mind, Mr Shapiro – that whatever he's done you'll look after him. You won't let anyone hurt him.'

Could he promise that, Shapiro wondered. Whatever he's done? If he's laving his grief right now in Donovan's blood? This was a man Shapiro had known for eight years, who'd driven him mad for eight years but who had also earned his gratitude and respect. He thought, What if we find him how we found Mikey? If we find him dead? If Roly's killed him? – tortured and killed him? What price then my promise to Thelma?

Actually, it would alter nothing. Once Roly was in custody it was Shapiro's job to protect him, and he would have no qualms about doing it. 'I promise. Once he's under arrest he's safe: my word on it. But first we have to find him. Can you think of anywhere he'd go if he needed not to be disturbed?'

'I'm a bit out of date with these things,' admitted Thelma. 'But he wouldn't come back to The Jubilee. You can't do anything here without being seen, and not everybody turns a blind eye. Walshes wouldn't – Walshes'd let you know, if only to do Roly a bad turn. Even some of our people'll think he's gone too far this time.' She gave a dry chuckle, a little desperate sound. 'If his own mother's prepared to grass him up—!'

'It isn't like that,' Shapiro said quietly. 'The state he's in, he needs help as much as Donovan does. If he was himself he'd know this was a bad mistake. He needs you to do his thinking for him.'

224

She didn't really need convincing, but she appreciated it just the same. 'Maybe he wouldn't go anywhere
in particular. I mean, he doesn't need to. He's got the
Transit with him, you could entertain half Queen's
Street in there. Maybe all he needs to do is drive out
into The Levels and park off the road somewhere. It
could be days before someone stumbles across them.'

Shapiro knew the big black van she was talking
about. She was right: it was as near a Black Maria as
you could get on the open market. Maybe better:
they moved even top security prisoners by hire coach
these days. It wouldn't be soundproof, but then he
wouldn't be parking it in Castle Place. Deep in the
woods, or out on The Levels, they could make all
the noise it took and no one would hear. A Transit
van was good enough for his purpose, for as long as
whatever Roly had in mind would take.

'I'll start looking for it,' he said.

'Tell your people,' said Thelma, the thin old voice
insistent. 'Tell them what you told me. That you'll
look after him. That he isn't to be hurt. Whatever he's
done.'

'I'll tell them.'

The same place he found the scalpel Roly had
acquired a family-sized reel of surgical strapping.
He'd bound Donovan's wrists behind his back with it,
and strapped his ankles together. Lengths of it
blinded and gagged him. He lay on his side, the only
movement he was capable of a sort of maggot wriggle.
Not that it got him anywhere. There wasn't much
room in here, he bumped into things almost immedi-

ately. Mostly he did it to check if Roly was still there, because he kicked him if he was.

Sometimes he was there, sometimes he wasn't. The only sense Donovan had left was his hearing, and he listened for the door as Roly came and went. But sometimes he got it wrong – Roly opened the door without going out, perhaps to check if there was anyone around – and then Donovan got a dig in the ribs to stop him fidgeting. He bore it stoically. It wasn't much of a dig, and the wriggling wasn't getting him anywhere anyway.

Worse than a bruised rib was not knowing what was coming. He hadn't seen Roly's face since this began: at first the blade under his jaw kept him from looking, then the tape over his eyes did. The man must have skipped a gear, which wasn't altogether surprising, but Donovan needed to know if it was only a temporary aberration. If an opportunity had presented itself and for just a moment he'd been crazy enough to take it; since when he'd been sitting with his head in his hands wondering how to get himself out of this mess. Or if the madness went deeper and he really meant to avenge himself on the man he blamed for his son's condition. If the eyes watching him were bestial with hate; if Roly had no thought for the consequences and the only reason he hadn't yet waded in was that he was brooding on what to do, how much and how quickly. Whether there was more satisfaction to be had from hurting him slow or fast.

Even without his eyes, Donovan could have made a fair guess if Roly had talked to him. Or shouted at him, or called him names. But he didn't. Instructions murmured in his ear until they were past the risk of discovery, and after that the only communication was between Donovan's ribs and the toe of Roly's boot. He might have provoked a response had he not been restrained by the sort of bondage usually associated with Tory MPs. He might hum, or sneeze, if he had a mind to but those were about the only freedoms left to him.

At some point, presumably, Roly would strip the tape from his mouth so he could answer questions. You couldn't beat a confession out of someone rendered mute. He would, of course, deny laying a finger on Mikey; Roly, of course, would not believe him. He'd set about making it easier to admit it than to hold out. It was important that Donovan didn't yield to the temptation. If this was about revenge, what Roly would do to a man who denied maiming his son was nothing to what he'd do to one who admitted it.

Donovan could take a beating. He had before, he could again. He could keep his mouth shut and take the punishment, and hope to wake up in Castle General with only some interesting new scars to show for it. But if he made the mistake of thinking a free and frank confession would end this, he wouldn't wake up at all. If the situation deteriorated that far, denial to his last conscious breath was his only hope.

Shapiro would be looking for him. He wouldn't know where to look, so he'd pull in every favour he'd ever earned to amass enough manpower to look everywhere. If Roly purposed his death, he clearly didn't purpose it right now or he'd have made a start. Time was on Donovan's side. It might not always feel like it, particularly once Roly started hurting him, but time was his friend.

The door opened and closed again. Donovan waited, feeling his nerve endings sharpen and twitch.

Roly's big hands fastened in his clothes and propped him upright. Thick strong fingers fastened in his jaw. He could feel Roly's breath on his face. When Roly ripped the tape off his mouth it took with it two days' growth of beard.

The man's voice was low and measured, oddly precise, as if Roly was choosing his words with uncommon care. 'Now, Mr Donovan, let's see if we can get to the bottom of this.'

Chapter Three

'First we need to set the ground rules,' said Mikey Dickens' father. 'The ground rules are, you answer my questions or I thump you. You lie to me and I thump you. You tell me the truth and—' He paused a moment, considering. 'Well, I might still thump you,' he admitted, 'depending on what the truth is, but at least you've got a chance that I won't. Clear?'

Donovan's mouth was dry. He'd lost track of how long he'd been lying here, gagged, blindfolded and trussed like a chicken, but it felt like hours. He croaked, 'Makes the Marquis of Queensberry look like Mother Teresa.'

That rumble low in Roly's jowels was a chuckle. But Donovan didn't read any more into it than that. The man hadn't come so far with this only to give up at the first smart remark. Besides, he might have earned a chuckle this time; next time he said something smart he'd probably get thumped.

'You know why?' said Roly. 'The Marquis of Queensberry was a sporting man. I'm not. He was looking for a fair fight; I'm not. He wanted to be entertained; I don't. I want to know who beat Mikey. I want to know if it was you, and if it was—' He stopped. This was a man who ran his business on the basis of casual threats, following up just enough of them to keep people in line, and he was reluctant to say what he would do to the man who beat his child. That told Donovan more than any threat.

He said, 'It wasn't.'

Blinded by the tape, he got no warning. Roly hit him across the mouth with enough force to snap his head over. The unexpectedness of it was shocking. He felt blood trickle down his chin.

'Sorry,' said Roly calmly, 'forgot one. You bullshit me, and I thump you.'

He knew what he was risking but it seemed important to Donovan to set some rules of his own. When his breathing steadied he said thickly, 'It still wasn't me beat up on Mikey.'

He waited for Roly's fist, his nerves screwed tight, but nothing happened. 'Well,' said the big man thoughtfully, 'we'll come to that. Let's start with an easy one. What were you doing in the hospital?'

'Visiting,' said Donovan after a moment. 'It's what you do when people are sick.' As always, fear made him querulous.

'Mikey's been sick for five days. You haven't been near him before.'

'I've been busy.' Did Roly also forget to mention that offensive answers, however accurate, would get him thumped? Donovan waited; but apparently not.

'So what changed?'

'What changed is—' He realized just in time what this was going to sound like and stopped, wondering what to do. While he was still wondering Roly's fist arrived, a knot of bone like a cow's knuckle spilling him across the floor.

The big man's voice was still ominously, unnaturally calm, prompting him. 'What changed is—?'

With his hands and feet bound Donovan couldn't sit up unaided. Whatever it cost, he was damned if he was answering questions in this position. 'Pick me up.'

'What?' It may have been the accent, which always thickened under stress, or it may have been the blood in his mouth, but Roly genuinely didn't understand.

'I said pick me up, God damn it!' Donovan raged in breathless, impotent fury. 'I'll tell you what I know, but not with my face on the floor.'

After a long second the big hands seized Donovan by the shoulders and propped him upright again. Roly picked up where he left off. 'And the question was, what changed?'

'I've been suspended.'

He heard Roly catch his breath. 'You mean, even Mr Shapiro thinks you did it?'

'I don't know what he thinks.' An edge of desperation snagged in Donovan's voice. 'But somebody's set me up well enough that he couldn't keep me on the job any longer.'

'You've been framed?'

As a defence, it usually provoked the same hooting derision from Donovan. His broken lips sketched a bleak grin. 'Pathetic, isn't it? You'd think a guy could come up with a better excuse than that.'

'What have they got on you?'

The man was asking him to hang himself. He could refuse to answer. He'd get thumped, but he still thought he could deal with that. More serious, more

231

of a threat to his long-term health, was that Roly would take his silence as proof of guilt. Why not? – in similar circumstances Donovan had. The facts were damaging; letting Roly see he was afraid of them could be fatal.

He took a deep breath. 'Plenty. *I'd* think I'd done it if I didn't know better.'

He didn't begin at the beginning: Roly knew what Mikey had done to him, he was more interested in what had been done to Mikey. He began with that sleepless night on *Tara* when he decided to take the dog for a walk.

Liz glanced at her watch as she turned into the school campus. The start of the lunch hour was a good time to catch a teacher: she wouldn't have to arrange cover for her class before she could talk.

She parked her car and headed for the staffroom. Mrs Taylor was going the same way: they met in the corridor. 'Is there somewhere we can talk?' said Liz.

'Now?' The other woman frowned. 'I was just going for lunch.'

'Skip the soup,' said Liz shortly. There was an empty classroom immediately beside them: she opened the door and waited till Pat Taylor joined her inside.

'There's a flap on,' said Liz, 'so I'd like to make this quick. I'd also like to clear it up once and for all. How many people were in the van that hit you?'

Annoyance flickered in Mrs Taylor's gaze. 'This is what I'm missing the minestrone for? Two. I told you: two.'

'So you did. The trouble is, that's starting to con-
flict with the evidence. The only other person who
said there were two is a proven liar.'

Her eyes flared. 'And who says there was one?
Your sergeant. The one who, if he hadn't been a
policeman, would have been charged with attempted
murder by now.'

That startled Liz so much that for a moment she
didn't know what to say. She was surprised that Donovan's situation was a matter of public gossip, at least
outside The Jubilee, more than surprised that Mrs
Taylor would throw it in her face like that. So she'd
had an upsetting experience; but even coming on top
of a bad time for her, that didn't justify her hatred for
Donovan. And plainly it was hatred, not unhappy
memories, that made her shun him before and speak
this way now. Why? – because he left her hanging in
her seat-belt for a few minutes while he rescued a
man from a fire?

'Is that what you want?' she asked quietly. 'To
ruin Donovan? Why?'

Expressions kaleidoscoped across Pat Taylor's
face. Liz glimpsed hate, sure enough; and loss and
pain. There was a mass of anger, and behind that
there was grief. She wouldn't meet Liz's gaze. At last,
and it was an effort to get it out, she said, 'He should
have helped me.'

'He *would* have helped you, if he could. Mrs
Taylor, we've been through this – he had two people
in trouble, one was frightened, the other was in
immediate mortal peril. He'd rather have helped you
than the boy – it would have been safer and more
rewarding – but he didn't have any choice. He did

what was required of him. It's most unfair that, with all the trouble he has right now, you're still trying to make him pay for that.'

'Unfair? You call that unfair?'

Which was the wrong answer from someone who was telling the truth. But Liz wasn't content to prove her a liar: there had to be a reason. She said quietly, 'Will you at least admit that you may have been mistaken about the passenger?'

It was like drawing teeth. Mrs Taylor clutched her grievance to her and held her tongue. Liz said nothing more: nothing that would help her out, nothing that would help her change the subject. She just waited, her eyes on Pat Taylor's face.

Finally, as if the very silence was a goad whose urging could not be resisted forever, Mrs Taylor stumbled out, 'I – suppose.'

Liz vented her breath in a sigh. She may have seemed certain, obdurate and enduring, but inside she'd been ready to give up. 'I see. All right. Well, it can go on file as Anyone-can-make-a-mistake. But I'd like to understand. I don't know why you'd treat a decent man that way.'

And then she did. Perhaps the answer passed intuitively from one woman's mind into the other; or perhaps deep in the synapses of her brain Liz was working on the puzzle unknown even to herself. However it was, connections were made that completed the chain of motive and action, of cause and effect. Some of it she knew already; the rest she guessed.

Shaken, she sat down abruptly on a desk. 'Oh

Pat. Pat, why didn't you tell me? Why didn't you tell somebody?'

Pat Taylor's voice was a whisper. 'How did you guess?'

Liz shook her head with shock and compassion. 'There had to be something – something like that, something big. You're not an irrational woman, there had to be some reason for you to hate him that much. And then, when I called at your house, you had a hospital appointment but you didn't want a lift into town. You weren't going to Castle General, were you? You were going to the Feyd Clinic. Had it already happened?'

Mrs Taylor gave a fractional shake of the head. 'I thought I'd got away with it. I told the hospital I was two months pregnant, and they checked me over and said everything seemed all right. They said to come back if I had any symptoms, and to see my own doctor in the next few days. That's where I was going when you called. The clinic knew my history, they'd finally succeeded in getting me pregnant – if anyone could save the baby they could.'

She sat down on the next desk. 'I was there when the bleeding started. They said not to worry, there wasn't much, it would probably stop in a little while. They put me to bed and gave me an injection.

'But it didn't stop. Then late in the afternoon . . .' Her voice tailed away. Liz stole a glance at her face and was stunned by the pain there. She didn't dare speak, could only wait until Mrs Taylor was able to continue.

'After everything that had happened, it wasn't such a surprise. I was where I needed to be, people who knew what this meant were looking after me. But oh! the wrench of it. It wasn't a pregnancy, it was a baby. It was *my* baby, the only baby I ever conceived, the only chance of a baby I'd ever have, and my body was pushing it out as if it didn't want it. I'd spent ten years fighting for that baby, and now my womb was throwing it away. I wanted to stab myself. I thought, maybe if I stabbed myself it would give my body something else to worry about and it would leave my baby alone. If I'd had something to do it with I would have.

'And then it was too late. It was all over. I felt – empty. As if my insides had been ripped out. They tidied me up, gave me a sedative. They said, All right, we'd been unlucky, but it was a good sign that I'd been able to conceive, maybe next time . . .' She barked a silent, mirthless laugh. 'Next time? This one took ten years. Now I'm thirty-eight, I don't have a husband any more, and even if they'd give me AID I couldn't afford it on my own. This was my one chance, my last chance. And it was gone because some little thug ran me off the road, and some stupid ignorant policeman thought his trashy life was worth more than my baby's!'

Liz had nothing to say to her. She'd known there had to be an explanation, something she was missing, something to explain that excess of anger, and this was it. God knew it was enough.

At last she stood up and touched Pat Taylor's hand. 'I'm so sorry,' she said. 'I do understand. It wasn't Donovan's fault, but I understand why you felt it was. I'll leave now. Call me if there's anything I can do; otherwise I won't bother you again.'

236

'And' – Mrs Taylor forced a thin smile – 'bearing false witness against a police officer?'

Liz shrugged. 'He's got more than that to worry about right now. Forget it, it's history. You were under a terrible strain and you made a mistake. It's cleared up now.'

Heading back into town she found a phrase rattling round in her head. 'His line was broken...' Shakespeare, the Bible? – most expressions you'd heard and couldn't place were one or the other. Until now it hadn't meant anything to her: she'd understood the meaning, given no thought to the import. Now the enormity of it bore in on her. The line of Clifford and Patricia Taylor was broken. A thousand generations had gone into making each of them; but their line ended here, their last chance stolen along with Ash Kumani's weekend takings.

The thief's line had ended too. The line of Roly Dickens would go on, he had more than enough children and grandchildren to ensure it, but the unique combination of DNA that was Mikey Dickens would not now contribute to the next generation. His line was broken.

As, for that matter, were the lines of Brian and Elizabeth Graham. To be sure, they'd had more choice in the matter than either Pat Taylor or Mikey Dickens, but the magnitude of the choice momentarily troubled her. There were no Graham children, and no Ward children either: Brian had had a sister who died of leukaemia in adolescence, Liz was an only child. Four lines – those of her parents and those of his – had combined in the hope of succession and had been disappointed.

Common sense kicked in. There was nothing so extraordinary about any one of them that their genes should have passed down undiluted. And there were plenty of children in the world, and the way sex worked there could be no shortage of those sporting ancestral Ward and Graham genes. They had heirs, and as much stake in the future as anyone else. They'd chosen – she'd chosen – to eat the cake, she couldn't now complain that the cupboard was bare.

But she could still find it in her to envy Frank Shapiro his three. In them his immortality was secure; through them he was made someone of historical account, and would have been if he'd achieved nothing more. He would live in them, and in their children, long after the small accomplishments of DI Graham were forgotten.

She was getting maudlin. There was another saying: Take what you want, says God, and pay for it. Nothing was for nothing; at least, nothing worth having. She still considered what she'd chosen was worth what she'd given up.

Shapiro was back in his office. She knew by his face that there was no news. She told him where she'd been. 'There was no passenger in the van. Pat Taylor made that up, to avenge herself on Donovan.' She told him why. 'Oh, and Jade Holloway's volunteered to give her fingerprints. Which means, of course, it wasn't her that handled the baseball bat. Frank, I think we're right back where we started. What do we do next?'

'I don't know what to do.' Liz wasn't sure but it

might have been the first time she'd heard him admit defeat. 'We've searched the hospital, we've got people looking for Roly's van, I even got his mum to say she'd call if *she* hears anything. I don't know what else we can do.' He looked old; old and tired.

And for the first time Liz felt that maybe she could do something he couldn't. She sat down, taking determination deep into her lungs. 'If we can get at who did what Roly Dickens is blaming Donovan for, maybe we won't have to find them – maybe Roly'll give it up. He'll have no reason to hurt Donovan once he knows.'

Shapiro's eyes were dull. 'If we can get at it. If it isn't already too late.'

'Don't think like that,' Liz said fiercely. 'As far as we know there's still everything to play for. Start thinking it's a lost cause and we'll get careless, we'll miss things. I can't guarantee we'll find him if we keep looking, but I'm damn sure we won't if we don't. Don't you dare give up on Donovan! He wouldn't give up on you.'

One of the few drawbacks to being a Detective Superintendent was that people didn't often speak to you like that. Only someone who'd known Frank Shapiro as well and as long as Liz would have done so now; but it was what he needed. He shook himself like a Labrador emerging from a pond. 'You're right. I'm sorry, I just – lost it for a moment. All right. Nobody's giving up on anybody. Maybe we need to split our resources. You concentrate on who attacked Mikey. Take who you need and what you need to do it. I'll stay with the search; I can use uniforms for that. We need a break – desperately, and soon, but we only need one. Don't tell me we haven't earned that much.'

Liz knew it didn't work like that but she wasn't going to say so. 'Damn right we have.'

'Then let's get out there and collect.'

Back in her own office, though, she let the optimism slip. Concentrate on who beat Mikey? She'd been doing that since it happened! She had no new ideas to explore, no leads to pursue. Between them, she and Donovan had interviewed everyone they could think of who might know something about the episode. All their questions had been answered, and if the answers were less than helpful that was because they weren't asking the right questions of the right people. Somebody knew what happened to Mikey, but Liz had no idea who; and if Donovan had had a suspect he wouldn't have kept it a secret while the evidence against him mounted until even his colleagues doubted him.

She couldn't think of anyone else she could talk to, or any new questions she could put to those they'd already seen. Sitting at her desk, with the statements they'd taken and various notes and jottings she'd made ranged in front of her, the bustle of the building coming to her as a rumour through the shut door, the awareness grew upon her that that might mean something. Beyond the perennial, frightening possibility that she was missing something and someone was going to get hurt because of it.

What it might mean was that all the pieces were already on the table. If she'd searched under the rug and round the back of the cushions and found nothing, maybe that meant all the bits of the jigsaw were there in front of her – she just wasn't recognizing their significance.

The facts were all here. There was something in one of the statements that they were misinterpreting. Something Vinnie had said; something Desmond Jannery had said; perhaps something Mikey himself had said. He told Vinnie he was going to meet Donovan. Either he was lying, or telling the truth, or had himself been misled.

No. Actually, he *didn't* say he was going to meet Donovan. If Liz remembered correctly – she flicked through her notes to confirm it – he said he was going to meet The Filth, and he hoped it would be as entertaining as last time. What else could that mean? Another policeman?

A policewoman?

She felt a little quiver of recognition, like a blip on a Geiger counter. They hadn't understood why Mikey would risk meeting Donovan. But maybe he went to meet someone who was less likely to lose her temper and would do less damage if she did. They knew a woman was involved: what if she'd set up this meeting not in Donovan's name but in Liz's? Mikey would have met DI Graham at Cornmarket at midnight without a thought for his safety. She wasn't going to beat him up, and she wasn't going to arrest him, not that way. All she could have in mind was to ask him to give Donovan a break. He'd have met her just for the pleasure of saying No.

'All *right*,' Liz whispered to herself.

She fanned the papers out again, went over the statements they'd taken. The answer was in here somewhere, if only she could recognize it.

Or just maybe it wasn't. Some of the statements were missing. The dossers Donovan had talked to immediately before the baseball bat turned up: there was no record of what they'd said. Of course, right about then the excrement met the air-conditioning. He'd gone back to Queen's Street, Shapiro had taken him to the interview room and he'd left there on suspension. Even if there'd been time, committing the thoughts of a bunch of winos to paper would not have been a high priority when Donovan was trying to explain his fingerprints on a weapon of murderous attack.

So the only place a record of those interviews currently existed, apart from Donovan's head, wherever and in whatever condition that might be, was his pocket-book. If he'd taken it with him its contents were no more accessible. But he might not have done. Strictly speaking, Shapiro should have asked for it before sending him home.

Liz tapped his door. 'Frank, when you sent Donovan home, did you keep his pocket-book?'

'Mm.' Shapiro had felt badly about that but it was good procedure, it was on the list of things he wasn't going to do differently for Donovan. He'd dropped it into his desk drawer and not looked at it since. 'Here.'

Liz studied it, trying to read the scrawl. Alongside what he'd written was a sketch of Cornmarket tagged with the positions of the various parties. Mikey, Desmond, someone called Leslie back at the fire, someone called Wicksy and a woman called Sophie. Also a car located in the middle of the canal, a snake, and a circular feature he'd labelled UFO. Liz could make nothing of it. 'I think he's lost his marbles.'

'Let me see.' Shapiro concentrated on the spiky, angular writing. He found Sophie's snake, and Wicksy's UFO, and the car which Leslie insisted had driven in from The Levels despite the inconvenient absence of a road. He gave a disappointed sniff. 'It's nonsense. Of course it's nonsense: they're winos, they're describing their bad dreams.'

But Liz still thought there was something important here. She reread the notes, looked again at the scribbled diagram. And very slowly she began to see a grain of sense in it.

'Something happened,' she said. 'Something unusual. They heard and saw something that isn't a regular feature of the Cornmarket night-life. One of them thought it was a car, one of them thought it was a spaceship and one of them thought it was a snake. But they all put it in the same place at more or less the same time – by the canal round about midnight.'

His interest captured, Shapiro came round the desk and peered over her shoulder. 'By the canal? Or on it?'

Liz didn't understand. 'On it?'

Shapiro was nodding. There was a light in his eye that said he'd got ahead of her. 'What sounds like a car, looks like a snake, contains men from outer space *and* travels on water?'

'A boat?' At least it met some of the criteria.

'Of course a boat,' said Shapiro. 'It had to be. He didn't come up Brick Lane or by the towpath, by car or on foot. He came by the canal. Donovan didn't see him because he never passed *Tara*: he came in from The Levels. If he'd come up from town Donovan would have heard the engine, whether he was at

243

home or already on the towpath. It wasn't a car Leslie heard, it was a motorboat.'

'And the spaceship? The snake?'

'It was dark, yes? Just a bit of moonlight? A motorboat leaves a wake.'

Finally Liz caught up. 'And the wake reflected the moonlight, and followed the boat down the canal like a silver snake!'

'About the UFO, I'm not sure,' admitted Shapiro.

Liz imagined the scene. 'This is someone who owns his own boat. You couldn't hire one at midnight in the middle of winter, and anyone you tried to borrow it from would ask too many questions. So he's a canal buff. He also owns the rest of the gear – waterproofs, a life-vest, maybe a sou'wester. If *you* bumped into somebody shaped like the Michelin man wearing oilskins in the middle of the night at Cornmarket, particularly if you'd been knocking back the meths, *you'd* think the Martians had landed!'

Shapiro was remembering something. 'There was a motorboat on the canal when Donovan found the bat. He said that's why he didn't immediately spot what the dog was playing with – he was watching the boat instead.'

Liz let out a silent whistle. 'He said he was being framed. I didn't really believe it. But he was right, wasn't he? It was no accident he found the bat when he did – whoever used it on Mikey brought it back a few days later, put it where Donovan would find it and stayed around until he did.'

Shapiro was shaking his head in wonder. 'I never considered the canal as a way of getting about. But that's what the damn thing was built for! You can

244

still get almost anywhere in the country by inland waterway.'

'Like where?' said Liz. There was an odd tone in her voice. 'Like where exactly?'

They unpinned the map from his wall, spread it on his desk. The Castle Canal was a blue line trailing away eastward through The Levels towards the greater expanse of Cambridgeshire and the fens.

Long before that, though, it looped round by Chevening.

Chapter Four

Donovan felt himself weakening. He'd been hit harder, and hurt more, by men who manipulated pain as if it were an art form; but none of them had had as much reason to hate him as Roly Dickens, and none had had the same patience. The sheer repetition of that ham-bone fist arriving out of the dark was taking its toll. He felt his brain slowing and growing woolly. He was getting punch-drunk. If he couldn't talk his way out of this with all his wits about him, he hadn't much chance with them dripping out of his ear.

Roly mightn't like his answers but at least they were still coherent. Donovan wasn't sure how much more of this he could take before he started rambling on about beach holidays in Ballycastle and the price of fish. You could bounce a man's brain off the inside of his skull only so many times before the damage became permanent. Maybe that was what Roly intended. Maybe that was the only fitting revenge: to put the man he blamed for his son's coma into an adjacent bed in ICU, plugged into the same machines, kept alive by the same tubes.

He found he'd been thinking about that while Roly was waiting for an answer. But Roly didn't hit him again; instead he shook his shoulder. His voice

came through the darkness and the fog with an incon-
gruous note of concern. 'Mr Donovan, are you all
right?'

Donovan gave a frail, breathless laugh. 'Since you
ask, Roly, no. Somebody's using my head as a
punchbag.'

Roly peered closely at the policeman's face. There
wasn't much light in here, he'd blindfolded Donovan
more for psychological effect than because there was
anything he wanted to keep secret. But from close
up he could see the damage he'd done, and he was
surprised because he didn't remember hitting
Donovan that many times. He sat back, breathing
heavily – with exasperation, and because he didn't
often take this much exercise. 'If you'd just tell me
the *truth*–!' he complained.

'I am, Roly,' Donovan groaned. 'You're just not
hearing it.'

'But you're making no sense!'

'That's my fault?' He thought for a moment.
'Listen, Roly. Go to the library if you want to read
about crimes that make perfect sense. The motive's
convincing, the timing's spot on, and when the criminal's nailed in the last chapter you knew it was him
all along. But Roly – and I'm surprised at having to
tell you this – the real thing isn't like that. People get
knifed over a packet of crisps. If you're looking for
sense you're going to be disappointed. Settle for the
facts. And try to recognize them when you hear them.'

There was a pensive silence. Donovan didn't
know if Roly was thinking or lining up another swing
at the punchbag.

'You want me to believe that you were angry at

Mikey, you threatened him, you were there when he was found and your prints were on the weapon he was beaten with, but it wasn't you beat him up?'

'*Yes*,' said Donovan heavily. 'That's exactly what I want you to believe.'

'But you can't prove it?'

'No.'

'And you're being framed, but you don't know who by?'

'No.'

'And even Mr Shapiro isn't prepared to take your word for it?'

Donovan would have given anything to be able to say that, however bad it looked, his superintendent continued to have faith in him. A ragged breath rasped in his teeth. 'No.'

'I'm sorry, Mr Donovan,' Roly said severely, 'but Cushy Carnahan would convict you on evidence like that.'

Donovan chuckled, stopped when it started getting away from him. The controls were beginning to slip. Partly it was exhaustion and partly it was fear, but some of it was concussion and that was only going to get worse. At least in the short term; maybe in the long term too.

He was worrying about the long term? When any minute Roly would decide that the reason Donovan's story made no sense was that he was lying in his teeth? 'I dare say he would,' he slurred. 'But I don't think he'd tie me up and beat me to death because of it.'

'He might if it was his son in Intensive Care,' said Roly; a devastatingly simple argument which even those who knew the judge in question would hesitate to rebut.

Defeated, Donovan slumped back. 'There's no other way I can put it, Roly. I didn't hurt Mikey. I can't prove it, but I didn't. But I can't make you believe me, and I can't stop you beating my head in if that's what you want.'

In fact Roly Dickens didn't know what he wanted to do. He'd begun this in a passion so high that if Donovan had confessed and thrown himself on Roly's mercy the big man would have cut his throat without a moment's hesitation. But that was hours ago, he'd calmed down a lot since then. Also, talking to Donovan made it harder. It wasn't what the man said that drew Roly's venom, any more than it was his sunny personality and self-evident innocence. It was simply that: talking to him. Stripped of his authority, without the trappings of power, he was just another man. Oddly enough, that made him harder to hate.

'But if it wasn't you, who was it? Even Mikey can't have annoyed many people this much.'

It was the first glimmer of light at the end of the tunnel. Donovan held his breath, scared that someone might turn it out. But Roly was waiting for a response, and maybe this time he wouldn't hit him if he didn't like it.

'It has to be someone who hates Mikey and me both. And that's crazy. People who hate me send Mikey Christmas cards.'

'This wasn't anyone from The Jubilee,' said Roly with conviction. 'Nobody who knows us would be that stupid.'

'Who says it was stupid? They've got what they

wanted, haven't they? – Mikey in the hospital, and you beating seven bells out of me. That's not stupid, it's clever.'

'All right,' conceded Roly, 'then it's too damn clever – for Walshes or anyone else I know. This was nobody from the six streets. They couldn't have kept it from me if it was.'

He was probably right about that. 'So it's somebody who never did anything like this before, and never would have done except that somehow Mikey and me both, together or separately, wound him up enough.'

'Wound him up?' Incredulity soared in Roly's voice. 'How do you wind somebody up enough to make them want to beat you to death?'

Donovan barked a desperate laugh. 'Jesus, Roly – you're asking me?'

Momentarily that knocked the wind out of Roly Dickens. For a second he saw himself through Donovan's eyes: a thug and a madman, dangerous and unpredictable, so warped by anger that no brutality was beyond him. It was not a flattering picture; it wasn't how he saw himself. All right, he'd broken a few legs in his time, but that was business. He never hurt anyone who didn't deserve it. He was a fair man. People didn't cross him, they made a point of laughing at his jokes, but they weren't scared of meeting him in a dark alley. He was more respected than feared.

But Donovan was afraid; with good reason. Roly would have been afraid in the hands of the man this had made of him.

When he spoke again his voice had dropped to a thick growl. 'You took something from him that

mattered more than his freedom, more than his conscience, maybe more than his life. You hurt him more
than he could bear. You took something that he
couldn't get back, that he couldn't replace and that
he couldn't be compensated for. Somehow you ripped
the very heart out of him. Mr Donovan, you *must*
remember doing that to someone.'

'But I don't.' Deep as he dug, his memory held
nothing like that. He'd angered some dangerous men
in his time but every one of them would have taken
the baseball bat to him, not Mikey. 'Roly, I swear to
you, I didn't do that to you and I haven't done it
to anyone else. What about Mikey, has he ever—?'

Donovan couldn't see the disgust in Roly's eyes
but he could hear it in his voice. 'Mikey's a thief.
He steals from people. That's all. To the best of my
knowledge he's never hurt anyone more than enough
to separate them from their belongings. A black eye,
maybe a cracked rib or a broken nose. This wasn't
about a broken nose.'

'Then what was it about?'

Roly thought about it a little longer. His voice
came back iron-hard, Siberian cold. 'Maybe it was
about a man seeing his credibility, his career, even
his love-life heading down the tubes thanks to some
cocky kid who wasn't old enough to know that everybody – everybody – has a breaking point. Maybe that's
all it was about all along.'

The blood froze in Donovan's veins. He had to
force words past a constriction in his throat. 'No. Roly,
I swear to you. For Christ's sake, Roly! Don't—'

*

Neither of them altogether believed it. They talked about it almost in the hope of dissuading themselves. But they kept not quite succeeding.

'Consider the profile of the people we want for this,' said Shapiro. 'We want someone strong enough to beat Mikey, and someone with small hands to prepare the weapon. It doesn't have to be but was probably a man and a woman. They have to hate both Mikey and Donovan with equal passion. The Taylors had just lost a baby they'd been trying for for ten years, in a crash that happened because Donovan was pursuing Mikey.'

'They were living apart,' Liz objected faintly. 'Would they have tackled something like that together?'

'In a rational state of mind, probably not. But they weren't, were they? Whatever Taylor said, it was natural that they'd get together again after the miscarriage. They were upset, they were angry. And they're two intelligent, educated people, well capable of working out an act of vengeance if that's what they decided on. They just had to stay angry long enough to carry it through.'

'So Pat set it up – phoned Mikey, pretended to be me, asked to meet him – and Clifford went to Cornmarket armed with a baseball bat?' Liz shook her head, still not quite convinced. 'I'd have *sworn* he was being straight with me.'

Shapiro shrugged. 'He's an accountant. He couldn't do the job if he blushed every time he had to tell a lie.'

Clifford Taylor was picked up at his office, Patricia Taylor at the school. They were fetched in separate

cars and shown into separate interview rooms.
Neither was informed of the other's presence.

Had time pressed less urgently, given the serious-
ness of the allegation Shapiro would have interviewed
them both himself. But that could waste an hour, and
Donovan mightn't have an hour to spare. Shapiro took
Taylor, Liz took his wife.

Taylor was obviously anxious, but everyone is if
a squad car comes for them. He asked what it was
about. Shapiro gave one of the stock answers designed
to convey no information, and Taylor didn't ask again.
Perhaps he was reluctant to make a fuss; perhaps he
already knew.

'Do you own a life-jacket, Mr Taylor?'

The man looked at him as if he was mad. '*What?*'

'A life-jacket. A buoyancy aid. Keeps you afloat in
water – you know the sort of thing. Do you have one?'

Taylor knew what a life-jacket was. He didn't
know what possible interest such a thing might hold
for the detective. 'No. *Why*, for heaven's sake?'

'How about a set of oilskins?'

'I've got some waterproof trousers that I play golf
in. Does that count?'

'Could do, could do,' Shapiro nodded slowly. 'And
a sou'wester?'

'No! Superintendent—?'

'What about a boat?'

'I don't have a boat,' Taylor said with a kind of
desperate clarity. 'I don't have a boat, or anything to
do with boats. I don't know anything about boats.'

'Really? But you keep two at home.'

Taylor blinked. 'Oh, those – Yes, I suppose. All

right, yes. But I don't live there any more, and I hardly used them when I did.'

'I hardly use my lawnmower, but I wouldn't deny owning one.'

'They came with the house, I never thought of them as mine.'

'What are they?'

Clearly Shapiro knew or he wouldn't be asking these questions. Taylor answered anyway. 'One's a rowing boat, the other's got an outboard engine.'

'Works, does it?'

'I have no idea.'

'When did you use it last?'

'Ages ago. Years. Maybe the summer before last.'

'So if it was in use recently, that wasn't you.'

'That's right.'

'Came with the house, hm?' mused Shapiro. 'Left you some gear too, did they?'

Taylor thought. 'I believe they did. In the shed. I don't know what.'

'A life-jacket? Oilskins?'

'Possibly.'

'A sou'wester?'

Taylor closed his eyes for a moment. He knew this wasn't routine questioning. He was being accused of something. But this was a man who took on the Inland Revenue for a living, he wasn't going to crumble in the face of disbelief. 'Superintendent, at the risk of stealing your next line, we can do this the hard way or the easy way. The easy way is where you tell me what I'm suspected of and I try to show you you're mistaken. The hard way is where you keep talking double-Dutch and I send for my solicitor to translate. I'll answer any question that I understand, but I'm not going to answer any more that I don't.'

Behind the careful blank of his expression Shapiro found himself agreeing with Liz. The man seemed straight. He was protecting himself just enough and not too much. If he'd come in here with a battery of high-priced lawyers it would have suggested he had something that needed careful explaining. If he'd waived his rights under the Police and Criminal Evidence Act in selfless determination to assist in the inquiry at whatever cost to himself, Shapiro would immediately have been suspicious. No, this was a good performance. If it was a performance.

'All right,' he said. 'Cards on the table? We know what the incident involving your wife's car cost you. Inspector Graham guessed and Mrs Taylor confirmed it. I'm very sorry. You must feel intensely bitter towards the young man responsible. Bitter enough to put him in the hospital? Bitter enough to cast suspicion for that on Detective Sergeant Donovan? – because he might have prevented the tragedy if he hadn't left Mrs Taylor upside down in her car?'

Clifford Taylor regarded the policeman across the table for what seemed a long time. His eyes were steady. At length he said, 'On the whole, I understood better when you were talking about boats.'

'We're in here, Mrs Taylor,' said Liz. 'Could you—?' She was carrying an armful of things she didn't need so that Pat Taylor would open the door of Interview Room 2 for her. She couldn't be sure that a viable right thumbprint would be left on the knob but it was worth a try. Pat Taylor wouldn't accede to a request, and obtaining a warrant to take her fingerprints without consent would take time. As she settled herself at the table and started the recording equipment she could hear Sergeant Tripp unpacking his dusting kit in the corridor outside.

'I don't understand this,' said Pat Taylor tersely. 'You said you wouldn't bother me again.'

'Yes,' agreed Liz bleakly. 'Things have moved on. I now have reason to suspect that your involvement with Mikey Dickens didn't end at Chevening roundabout.'

'I don't know what you mean,' said Mrs Taylor.

'I assume it was Clifford's idea,' said Liz untruthfully. 'It was his baby too, there's no reason he'd feel any less strongly about it. He'd invested ten years in it too, he knew as well as you did there'd only ever be one chance. When you told him it was gone he must have been beside himself with grief and rage.'

'Clifford,' said Pat; and there was a hint of a question in it, as if she wanted to make sure they were talking about the same man. 'Clifford and I are separated.'

'That would look better,' nodded Liz. 'Even if you planned on getting together later, it might be wise to wait a while. If people aren't thinking of you as a couple right now they won't suspect you of anything needing two pairs of hands.'

'Such as?'

Pat Taylor was not an easy woman to interview. She was always tense, which made it difficult to know if she was more than reasonably anxious now. When interviewing suspects it was useful to watch what they did in the pauses. People who were hiding something relaxed a little when the pressure was off. People who weren't wanted to get on with it, wanted to prove their innocence: a long silence worried them. Pat Taylor just sat there, bolt upright, with the same stern expression whether Liz was speaking or not. Her manner was like a thin cloak of icy disdain folded about a fierce outrage, and it was hard to be sure whether she was angry at being accused of something she hadn't done, angry at being caught, or just angry at the things which had gone wrong with her life.

'Such as laying a trap for a young thug neither of you could have dealt with alone. Such as manipulating the evidence to incriminate someone else you thought you had reason to hate.'

'I've no idea what you're talking about, Mrs Graham,' said Pat Taylor coldly.

Liz waited for her to say more but she didn't. More than anything, that iron restraint persuaded her that this time they were on the right track. No one accused of a violent crime kept that quiet without a very good reason.

She wished Sergeant Tripp would hurry up. One firm connection between this woman and any aspect of the crime, and they were in business. She would get all the detail then because there would be no further point in concealment. No jury would miss the fundamental significance of Pat Taylor's fingerprint at one end of the baseball bat and Mikey's blood at the other.

But Liz couldn't wait while SOCO performed his alchemy with dusting-powder and magnifying-glass. She had to make a working assumption and press on.

'I imagine Clifford wore gloves,' she said. 'Anyway, it was a beat-up old bit of wood, he'd hardly have left prints if he hadn't bothered. Then he returned home – not to his flat in town, to your house, using the boat moored at your landing – and you helped him with the next phase, which was shifting the blame on to Donovan. The tape was a good idea: you did it because Clifford's hands were shaking. Attempted murder does that to a man; the first time, anyway.

'When you'd finished you wiped over the tape to remove any prints. But in handling the tape you'd left a print on the inside, the sticky side. That print will tie you to this crime, and there's nothing you can do about it.'

Again she waited. But she wasn't expecting Mrs Taylor to collapse in tears and confessions, and she didn't.

'Except for one thing,' Liz continued, 'which is help me now. Tell me what happened, while there's still time to save Donovan's skin. I have to tell you, that's the single most important thing you can do in your own best interests. The judge will recognize that, in the end, you tried to limit the damage you'd done. He'll also bear it in mind if you don't.'

Pat Taylor said, 'Save Donovan?'

Liz breathed heavily. They hadn't time for this; but she couldn't force a confession out of the woman, if she insisted on playing the fish Liz would have to act the angler. 'Mikey's father has him. Roly Dickens is a professional criminal, a man who keeps other criminals in line by brute force, and right now he's feeling how you felt when you lost your child. He thinks Donovan beat Mikey's head in. When you lost your baby you wanted to kill the man responsible. I imagine Roly Dickens feels the same way.

'I can stop him if I can get word to him that the people who attacked Mikey are in custody. An honest statement from you is Donovan's best chance, but it has to be now. He may be hurt already: the longer this goes on, the likelier it is it'll end in tragedy.'

She was determined to say no more. She watched Pat Taylor's face and waited for a response. The woman must know by now that she wasn't going to leave here. She hadn't yet given the fingerprints that would confirm her guilt, but she must know she would have to. She wasn't even bothering to protest her innocence. She was going to pay for what she'd had a part in, all she could do now was haggle over the bill. She was cornered, there was nowhere else to go.

Liz saw her eyes clear, saw the resolution there. Her decision was made. She gave a faint ghost of a smile. 'Good.'

Chapter Five

Not for the first time in CID history, necessity was the mother of detection. Benighted by his blindfold Donovan had no idea where Roly was or what he was doing, he felt only the chill of his hatred when he leaned close. He believed that he was facing death. For all he could tell Roly's sandbag fists were already on their way, and if the big man had decided that nothing Donovan said could be trusted he would have no interest in coaxing more words out of him. Before, Roly had a reason to keep Donovan alive, conscious and lucid. That reason seemed now to have gone.

He needed another one, quick.

The words blurted out of him. 'Roly, wait! I know how it was done!'

'*I* know how it was done,' grated Roly Dickens, close to his ear. 'With a baseball bat.'

'I mean, how someone got to Mikey and got away again without being seen. How no one came down Brick Lane and no one but me was on the towpath.'

'I think I know that, too,' said Roly.

'No, you don't. Jesus, Roly, *listen* will you? It wasn't me. It was someone who came by boat.'

'Boat?' If his youngest child hadn't been dying in

ICU he'd have found the idea of Mikey being beaten up by Captain Pugwash laughable. 'Who?'

'I don't know,' admitted Donovan. 'But I think I saw him. Not then – yesterday, when the bat turned up. When the dog found it on the towpath there was someone in a boat off *Tara*'s stern. I noticed because you don't see many people on the water in January. I couldn't see who it was, he was muffled up to the eyebrows, then as I picked up the bat he started the outboard and headed off. That's what he was there for – to make sure I put my prints on the weapon that was used on Mikey. Once I had he left.'

Roly sounded deeply mistrustful. 'It could have been anyone.'

It could. But Donovan couldn't afford for him to think so. 'Don't you see, it's the only way it could have been done. That's what was puzzling us, why Shapiro couldn't take my word that it wasn't me. Whoever attacked Mikey had to get there and had to leave. He could have been waiting a long time, but he had to leave after I was already on my way to Cornmarket. If he'd come up the towpath I'd have seen him; if he'd left by Brick Lane he'd have been seen there too.

'But who'd see him come by boat? Who'd stop him as he left and find the weapon still on him? He could afford to take it away, and bring it back later, because there was no chance of him being stopped and searched. He slung it on to the path when he saw me coming, waited till the dog brought it to me, then he started his engine and left.' The breath left him in a shaky sigh. 'Jesus, Roly, that's how he did it. That's how it was done.'

'Who? Who did it?'

'I don't know.' But in the moment of saying it he did. He knew where he'd seen that boat before. He remembered Pat Taylor's eyes when she looked at him and before she looked away. He didn't know why, but he knew how and now he knew who.

And if he told Roly Dickens, the big man would leave him here, bound and gagged, and go to the house on the canal at Chevening. Would his fury be in any way lessened by the fact that the attack on his son was carried out, or at least instigated, by a woman?

Donovan was Irish and therefore sentimental. He didn't believe that a woman's body could take the kind of punishment his had had to. He thought that if Roly got his hands on Pat Taylor he'd kill her. He thought that if he told Roly what he believed he'd be responsible for a woman's death. If he was right, Donovan had every reason to despise Pat Taylor for what she'd done to him. But he still couldn't bring himself to send Roly Dickens to her door.

'Roly – please – I can't tell you that.'

Roly's voice was as cold, hard and unyielding as the creak of a glacier. 'Wanna bet?'

This was harder than before. Before he had only his wits to defend him from Roly's anger: now he had something to buy him off with. He had no illusions about how serious this was: it was literally a matter of life and death. He thought probably, at least on this occasion, he deserved to live more than Mrs Taylor did: whatever her motive – and all he knew was that she'd lost her car – she'd reduced one man to a vegetable and set out to destroy another. It was she, not Donovan, who had sewn the wind: he knew of no law, common, statute or moral, that compelled him to reap her whirlwind.

And yet. It was his job to protect the weak against the strong, and it remained his job even when doing it meant getting hurt. He'd risked his life for his job before – every policeman had at some time or another. In essence, this was another situation like that. He could keep a dangerous man here, or he could let him go to hurt a defenceless woman instead. When you got right down to it, that was the issue: not what that woman was and had done, or even what Roly was, but what Donovan was.

Right now Donovan was scared for his life, and too damn stubborn to buy it with the only acceptable currency. With a tremor in his voice that someone much further away than Roly couldn't have missed, he said, 'I can't, Roly. Don't you understand? – I can't. I don't have the privilege of a choice.'

Someone tapped at the interview room door. Liz was expecting Sergeant Tripp, but he was only the first in a queue: Shapiro was coming down the corridor from Interview Room 1 with WPC Flynn bobbing in his wake, trying to attract his attention.

Tripp could be dealt with in three words. 'Well?'

'Yes.'

'Great.' She sent him back to his witch's kitchen and Shapiro took his place.

'Is she talking?'

'They did it, all right. But no, she won't say as

much. She likes the idea of Roly kicking Donovan's head in.'

Shapiro stared at her, appalled. 'Is she crazy?'

'If you mean, is she in control of her actions, then yes. She blames him as much as Mikey for her miscarriage. The husband dealt with Mikey, she's dealing with Donovan.'

'Is that what she said? That Taylor beat Mikey?'

Liz shrugged. 'She hasn't said much of anything. She didn't try to deny it. That *was* her print inside the tape, incidentally – I just got confirmation from SOCO.'

Shapiro had both hands shoved deep in his pockets. It gave him the round-shouldered profile of a dyspeptic bat. 'Liz, I'm not sure Taylor was part of it.'

Liz stared at him. 'Then who do you think helped her?'

'Maybe nobody.'

Since suspicion first settled on the Taylors Liz had assumed that Pat had set it up and Clifford carried it out. But if Clifford wasn't involved . . .

Pat Taylor beat the living daylights out of Mikey Dickens with a baseball bat? The head of the English department at Castle High stood over a nineteen-year-old boy and pounded away at his head until her oilskins were spattered with his blood and fragments of his skull and brain?

Actually, there was nothing a woman couldn't have done, if she was angry enough. Liz's mind flashed back to little Bella Willis, tackling with her bare hands the man she thought was threatening her baby. That maternal drive went down deeper than reason, deeper than fear or even self-preservation, tapped into a well of primal savagery nothing else reached. If Kevin Tufnall had actually stolen her child, had in fact killed him, nothing on God's earth would have prevented Bella from taking him apart.

That surfeit of anger, the disabling of normal inhibitions, was the key. Given that, there was nothing so physically demanding about the demolition of Mikey Dickens that a middle-aged woman couldn't have accomplished it; except for one thing. 'Frank, the attack on Mikey was three days after Pat Taylor's miscarriage. I don't think she'd have been strong enough to do it. To help Taylor, certainly. But to play baseball with a man's head?'

Shapiro caught his breath. He'd missed the significance of the timing. 'God damn!'

'Look,' said Liz, 'maybe just how she did it doesn't matter as much as the fact that, with or without help, she managed somehow. Because if she did it, Donovan didn't. Isn't that enough? For Roly, I mean.'

That was the crucial point. Shapiro nodded. 'If we can find him.'

WPC Flynn finally succeeded in catching his eye. 'Call from PC Stark, sir. He's found Roly Dickens's van, on a track in the woods near Hunter's Spinney. He can't see anyone, but he says they must be inside because he can see it rocking from fifty yards away.'

Liz knew what that meant. 'Oh Christ!'

Shapiro said, hard and fast, 'Tell Stark not to approach until we get there. He can't take Roly on his own, he can only get hurt too. We'll be there in six minutes – tell him to wait till then.'

'Sergeant Bolsover already has, sir,' said Flynn. 'But I'm not sure he will.'

Jim Stark was a born policeman. He was a strong man but he didn't throw his weight around; he was brave but not foolish; he did a good rugby tackle if a suspect tried to leg it but was equally happy seeing old ladies across busy roads.

If he had a weakness, it was that he was too kind. He was a sucker for tramps wanting a hot meal and small children claiming to be lost. He had no illusions about his ability to arrest, single-handed, a man four stones heavier than him, with huge well-practised fists and boots, fuelled by a deadly rage taking him to the brink of madness. He knew that in any confrontation with Roly Dickens he'd come off worst. It made no difference. He couldn't hide in the trees while Roly's van bounced on its suspension and grunts and choked cries attested to the violence of what was happening within. He turned off his radio and came up the track at a run.

They were in the back: there wasn't room for this in the front. He went to the back doors and snatched them open, and kept moving forward in the hope of forcing Roly off the target of his fury before his own impetus ground to a halt.

He found himself sprawled on top of two naked bodies that were so involved in what they were doing they didn't even stop.

By the time the cars arrived the naked bodies had calmed down and found some clothes, PC Stark had recovered his composure and his message had been relayed to Shapiro. So the superintendent already knew it wasn't Roly and Donovan in the van but two seventeen-year-olds who'd despaired of finding an empty room in either of their houses.

But it was still Roly's van, and it was vital to establish where they'd acquired it and when.

'A couple of hours ago,' said the girl. 'It was sitting in the car-park with the doors unlocked and the keys in the ignition. We reckoned anybody that stupid would probably think he'd forgotten where he parked it. We were going to put it back later, then nobody'd ever believe it went missing.'

'What car-park?' demanded Shapiro tersely.

'The one at the hospital.'

'They never left the hospital.' Shapiro sounded stunned. His mind was desperately sifting information, trying to work out if the clues had been there and he'd simply missed them. He glanced at his watch: two o'clock. 'They've been there all along. We searched but the place is a rabbit warren. Roly must have found somewhere he wouldn't be disturbed, and they've been there for five hours. They're still there.'

Liz's eyes were enormous. 'If we have to search every storeroom, every side room, every maintenance area and staffroom and repository on the site, it'll take another five hours.'

'We've no alternative. Basically, we have to open every door in the building because they could be behind any one of them.' Shapiro became aware he didn't have Liz's full attention. 'What?'

She blinked. 'I'm just thinking. We know how Roly

feels about Mikey – look what he's done to prove it. Give or take the odd hour, he's sat by his bed for five days. Now he's got Donovan with him he needs some privacy so he's gone somewhere else. But if you were hiding in a quiet part of the hospital, and a child of yours was maybe dying in another part, wouldn't you slip away and see him from time to time? And Roly doesn't know we're looking for him. He's no reason to suppose we're even looking for Donovan yet.'

'How can you slip away from six foot of bad-tempered detective?' objected Shapiro. 'No, don't answer that . . .'

Liz shook her head. 'If Donovan was dead there'd be nothing keeping Roly away from ICU, and he hasn't been seen since before nine o'clock. I don't think he'll run, whatever he's done. While Mikey's in ICU Roly will be nearby; and he's not going to sit in a storeroom all day and never know how the boy's doing. If we watch Mikey, sooner or later we'll spot Roly.'

'If he doesn't spot us first.'

'Mary Wilson will look good in a nurse's uniform,' said Liz. 'He won't be worried about the odd nurse seeing him.'

'What do you suggest – we all hide in the sluice-room and jump him when she gives the word?'

'We could,' agreed Liz politely. 'But it might be better to follow him. We'll find Donovan quicker than way, which might matter if he's hurt.'

'Do it,' said Shapiro. 'I'll organize some fire power.'

An arched eyebrow signalled Liz's surprise. 'Do we know Roly's armed?'

'We don't know he isn't.'

268

It didn't seem enough. 'That's grounds for issuing firearms?'

'Not if it was Mikey holed up in there, or almost anyone else,' said Shapiro. 'But I've known Roly Dickens a lot of years, and I worked with officers who'd known him longer still. He was a bare-knuckle fighter in his youth. I bet you thought that went out with compulsory education and the Welfare State, didn't you? – but not round here it didn't. Round here it went out when there was no one left who was prepared to take on Roly Dickens.

'It's a long time ago but it shows what he's capable of. He's not much younger than me, and he's even fatter, and still I have no doubt that in his present mood he could kill a man with his bare fists. On my reading that makes him armed and dangerous. I hope we won't have to use guns, but it would be foolhardy not to have them in support.'

She didn't know whether to say anything more or not. Shapiro realized what she was thinking and grimaced. 'I know: I promised Thelma I wouldn't hurt him. But we were talking about when he's in custody. I said he'd be safe at Queen's Street, and I meant it. I didn't say I'd stand by and watch him cut Donovan's heart out. If that's my only choice I will cheerfully blow his God-damned head off.'

Chapter Six

WPC Wilson made a fetching nurse. She wasn't a big girl, people who didn't know her wondered if she was tough enough to be a police officer, and the blue gingham uniform suited her. She installed herself at a desk in the next bay to Mikey's, with a clear view down the corridor. If Roly got close enough to see his son, Mary Wilson would see him.

Liz waited in the nearby staff-room with Dick Morgan, and Shapiro with another three officers, two of them armed, in an empty office on the ground floor. They knew they could be there a while, and strictly speaking there was no need for both the town's senior detectives to be at the scene. But neither was prepared to sit it out at Queen's Street, so they sat with their radios and waited. And waited.

When rough hands grabbed Donovan's head, fear burgeoned through him. But Roly was only snatching off his blindfold.

It took time for his eyes to adjust but when they did he recognized two things in quick succession: the broad face of Roly Dickens, flushed with anger and thrust forward on the bull neck until it was only inches from his own, and the scalpel that he'd used to get Donovan down here. Its lancet tip was at his left eye. When Donovan blinked his lashes brushed it.

'Donovan,' spat the big man, 'I will use this. To get the man who maimed my child I will carve you; I will blind you if I must. Whoever he is, he's not worth that. You've held out as long as anyone could: now tell me. No one'll blame you. I'll give myself up as soon as I'm done – I'll send them here and they'll see you were all out of choices. Don't lose your eyes for a man who'd beat a boy with a baseball bat.'

'Jesus, Roly.' Donovan began to shake. 'Think about this, will you? This – man – is going to pay for what he did to Mikey. You don't have to do anything more. He's going to jail: he's going to be old before he gets out, if he ever does. Isn't that enough for you?'

Roly shook his head. 'You've seen Mikey, you've seen what he did to him. He's never getting out of that bed. It's only a matter of time before the doctors start sounding me out about pulling the plug on him. This is my *child* we're talking about, my youngest son, and I'm going to have to say it's all right to kill him.' The pain and the fury in him were incandescent. Watching him was like seeing a star go nova.

He was panting as if with exertion. 'But if you think I'm going to watch him die, and afterwards I'll be content for a court to say what happens to his killer, you know nothing about me. I'm an Old Testament man, me – an eye for an eye, a life for a life. He destroyed my son: I am the *only* one qualified to judge him. After that, a court can decide what happens to me.'

'Roly, I understand how you feel.' Donovan had given up any attempt to disguise the tremor in his voice. 'But I can't give you what you want.'

'You can. You will.'

'No. You may take it. Someone with a cast-iron stomach and enough time can probably get anything out of anyone. Sure you can hurt me. You can blind me; and probably by then I'll be ready to do anything, to say anything, to make it stop.' The words were coming faster and faster, out of control, almost too fast to follow. He clenched his jaw, struggling for command. 'But you'll have to do it. Do you understand? – you have to *do* it. The threat isn't enough. You'll get what you want eventually, but I'll take a fair bit of punishment first. Is that what you want? Is that what you want to go to prison for – torturing information out of someone who couldn't fight back? I know you can do it, Roly. But you'll regret it.'

'I can do my time,' Roly said thickly.

'Jesus, I know *that*!' exclaimed Donovan. 'That's not what I mean. There are people in this town look up to you. Admire what you've achieved. Today, right now, the worst anyone can say is that you're a professional criminal, and I don't suppose you'd mind having that on your tombstone. This is different. People may understand, in a way, but a lot of rooms'll go quiet when your name comes up in the conversation. Even apart from that, you'll be sorry. You won't believe you sank this low. I'm not your enemy, Roly, you know that. I know you want the name, but you can't justify what you're going to have to do to get it.'

'My son is all the justification I need!'

272

Donovan shook his head. Droplets of sweat flew off the rat-tails of his hair. 'No. We've had our differences, Roly, but I never thought you were capable of this. In your right mind I don't believe you would be. And when it's over, when your head's clear and you know the whole story, you'll wish you hadn't. You'll wish to God you'd stopped when you had the chance. Now, Roly. You can stop this now.' His mouth was dry. He swallowed. It was like swallowing ashes.

For as long as Roly Dickens said nothing, staring at him from a range of inches with anger and puzzlement and respect and, yes, regret in his eyes, Donovan thought there was a chance that he'd done it – that he'd saved both himself and Pat Taylor from the big man's wrath.

Then Mikey's father said bleakly, 'You're a good man, Mr Donovan. It's a pity it's always good men who get hurt.'

Liz's nerve broke before Shapiro's did, but it was a close thing. If she'd delayed calling him another five minutes he'd have called her.

'This is crazy!' she said. 'He isn't going to come. He's holed up somewhere, God knows what he's doing to Donovan, and we're not even looking for them!'

It had been a calculated gamble. If the hospital had been crawling with police officers opening doors and checking under beds, Roly would have seen them before they saw him. If he meant to kill Donovan he would have all the opportunity he needed. But she was right. If he wasn't going to come, too much time was going to waste.

'All right,' decided Shapiro, 'Plan B. We search the building from top to bottom. Well, bottom to top – we'll start in the basement, drive him upwards. Less chance of him slipping out through a side door.'

'Do you want me to come down?'

'No, stay where you are. You might get lucky before we do.'

Shapiro surveyed his team. Four of them wasn't enough to search a large, complex building but getting more would mean waiting and suddenly he felt they'd waited too long already. 'Be careful. I don't want to overstate the case, but Roly Dickens in his current state is a deeply dangerous man. Nobody tackles him alone. You find him, you even think you've found him, you pull back – quietly – and call me. Clear?' There was a muttered chorus of assent. 'All right, let's do it.'

Nothing she could have been doing, even snatching open doors that might conceal a homicidal maniac, would have been as hard on Liz's nerves as doing nothing. She looked to DC Morgan for signs of a similar frustration, but Fenmen like Morgan could give lessons in patience to a stone.

Finally she got to her feet. 'It's no good, I can't—'

The radio on the table beside her burped as Wilson tapped hers with her pen.

Hope flared in Liz's eyes. 'She's spotted him!' She picked up the radio. 'I'll let Mr Shapiro know.'

'All *right*,' exclaimed Shapiro. He raised his voice, no longer afraid of being overheard. 'Roly's upstairs. So let's get Donovan found while there's no risk of meeting him. Liz, you'll let me know as soon as he leaves?'

'Of course. We'll be right behind him.'

They hadn't expected Roly to stay in ICU, just stick his head in to see if anything had changed before returning to where he'd been for the last several hours. But it seemed the big man was no longer concerned with concealment. He trudged across the ward, cumbrous and tired, pulled out the chair beside Mikey's bed and sat down heavily. He looked as if he was there for the duration.

Unable to make sense of it, Liz radioed downstairs again. But Shapiro didn't understand either. Unless, and he wasn't going to say this aloud, it meant there was nothing for Roly to go back to. 'I'm on my way. We'll have to ask him what he's done with Donovan.'

Just then, though, Roly looked up from the bed, looked around and heaved himself to his feet. The big body rolling slightly, he walked over to the sister's desk.

'If Mr Shapiro's anywhere handy, tell him I'd like a word.'

Liz was with them in a few quick strides. 'He's in the basement, Roly. Shall I get him up here?'

Roly shook his head. 'We'll meet him down there.'

Shapiro had thought he'd need guns to make a safe arrest, but two women and a middle-aged man without a Swiss Army penknife between them proved a wholly adequate escort. Roly wasn't going anywhere. Whatever had happened, it was over now.

Liz fought the urge to question him. She'd know about Donovan soon enough, but while Roly was trudging docilely beside her and help was two floors below she wasn't going to open a line of inquiry that would make both of them angry.

Shapiro met them at the foot of the lift-shaft, nodded a wary greeting. 'Roly. I believe you've got something we're looking for.'

There was no reading Roly Dickens's expression. His eyes were as blank as ball-bearings: the adrenalin storm had passed, leaving him drained. He led them past the emergency generators and the laundry and into a side corridor.

Liz kept her voice flat. 'Are we going to need a doctor?'

The big man considered, then nodded. Mary Wilson took off back the way they'd come.

Roly stopped at a shut door. Shapiro couldn't imagine how he could tell it from a dozen others. 'He's in there. Before you go in, I'd better warn you. I had to hurt him.'

Liz pushed past him, fear and a helpless fury beating a turmoil in her breast, and flung open the door.

It was a small concrete box of a room with one small, high window. Dusty crates and boxes suggested it had no particular function except as a repository, for things that were broken or finished with.

At the back of the room, under the window, a body spilled across the dirty floor. That long and thin, and dressed for a tanners' funeral, it could only be Donovan. He was on his side with his back to her and his wrists taped behind him. He lay quite still. There was blood on the floor.

She hesitated, his name thin on her lips. Then she steeled herself and bent over him.

His face was battered almost past recognition. Blood trickled from his mouth and his nose, and his eyes were swollen shut. A painful whisper of breath rasped between broken lips. He was unconscious, but not so deeply unconscious that the hurt couldn't reach him. It wouldn't be long before he was back.

On a crate beside him lay the scalpel Roly had taken from ICU. It was clean. Except to cut lengths of tape, he hadn't used it.

Shapiro vented his breath in a ragged sigh. 'All right. Liz, stay with him till the doctor gets here. Roly, time for you and me to talk back at Queen's Street.'

The superintendent went to lead him away; but Roly stood his ground for a moment, half turned in the doorway, looking back over his shoulder. His voice was gruff. 'I'm sorry about this, Mrs Graham. I had to lay him out. If I hadn't I'd have done something we'd have both regretted.'

Liz looked up at him, caught between tears and a smile. Donovan's face was a bloody mess, but he'd heal. It could have been so much worse. 'I think he'll be all right.'

'He'd better be,' grunted Roly. 'He knows who beat up on Mikey.'

'He does?' Shapiro couldn't have looked more startled if someone had hit him with a kipper. '*How?*'

Roly shrugged. 'I dunno. Something to do with a boat, I think.'

Liz gave a shaky chuckle. 'Figures.' She looked at Shapiro. 'Can I tell him? It won't make any difference now.'

'Go ahead.'

She stood up. 'We're not sure of the detail yet, but

we have two people helping with our enquiries right now. As Mikey's father, I think you're entitled to know that.'

'Someone I know?'

Liz shook her head. 'Even Mikey didn't know them. The woman was in the car he turned over the night of the robbery. She miscarried a baby she'd been trying for for ten years. I think it drove her a little mad.'

'A *woman*?' Roly sounded astonished. He thought about it. 'A woman. And that's why . . .' He nodded at Donovan, still senseless on the floor.

Liz's lip curled. 'You played right into her hands. She blamed them both: Mikey for the crash, Donovan for saving him instead of helping her. This was her revenge. She wanted you to kill him.'

Roly wasn't accustomed to being used. The thought of what this woman he'd never met had nearly made him do made him feel ill. His voice was thick. 'Yeah? Well, tell her something. Tell her he took that for her. Tell her he was ready to take more.'

Liz was glad when they went. She didn't want Donovan waking up as the main attraction in a three-ring circus.

In fact they were alone when he surfaced. He didn't open his eyes: they were too bruised. He mumbled, 'Roly?'

'No, it's me – Liz Graham.'

She'd freed his hands. They were numb after five hours lashed behind his back. He moved one towards his face, but he had neither the co-ordination nor the feeling in his fingers to be sure. 'My eyes?'

Understanding rocked her. So that was what Roly

meant. She guided Donovan's hand and touched his fingers to his eyes. 'They're fine. A bit puffy, you look like the morning after the night before, but you're OK. There's no damage done.'

For a minute longer he just lay where he was, absorbing that. Then he sucked in a deep breath and struggled to sit up. Liz helped him. 'I know who did it. I know who beat Mikey.'

She could have lied, but he'd have found out soon enough. She chuckled sympathetically. 'Sorry, Donovan – so do we. The Taylors. We picked them up this morning.'

Donovan would have been angrier if he'd been stronger. He stretched his forearms across his knees and rested his head on them. 'Oh, bugger,' he muttered wearily.

Chapter Seven

Dealing with Roly Dickens took priority. Shapiro spared little thought for the Taylors until he had the big man tucked up comfortably in a cell.

Roly gave no further trouble. He didn't want his solicitor, he didn't ask for bail, he made no attempt to put a gloss on what he'd done. He was sorry for what he'd done to Donovan, but mostly he regretted being in a police cell when he should have been at his son's bedside.

'I promise you, Roly,' Shapiro said, 'if there's any change you and I will go back to the hospital. I let them know you'd be here, they'll call me if there's anything to report.'

''Preciate that, Mr Shapiro,' rumbled Roly.

Shapiro regarded the old battler with compassion. 'I do understand, you know. I can't ignore what's happened, but I understand where it came from. You had your strings pulled at a time when you were desperately vulnerable. I'm not saying anyone would have reacted the same way, but in all the circumstances things could have been worse. We'll sort it out, Roly. Nobody wants your head on a platter.'

'Mr Donovan might.'

'I doubt it. Or if he does now, he won't for long.

Leave it with me, once he's feeling better I'll talk to him.'

'I could have done it, you know.' A little peak of wonder rose through the dull monotone of Roly's voice. Already the thing was beginning to seem unreal, like a nightmare he'd woken from, but he remembered with a kind of horror how he'd felt. 'I shouldn't be saying this, should I, but it's true. I wanted to kill him when I thought he'd beaten Mikey. Even when I knew he hadn't – I saw it come together in his face, nobody's that good an actor, I saw him work out who did it and then realize he couldn't tell me – I was ready to hurt him to get the name. I threatened to blind him, Mr Shapiro. I could have done it. I was this close.' The finger and thumb he held just barely apart were as thick as sausages.

'Roly,' said Shapiro firmly, 'neither of us knows for sure what you could have done. We only know what you did. I know what you threatened to do, but whether you'd have done it is something else. The facts are that for five hours you held a man you believed responsible for your son's condition, and all you actually did was thump him. All right, several times and quite hard, but people get worse injuries in boxing matches.

'Forget what might have happened. Yes, you could have killed him, or blinded him, but if you hadn't got round to it in five hours it's my guess you never would have. Talk's easy, but it takes a particular type of man to brutalize someone who can't defend himself. Whatever our differences, Roly, I don't think you're that kind of man.'

'Mr Shapiro,' said Roly with a slow smile, 'did you ever think of going into criminal defence work?'

Shapiro gave a little snort of laughter and left him alone.

The Taylors were still where he'd left them. Sergeant Tomlinson was the Custody Officer: Shapiro checked that no problems had arisen during his absence.

'No, sir. But Mr Taylor made a phonecall about an hour ago.'

Shapiro wasn't surprised. 'His solicitor?'

'No, sir, his doctor.'

That did surprise him. 'He's ill? Why didn't you call Dr Greaves?'

'He wasn't ill,' said the sergeant stoically. 'And Dr Greaves may be an excellent police surgeon but I doubt he's a fertility expert.'

Shapiro enjoyed being enigmatic; he wasn't keen when other people got enigmatic back. He squinted over his shoulder at Sergeant Tomlinson as he headed up the corridor.

Clifford Taylor looked up quickly as Shapiro came in. There was a cup on the table in front of him: he'd drunk about half of it. Not too anxious to drink at all, nor so relieved at being left alone he could have managed a square meal. In his gut Shapiro didn't believe this man had done anything as dreadful as bludgeoning a nineteen-year-old boy.

'Did you find your sergeant?'

Though he was a bit taken aback, Shapiro knew how difficult it was to keep secrets in a police station. He saw no reason not to answer. 'Yes. He's all right – a bit of concussion, some pretty spectacular bruises;

I left him at the hospital but I'll get him back in a day or two.'

'The boy's father had him?'

'He thought Donovan put his son in ICU. Which is what he was supposed to think.'

'Somebody' – the accountant gave an awkward shrug, too embarrassed to use slang he'd only ever heard on television – 'made it look that way?'

Shapiro breathed heavily. 'Mr Taylor, you *know* somebody made it look that way. You also know who. If it wasn't you and your wife together it was your wife alone.'

Taylor's gaze flicked up briefly and then returned to the table-top. 'I made a phonecall. While you were out.'

'I know,' nodded Shapiro. 'Do you want to tell me about it?'

'I called the clinic. The Feyd Clinic, where we were having fertility treatment.'

'Oh yes?' Shapiro was puzzled. Guilty or innocent, he'd have thought the man would have other things on his mind.

'Pat didn't have a miscarriage.'

The superintendent stared at him. 'You mean, she's still pregnant?'

'I mean, she never was pregnant.'

All Shapiro's experience told him that women didn't lie about something like that. 'What makes you think so?'

'The consultant. I asked him if she miscarried, and he said no.'

But it made no sense. What Pat Taylor had done, the lengths she'd gone to – the extreme lengths, if her husband hadn't helped – were beyond belief if all she was mourning was her battered car.

The possibility remained, of course, that what Taylor was trying to do was wriggle off the hook, and that he'd say anything about anyone to do it.

'I'm surprised the consultant was willing to discuss it with you.'

'I'm not,' said Taylor tersely, 'I bought him his Rolls Royce. As far as he's concerned, I'm still a patient. Pat and I went there as a couple, she never told them we'd split up. I think she was afraid they wouldn't treat her alone.'

'In that case your consultant should be prepared to speak to me, with your consent. Will you give it?'

'Oh yes,' said Taylor. 'Superintendent, don't misunderstand me. I'm not trying to persuade you of my innocence by convincing you of Pat's guilt. But I think she needs help – not medical, psychiatric – and until the facts are known she's not going to get it.'

That seemed reasonable. Taylor didn't need to throw suspicion on his wife, and he wouldn't succeed in averting it. 'And the consultant was quite sure there was no pregnancy?'

Taylor ground his knuckles into his eyes. 'She went to the clinic after the accident. She told them what had happened, and what she was afraid of – that she was carrying a child and it had been harmed. They ran the tests and found what they expected. There was no evidence of pregnancy.

'When the consultant told her she became hysterical. They put her to bed for a couple of hours until she was feeling better, then they sent her home. I asked if she could have got confused, if she could have miscarried at home either before or after visiting the clinic, but he was adamant there was nothing to miscarry.'

Shapiro was still trying to get his head round it. 'Then what on earth was it all about? Why have we got one man dying in the hospital, one sitting in the cells here, and one who could have been in the next room to either of them if things had gone just a little differently? If she wasn't avenging a lost baby, what *was* she doing?'

'I asked that too.' Taylor swallowed. This wasn't easy for him. He was talking about a woman he'd loved for half his life. In spite of everything, what he felt for her was still closer to love than anything else. 'I told him she was behaving irrationally and blaming it on the loss of a pregnancy. The consultant reckoned that by now she'd convinced herself it was true. That his tests were wrong, that she really was pregnant and she lost it because of the accident. He said what she was really mourning was her fertility, her ability to have a child. When she finally realized it was never going to happen, she felt bereaved.

'She needed to grieve, and she did it by thinking of it as a child she'd lost. The rest followed from that. If there was a child and she lost it because of the crash, that was the fault of the boy who ran her down and the policeman who could have rescued her before the baby was damaged. She believed that between them they'd killed her child.'

And she wanted revenge in the same fierce, regardless-of-the-consequences way that she'd spent ten years trying for a baby. Liz had been worried she'd have been too weak from the miscarriage to do

285

all she'd have had to, but that wasn't a problem if there never was a pregnancy.

'Let me get this straight,' said Shapiro. 'From start to finish she was acting alone? You didn't help her with any of it, not even inadvertently?'

Clifford Taylor shook his head. His eyes were hollow. 'Incredible, isn't it? For twenty years people have been leaving their children with Pat in the absolute belief that she could be trusted to look after them. As far as I know she's never so much as smacked one round the head with a ruler. And then, almost out of nowhere, she took a stave to a nineteen-year-old boy and hit him until she thought he was dead. And not in the heat of the moment – she had to plan it like a military manoeuvre, and then to plan some more how she was going to lay the blame on your sergeant. God in heaven, Superintendent – is it even possible?'

It was possible. In thirty years Shapiro had seen all manner of people do all manner of things that others had thought beyond them. Bella Willis defending her baby from Kevin Tufnall. Other mothers and fathers walking through fire to rescue their children. Other men and women, equally ordinary to the casual eye, conceiving and carrying out difficult and complicated schemes to get what they wanted – money, somebody else's spouse, their own freedom.

And these were the cases that Shapiro knew about, the ones where something went wrong and it all came out. As a realist he knew there must be others who'd been clever enough to get away with it. With just a little less ambition Pat Taylor could have been one of them. If she'd settled for punishing Mikey she would never have been suspected. Unless he recovered enough to point the finger, which was looking less and less likely, the attack on him would have remained unsolved. Greed was her undoing. She wanted them both, but her efforts to implicate Donovan started her careful construct unravelling.

Shapiro nodded wearily. 'Oh yes. More than that: one step at a time it wasn't even very difficult.' Murderers were often surprised at how easy it was to end a human life. Beforehand they worried they mightn't have the strength or the stomach to complete the task. But when the time came they had no trouble inflicting enough damage to kill the victim three times over.

'The hardest part would be working it all out, and that was an intellectual exercise she was well equipped for. She made a phonecall, and a couple of boat-trips, and beat the living daylights out of a boy she blamed for the loss of her baby. None of that was beyond her once she'd decided on the sort of revenge the courts are no help with, that you have to take for yourself.'

For all the mayhem she'd caused, Shapiro couldn't help feeling sorry for Pat Taylor. She'd acted on emotions as powerful at a genetic level as self-preservation. If she'd been made to kill at gunpoint they'd have been talking inculpable homicide. Perhaps Mrs Taylor had had no more chance of resisting the demands on her than if she'd had a gun in her back.

In a way, whatever they decided, what happened to her now was academic. Her life was wrecked as much as Mikey's. If she continued to believe that she'd lost a child, the refusal of the rest of the world to acknowledge that loss would be an enduring torment. And if at some point she came to understand that there never was a child, that she'd destroyed one man and come within an ace of destroying another for a figment of her imagination, how would she feel then? They were all victims: Mikey, Roly, both the Taylors . . . In the end, and by the skin of his teeth, Donovan with his black eyes and his bloody nose had got off lightest of all.

He also had a certain amount of pleasurable satisfaction coming, in that his superintendent owed him an apology.

There was still Pat Taylor to see. Now Shapiro had all the material facts he hoped she would answer whatever questions remained. Both the objects of her hatred were beyond her ability to harm them further so she had nothing left to lose. Shapiro thought she would tell him now what she did and how she did it. He didn't think he'd ask her why.

The cup in front of her had been drained to the dregs. Whatever hags had ridden and continued to ride Pat Taylor, anxiety for her own future was not one. She knew she hadn't got one.

Her gaze was hard and fierce, a combination of fire and ice. Tiger eyes. She didn't care what happened to her now; she only cared what Shapiro might be able to tell her. She barked at him, 'Well?'

It wasn't the time and anyway he felt no inclination to gloat. He stood with his back to the door and his hands in his pockets. 'Detective Sergeant Donovan's being kept in hospital for a check-over but he doesn't seem to have come to much harm. Roly Dickens has been charged with assault.'

'*Assault?*' She spat the word at him as if she'd bitten into a strawberry and found half a worm. 'I wanted . . .' She stopped, the fanatic eyes disappointed.

'I know,' murmured Shapiro. 'But most people draw the line somewhere, even the head of crime in The Jubilee. Roly had a pile of grief and rage to deal with, but in the end he managed to cope with the loss of his son without destroying someone else's.'

Her chin came up. People who'd known Pat Taylor for years, people who'd studied the subtleties of Jane Austen and William Makepeace Thackeray with her, would not have recognized her now. 'You think that makes him stronger than me? How strange; *I* think it makes him weaker.'

Shapiro could think of nothing more pointless than arguing morality with her. 'I know what you did; I know pretty much how you did it. You could clarify a couple of matters.'

She no longer cared who knew what. She had more than half succeeded in what she'd set out to do. If that was something less than a triumph it was just enough to satisfy her need for vengeance. 'Such as?'

She had phoned Mikey at home, pretended to be Liz Graham – whom she knew just well enough to convince someone who knew her no better – and arranged to meet him at Cornmarket at midnight. She already had a weapon, it had been lying in the boot of her car since the last time she covered for a missing sports teacher.

'A baseball bat?' said Shapiro.

Mrs Taylor shook her head once, crisply. 'Rounders.'

She put it in the boat at her landing. The clothes she needed for a cold night on the water were a perfect disguise, and the blood washed off easily. It took her twenty minutes to motor to Cornmarket. She saw no one except the derelicts by the fire.

Mikey arrived late. Pat Taylor was waiting inside the ruins of the Inland Navigation offices. They didn't exchange so much as a word. She let Mikey pass her, then felled him with a knock that would have won her a home run in the World Series.

'And after that?' prompted Shapiro gently.

'After that I hit him some more. I kept on hitting him till I couldn't lift the bat any more.' By then she believed Mikey Dickens was dead. Giving the fire a wide berth she walked back to her boat, taking the weapon with her, and went home.

Phase two, she admitted, involved a little homework. There were things she needed to know about Donovan before she could make him a convincing scapegoat. Fortunately, she worked with a man whose wife knew him well.

'You must tell Brian Graham how helpful he was. He was always telling some new anecdote about his wife and her sergeant. I knew a lot about him already, it was easy enough to find out more. Where he lived, for instance.' That icy smile again. 'I was lucky there. I'd have managed somehow if he'd lived at the top of a tower block, but it was so much easier that he lived on the canal too.'

She prepared the weapon, returned to Broad Wharf at a likely time and waited for Donovan to take his dog for a walk. The animal wouldn't ignore something as intriguing as the scent of a man's blood on a stick left by its own front door. The first time she waited in the motorboat but they didn't show up and she had to go home. The second time it worked like a charm.

She hadn't anticipated Roly Dickens finishing the job for her. She meant to wreck Donovan's career, maybe send him to prison. When she learned that Roly too had pieced the clues together and come to the desired conclusion, the idea that he might do to Donovan what she'd done to his precious son seemed like a miracle. It was so perfect it *had* to happen.

Her lip curled. 'Now you tell me you've charged him with assault. I hoped he'd kill the bastard.'

'If it's any comfort,' murmured Shapiro, 'it's not your fault he didn't. He believed what you wanted him to; only in the end it wasn't enough for him to *do* what you wanted him to. He meant to, at least at the start. Fortunately, it's one thing committing murder in the white-heat of blind fury, quite another to stay angry enough for five hours. If Roly had really wanted Donovan dead he should have cut his throat when he found him asleep on Mikey's bed. It was always going to be harder after they'd talked.'

'I wouldn't have found it harder,' said Mrs Taylor.

'No?' Shapiro shrugged. 'But you didn't risk finding out, did you? You weren't prepared to talk to him.'

'I didn't think I could hide how I felt. And I had to, if I was going to do anything about it.'

'Maybe you were worried about giving yourself

291

away,' allowed Shapiro. 'Or maybe you were worried that if you talked to him you'd realize he didn't deserve your enmity. He was just an ordinary man doing a difficult job the best way he knew. He never meant you any harm, as far as he knew he hadn't done you any. You couldn't talk to him because you couldn't afford to see him as another human being with hopes, fears and problems of his own. To do what you intended you had to demonize him, and real human beings don't make good demons.'

Pat Taylor lurched to her feet behind the table so abruptly that WPC Flynn took a step forward, ready to intervene. But she wasn't going anywhere. Her face was crimson with a rage that nothing she'd done, nothing that had happened, had in any way diminished. Pure atavistic savagery shone from her eyes. 'They stole my baby,' she shouted, spit flying out with the words. 'They stole my baby!' Shapiro had no doubt that if either of the men she blamed had been there she'd have tried to finish the job, with her teeth if no other weapon presented itself.

Shapiro shook his head, but there was no point trying to convince her. Taylor was right, she needed professional help; though how much good it would do remained to be seen. He sighed. 'We'll need to get a statement at some point, but perhaps you'd like to rest now?'

She shrugged, returned to her chair. 'I'm not tired.'

But Shapiro was. He needed some fresh air. Mostly, he needed to be out of that room.

He was doing Donovan's thing, strolling by the canal behind Queen's Street, when Sergeant Bolsover hailed him from a back window. 'Phone, sir. It's the hospital.'

Roly Dickens had an appointment with the Magistrates that afternoon. Shapiro cancelled it. He helped the big man into his coat, waiting patiently while he went through the ritual of checking he had a handkerchief, his gloves and a scarf. It was displacement activity: if he did what he always did when he was going out, perhaps everything would be all right when he got back. Perhaps he wasn't really going to sit by a hospital bed and watch his youngest son struggle through his last few breaths.

'Ready?' asked Shapiro.

'Ready,' said Roly. Then he began to cry.

After a moment Shapiro stretched an arm around the broad, bowed shoulders and just stood with him as The Jubilee's answer to the Godfather sobbed brokenly into his spread hands.

Shapiro didn't want to rush him but there was a certain amount of urgency. As the great racking sobs abated, pity knotting up his stomach he patted Roly's arm. 'Come on. Let's go and give Mikey a proper send-off. See him safely on his way.'

They went down to Shapiro's car together, and as they passed the busy building fell silent around them.